Bounded Rationality
The Encryption

Bounded Rationality The Encryption

Humanity's Death Wish
Comes Close to Fulfilment

Kenneth Moore

Copyright © 2022 by Kenneth Moore.

Library of Congress Control Number:		2022912524
ISBN:	Hardcover	978-1-6641-0791-5
	Softcover	978-1-6641-0790-8
	eBook	978-1-6641-0789-2

All rights reserved. No part of this book may be reproduced or transmitted in any form or by any means, electronic or mechanical, including photocopying, recording, or by any information storage and retrieval system, without permission in writing from the copyright owner.

This is a work of fiction. Names, characters, places and incidents either are the product of the author's imagination or are used fictitiously, and any resemblance to any actual persons, living or dead, events, or locales is entirely coincidental.

Any people depicted in stock imagery provided by Getty Images are models, and such images are being used for illustrative purposes only.
Certain stock imagery © Getty Images.

Print information available on the last page.

Rev. date: 07/26/2022

To order additional copies of this book, contact:
Xlibris
NZ TFN: 0800 008 756 (Toll Free inside the NZ)
NZ Local: 9-801 1905 (+64 9801 1905 from outside New Zealand)
www.Xlibris.co.nz
Orders@Xlibris.co.nz
843389

Contents

Introduction ix

Chapter 1   Deep in interstellar space 1
Chapter 2   Conference Room, Hilton Hotel, Las Vegas....................7

A FEW MONTHS LATER

Chapter 3   Spring Valley Hospital, Las Vegas 18
Chapter 4   Office of *Las Vegas Sun* Newspaper............................34

TWO YEARS LATER

Chapter 5   Origins Of The Unidentified Starship.........................41
Chapter 6   Observatory, Atacama Desert, North Chile..................47
Chapter 7   La Moneda Palace, Santiago, Chile 59
Chapter 8   The Vatican..70
Chapter 9   Central Africa 87
Chapter 10   Central Africa 89
Chapter 11   Observatory, Atacama Desert, North Chile................103
Chapter 12   Office of *Las Vegas Sun* Newspaper..........................115
Chapter 13   Somewhere in the Western Australia Outback............127
Chapter 14   Place: Arnhem Land 146
Chapter 15   Place: Spatial Corroboree 152
Chapter 16   President's Oval Office, White House 175
Chapter 17   The Gathering 190

For my family,
immediate and distant.

Writing a book is harder than I thought and more rewarding than I could have ever imagined.
I must express all the gratitude and acknowledgement to all friends and family for their wise counsel and, above all, to my dear Trisha for her encouragement, which has made this book a reality.

Introduction

The concepts of science fiction form the basis for this book. What is science fiction? Indeed, it is difficult to define briefly, but according to Wikipedia, the most appropriate description is

> *Science fiction is largely based on writing rationally about alternative possible worlds or futures. It is similar to, but differs from fantasy in that, within the context of the story, its imaginary elements are largely possible within scientifically established or scientifically postulated laws of nature (though some elements in a story might still be pure imaginative speculation).*

Thanks to our exposure to an abundance of cocktails of films and books that have come into existence since records began, we know the main characteristics with which we are familiar. These usually consist of myths operating outside the realm of the known laws of physics and the principles of nature. By these definitions, Shakespeare's play, *The Tempest*, would have to be classified as science fiction, amongst many other classics like Jonathan Swift's *Gulliver's Travels*. These can also be regarded as some of the true forerunners of science fiction. Even comics and films littered with superheroes are indeed labelled as science fiction as part of pure escapism. Bearing this in mind, it is necessary to clarify views even further by shifting our mindset into a different sphere of science fiction that involves primarily technology and scientific reasoning. It is safe to say the introduction of scientific awakening during the Age of Reason (or Age of

Enlightenment) of the 17th and 18th centuries has revolutionised the public's concept of science and technology.

This has pushed the scientific barriers by questing for rationality and truth of information, much to the discomfort of many religious beliefs. Nevertheless, it is caused by the public's general awareness and understanding of scientific discoveries somewhat 'superficially' that leads to the foundation of machine-originated stories in the late 19th century, as characterised by H G Wells' *Time Machine* and *The War of the Worlds*, along with Jules Verne's *Around the World in Eighty Days* and *Twenty Thousand Leagues Under the Sea*. It is interesting that even though they captured the public imagination, these stories are usually littered with various fictional elements that cannot be explained scientifically and are implausible. Many known laws of physics have been either bent or broken completely.

Fortunately, some degree of suspension of belief is often facilitated by the public or reader's minds to the fictional imaginations to set them into a form of escapism. In other words, 'Anything for a good story, do not let facts spoil it'. If we are to pause and consider the truer meaning of suspension of belief, it would probably better be described, with a tongue-in-cheek attitude, as suspension of intelligence! Nevertheless, for the sake of promoting fallacy, but in a humorous manner, we can highlight the strange occurrences where existing laws have become bizarrely unaccountable! We can examine this fallacy with one of H G Wells' classic novels, beginning with *The War of the Worlds*, where the aliens invaded the world and started single-mindedly the process of eliminating the human population globally. All form of resistance thrown up by humans proved to be futile, and consequently, all people were starting to despair, knowing there was a very remote chance of salvaging mankind but were saved unexpectedly at the last minute by simple single-celled organisms, which had managed to ravage the alien's immunisation system, decimating them. That is the story in a nutshell. However, what is really intriguing from the outset is the notion gleaned from this novel, that the aliens do possess an enormous engineering intelligence far superior to humans in terms of technology. This is evidenced from their invincible tripod machines, but somehow, they managed to overlook the universal dangers posed from exposure to another world's microscopic organisms, which had a completely different DNA. How was it possible that with all the intelligence they possessed, they could have overlooked this obvious fact? Perhaps it was because of their type of intelligence, possibly the psyche side of their mindset, that physics, then travel will require extremely long voyages, much longer than a human lifetime. Bearing this in our mind, there are four possible options:

1. Generational ships - whole mini-societies commit to voyages that only their descendants will complete.
2. Sleep ships - like in the movie *Avatar*, travellers go into hibernation (or induced coma?).
3. Relativistic ships - as near the speed of light, time compresses, so that travellers may experience only ten years while a hundred years pass back on Earth.
4. Download ships - suppose we learn how to copy human consciousness into some machine-like device. Such 'iPersons' would be able to control an avatar that could function in environments inhospitable to biological humans. They may not be limited to Earth like planets.

What about other speculative ideas such as 'wormholes' that would provide pathways through which we can travel? Implausible, as to keep the wormhole open, an enormous source of negative/positive energy would be needed to be generated. According to the late Prof Stephen Hawking, it would be unstable and, therefore, unusable. It is concluded that FTL travel of the sort of science fiction writers would like is almost certainly impossible given the current knowledge of the laws of physics.

Finally, we now move to the fourth and final fallacy, which concerns communication. It's quite amusing to see how humans managed to strike a conversation with humanoids or aliens they met for the first time in the far, far-flung world deep in space, starting the greetings in perfect English. 'Hello, haven't we met before . . . ?' or words to that effect. In the *Star Trek* TV series, it was mentioned a few times the crews of the spaceship *Enterprise* do have a universal translator device built into the badges worn on their shirts enabling them to communicate with other alien races who amazingly happened to possess very humanlike voice boxes. Again, some form of suspension of belief is required here, when considering that the characters' mouths move simultaneously in sync with the translated words and not the original language. Nevertheless, it removes the need for cumbersome and potentially intrusive and repetitive subtitles. (Or was it for the hearing viewer's benefit or deaf viewer's dismay?) It eliminates the rather unlikely supposition that every other creature in this galaxy or confined their thought processes to that specific structural machinery technology, rather than the biological or medical issues with which we are familiar? Naturally, there is bound to be some interesting debate on how this aspect can be addressed constructively within modern literature. The judges are out on this matter. Likewise, as seen in many films and books, it is very common to see many encounters between the human and alien species happening as matter of fact and casually with barely any reference made to immense nightmares ever present, with the attendant risks and dangers of biological contamination to the environment.

Moving on to fallacy no. 2, repeated consistently across the broad spectrum of books and films involving space travel is the significance of gravity. It is often laughable to see many people walking about in small spacecraft travelling through space as though gravity was ever present in 'normal' earthly levels. People tried to justify it by emphasising there could be some form of 'gravity plate' fitted to the floors as popularised with spaceships in the TV series *Star Trek*. Unfortunately, to achieve the effect of the concept of the gravity plate, the device must be compressed tremendously and colossally into some kind of super-dense material that is equivalent to Earth's mass and weight! Even if, with such a supposedly advanced form of engineering, they could create it and have it fitted in the floors, then in theory, people should be able to walk underneath the floor parallel to people walking on top!

Now shift attention to fallacy no. 3, which is speed and distance. As is known from Einstein's famous theory of general relativity, where nothing can go faster than the speed of light, it is absurd to see many spaceships travelling at extreme speeds, faster than light (FTL), for great distances and yet manage to hold communication in real time with Earth. Have they found a means to transfer signals faster than radio waves, breaking all known laws of physics? Doubtful. Above all, this is an extremely hard problem to resolve for two primary reasons: (1) the enormous energy required to drive far and fast and (2) the vast amount of time it takes to get anywhere in galactic terms, even at high speed. Perhaps with hindsight, it is one of the reasons that, so far, with no hard evidence to show otherwise, we have never been visited by aliens—ever. (Uncorroborated sightings of UFOs don't count). So the formula $E=mc^2$ does remain supreme and factual. It is intended to stick to this throughout the book to keep the narrative in it as close to known scientific facts as possible.

Then if we are to confine our concept of travel to the realm of standard beyond has gone to the trouble of learning English or any other major languages from this world.

Again, as previously mentioned, it is largely because of the reader's ability to maintain a degree of suspension of belief or intelligence that made it possible to have unobstructed enjoyment of science fiction without having to apply too much attention to the fields of natural or physic laws. However, in this book, it is intended to make a difference. It is a science fiction book, but it is where I have made serious efforts to make the novel plausible by restricting it as faithfully as I can to existing physics principles that are well known to us in our present days. There is no point creating unconstructive issues in it, saying one day there would be a new theory of physics cropping up that will make another existing one invalid and obsolete. It is akin to saying the universal Isaac Newton's Laws of Motion can be eclipsed into disrepute by a 'new set of physics laws' or whatever. I have chosen to play it safe and leave them as they are. Having done so, then hopefully, my readers' mindsets will go with the flow of the novel. Does that still mean there is no requirement for us to maintain a degree of suspension of belief? Well, not necessarily. We still do need it *sometimes* where it is required at odd times. Or in other words, some degree of rational thought is required here. For example, we will never know for sure what the actual anatomy of the aliens will be. This will ever remain obscure to us until one day when we can be sure our minds will be boggled!

My intention in writing this book is to create a thunderingly good read without my scientifically minded readers being constantly distracted by doubts as to feasibility issues. It remains, dear reader, to see if reading this book can be made enjoyable while remaining faithful to the laws of physics that we know exist today.

*　*　*

CHAPTER 1

28 September 2025

Deep in interstellar space

A metallic object was cruising deep in dark space at the speed of 17 kilometres per second (equivalent to 61,000 kilometres per hour). Upon closer inspection, it was possible to see it had a large antenna dish mounted on a rectangular base, which gave away the nature of its human creation. It had blasted off from Earth in the year 1977 and was called *Voyager 1*. It was launched about two weeks *after* its sister *Voyager 2*, which was commissioned on 20 August 1977. Why the reversal of order? The two were sent on different trajectories, and *Voyager 1* was put on a path to reach its planetary targets, Jupiter and Saturn, ahead of *Voyager 2*.

Mounted with an assemblage of 11 major electronic instrument systems, its primary mission was to capture digital images of Jupiter and Saturn at close quarters. It had no propulsion system and was totally dependent on gravity, as it had been since its launch, and had to rely on the gravitational pull of the giant gaseous planets as a means of slingshotting to propel it out of the solar system. Throughout its 48-year journey, it relied on its three-axis stabilised guidance systems. The antenna dish was focussed with extreme accuracy at the very small pale blue dot orbiting the brightest star. It takes no guesswork to identify the blue dot as being the Earth and the bright star as the dominant and life-giving sun. In the year 2012, *Voyager 1* had finally crossed the heliopause and entered interstellar space, making it the most distant that any man-made object had travelled outside the solar system. It took more than a day for the radio signal transmitted from *Voyager 1* to reach the giant radio dish on Earth. The strength of transmission was only 22 watts, which are about the equivalent of a refrigerator light bulb. By the time those signals reached Earth, they were about one-tenth of a billion-billionth of a watt which indeed made *Voyager 1*'s signal extremely faint.

At its current speed, it would take *Voyager 1* 40,000 years to reach another star known as Gliese 445. Alpha Centauri is the closest star to our own right now, but because the stars were also moving, *Voyager 1* would get within 1.7 light years from Gliese 445.

The remote possibility that the craft would ever encounter another created object or beings had been considered with the mission plan. Should the craft ever encounter aliens, a possible aid to communication in the form of a gold disc had been fixed to the side of the body of *Voyager 1*. This could reveal possible means of dialogue to any intelligent form of life. The sole purpose of this device was to assist decryption by any alien beings to the unaggressive humankind intentions. There were basic welcoming greetings made in 55 different human languages, including the pictures and natural sounds meant to show extraterrestrials a glimpse of life on Earth. Whether they could be interpreted by an alien with a different psyche mindset regarding intentions was anything but assured.

As the space probe *Voyager 1* continued cruising steadily through the deep dark interstellar space, with stars as the only source of illumination, it had three radioisotope thermoelectric generators (RTGs) mounted on a boom. Each MHW-RTG contained 24 pressed plutonium-238 oxide spheres. The RTGs generated about 470 watts of electric power at the time of launch, with the remainder being dissipated as waste heat. The power output of the RTGs does decline over time (because of the short 87.7-year half-life of the fuel and degradation of the thermocouples), but the RTGs of *Voyager 1* would continue to support some of its operations until 2025, when, by then, the available power would have drained down to its last microwatt.

Based at Pasadena, California, the team at the Jet Propulsion Laboratory, which operated and monitored *Voyager 1* and its sister *Voyager 2* at regular intervals, had taken predetermined steps for the last 30 years to conserve the ever-reducing power by turning off selected sensors one by one, with the last being turned off around 2025. After that, *Voyager 1* would cease to be operational. It would be a piece of metal junk floating at zippy speed, aimless and eternally.

For a moment, when its power was almost exhausted abruptly, the talismanic craft was lit by a series of blinding light pulses. Intense rays of red light beams scanned across the body of the space probe in the form of long straight grid lines and then started to move along the dish and the body vertically and then a moment later, horizontally. So intense were the beams that illuminated the space probe that it was like an enormous spatial display of the Northern Lights. Moments later, the beams suddenly switched off, and the blackness of space returned once again.

A few minutes later, the same thing happened again, bathing the space probe with intense blue laser beams, followed by a third scan with intense yellow beams. The deliberate process indicated a very precise measurement was taking place, but for what purpose? Measuring the mass, the speed, and the trajectory from where it came? At this stage, there was no apparent focus on the information displayed by the golden disc. A few seconds later, the pattern was repeated with the scanning beams again being switched off, leaving *Voyager 1* in total darkness.

The last remaining operating sensor aboard *Voyager 1* had been alerted to some changes in the environment and sensed spikes of charged interstellar particles and transferred the readings to the pitifully small computer with 60 kilobytes of memory sited deep inside the body. The computer used the last wattage of its battery power to do some data analysis before transmitting the encrypted data towards the brightest star. That would be the last transmission it made. The very faint signal would not be heard by Earth for another day, and even then, only if some being took the trouble to read it, having deliberate intent.

A short moment later, another laser beam flared across the whole body of the space probe, but it was of a massive destructive power this time. The probe disappeared, totally vapourised literally, in a blinding flash. There was no sound as the whole event had taken place in the vast vacuum of space.

Voyager 1 had ceased to exist, without any trace whatsoever remaining. In its place, a gigantic threat emerged.

***

The new arrival was travelling at a phenomenal speed by earthly comparisons, more than ten times faster than *Voyager 1*. There were two more identical objects in tandem immediately behind. This was the lead trio as there were no less than three more flights of three identical space traveller groups.

These crafts were equipped with a propulsion system that enabled each to select speed or direction independently. However, only the lead craft was using its power system. At the rear of each of the massive cylinders were the shuttered openings of the engines. Each craft could be operated independently, but when the engines were not in use, the reactive outlets were sealed.

A closer examination of one of the trios of these flights would show considerable external damage with some parts of the external fuselage missing. These had apparently been removed in a somewhat random pattern, giving an indication of travel wear and subsequent cannibalism. This evidence indicated there was an active process of repairs and that some being was involved in maintaining the starships deep in the hugeness of unforgiving and uncharted space.

The length of the cylinder of each *unit* was about 8 kilometres long and 5 kilometres wide. There were several ribs running lengthwise on the outside of the cylinders. These contained high strength magnetic materials. Their primary multipurpose was to create magnetic fields cocooning the starships protectively against all forms of cosmic rays encountered during their journey in deep space. The same magnetic system also maintains the distances among the three units in each group; there is no other physical connection.

The secondary purpose was to create electromagnetic propulsion that kept the secondary cylinder, which was occupied inside the outer cylinder spinning at high speed. There was a spatial cushion between these two-cylinder parts that created a frictionless property that an electromagnetic propulsion system creates. This would ensure prolonged longevity of the machines in operation. In theory, the maintenance could be kept down to an absolute minimum, which was ideally suitable for long-distance space travel.

With the secondary cylinder spinning inside at such a speed, the third major effect it had created was to create artificial gravity. There were several layers of floors inside the secondary cylinder, with the outer floor amassing strong gravity equivalent to 2.8 times the Earth's gravity. The floor closest to the centre of the cylinder, which spun relatively more slowly than the middle and outer floors, had much lower gravity matching the same strength as the Earth's. This is consistent with Newton's first law of motion, namely the Coriolis effect (force). This is like a roundabout at a park, where children try to keep themselves close to the axis of the roundabout, where the centrifugal force is relatively weaker than the outer rim from which they knew they would be flung off.

The starships were all looking slightly weather-beaten after being in space for such a long time. Space-beaten is probably a more appropriate term to describe their state.

An umbrella-shaped shield was mounted on a 2-kilometre thin tube extended centrally in front of the main cylinder. There were various probes and antennas protruding from the shield. There was a speck of fine meteoric dust covering it as would be expected after extended space travel. There had been many inevitable collisions with space debris, such as interstellar dust, micrometeorites, and asteroids.

The main functions of the antennas were to scan the region in front by emitting low-powered laser beams at intervals. When needed, some destructive force could be applied, such as laser cannons, to remove debris, but over such huge lengths of time, there were unavoidable collisions and some collateral damage that occurred and to minimise unavoidable damage, speed had to be compromised at times to avoid annihilation and self-destruction.

As the distance a spaceship travelled through space increases, so did the odds that it would collide with debris in its path, such as interstellar dust, micrometeorites, asteroids, dark matter, dark stars, etc. They had become something of a real nuisance and life-threatening objects to the starships, and they had taken extreme measures to avoid them by either steering around or annihilating them. If travelling at super-high speed through unforgiving and uncharted space, there was no way to know what was out there to impede or impact these remarkable craft. Unfortunately there had to be some form of gamble. Even if it was charted territory, debris was always flying through, sometimes at incredibly high speeds; there really was a paramount need for a rapid response detection system. After a certain distance, the odds are 100% that a spaceship will experience a fatal collision. As a result, these spaceships cannot go any faster than the required 'optimum speed' as a means of giving them increased opportunities to manoeuvre when required to steer away from these threats. Essentially, their speed was restricted severely for safety measures. It went without saying that risks had to be kept down to an absolute minimum.

Coupled with laser cannons for extra protection, they also had a big electromagnetic shield extending far in front of the ship that would attract and deflect small objects; most meteoroids were ferromagnetic, so they react and are deflected well by electromagnetic fields. Non-ferromagnetic fragments were not abundant, but whenever they were present, they were deposited on the front of the ships. Small space probes were sent outfitted with cleaning devices to the front at intervals as required to vacuum up the layers of dust off the skin of the umbrella shield. Some of the debris were then filtered down to essential materials that could be recycled as topping up the fusion fuel used for its nuclear propulsion system. Nothing was wasted. It was an essential design feature for the long distances to be covered during the equivalent of 24,000 Earth years that these ships had travelled so far.

* * * *

Chapter 2

29 September 2025

Conference Room, Hilton Hotel, Las Vegas

The crowd of some 300 people were mostly dressed in long evening dresses, and they were mingling freely, carrying drinks and chatting politely, but audibly louder than the soothing mood music playing in the background. There was a prominent stage to be seen at the far end of the room. Above it, there were three giant TV screens hanging in places for the benefit of the crowd. A few TV cameras could be seen at the corners being manned by journalists and reporters, all fiddling about while they were impatiently waiting for the press announcements to begin. World media interest was intense. On the TV screens' background, still pictures of the old space probes, *Voyagers 1* and *2*, were being projected.

A man sitting in a motorised wheelchair manoeuvred his leisurely way, snaking through the crowd as they moved apart in respectful acknowledgement. 'Well done, Edward! What an achievement!' someone hollered at him.

'Thank you', he repeatedly acknowledged.

His right hand rested firmly on a small joystick he manipulated skilfully to control his wheelchair. His face was thin and haggard, but he was beaming with pride and appeared very tranquil and content. He looked older than his actual age, and the wheelchair indicated that his physical state of health was severely diminished. But that was only the initial impression. His mind was still amazingly sharp as his eyes were piercing with intense razor-sharp intelligence. He went to the end of the room and up a ramp to the stage as people turned their heads to watch him. The reporters and camera crews started fiddling with their cameras and recorders, focussing their attention on the celebrated international figure on the stage. 'Ready when you are, Mr Stone', the event manager suggested.

'Please call me Edward. These people'—he pointed at the crowd—'are part of my family, my work colleagues, my team for nearly 50 years, so some informality is the order of the day, please'.

'Okay, Edward, I'll remember that', the manager said sheepishly, slightly in awe of this world-famous celebrity.

Edward laughed. 'Okay, here we go!'

He took a personal screen controller out of his pocket. Computerised options flashed across the PSC. He manipulated the device expertly and looked up expectantly at one of the three TV screens. An internationally recognisable face of a woman appeared. She looked fatigued from the long hours of work and stress.

'Good evening, Mrs President'. Edward smiled at her. 'It is an honour and greatly appreciated to have you taking time off from your responsibilities to address us all on this memorable evening'.

She perked up, beaming a big smile. 'No, Edward, it is *my* honour, and indeed a privilege, to share with you all this sad and historic occasion, marking the demise of the fabled *Voyager*'.

Edward nodded with his eyes becoming misty. A bittersweet event it was to be.

'So today is the day that has finally come for you to bid a fond farewell to the *Voyager*. All the staff at the Jet Propulsion Laboratory based in Pasadena will be sad because they will have nothing more to do!'

This drew a lot of good-natured laughter from the audience.

'I have run out of gas before in my car, but I never thought that a space probe would run out of nuclear power!'

This brought more chuckles.

'You are correct, Mrs President', Edward said. 'We cannot use it anymore, and it is time for us to wave it goodbye and say bon voyage and close down the whole project'.

She responded, 'It has been a really amazingly successful project, not just for the USA, but also for all our international collaborators. For the power on the *Voyager* to have lasted this long exceeded its planned duration. I wish my new electric car could last that long!'

The crowd murmured applause, laughing in agreement at the president's comments, which captured the mood of the event. They went quiet as she continued her speech.

'So the *Voyager* won't be operating anymore and will be flying like a piece of junk metal forever into space, and who on Earth knows where it will end up? I will end my address to you all by giving you and your team thanks on behalf of our grateful nation', the president said with evident enthusiasm.

'Thank you for your time, Mrs President. Indeed, it is a very expensive lump of junk!' Edward said, and there were chuckles at his humour. 'But let's hope something, somewhere will make use of the golden disc on the *Voyager* and take the trouble to decrypt it and let us know where it is, so that we might be able to find someone to buy the gold disc from us, and we could get some of the taxpayers' dollars back!'

The president took her cue from the notes in her handheld prompt. Her composure became more formal.

'Mr Stone, I would like to say it has been a great achievement for you personally to have masterminded the *Voyager* project since its launch back in 1977, and . . . ' She droned on for another 5 minutes on the list of achievements and how wonderful the team at Jet Propulsion Laboratory were.

Edward listened passively and nodded at intervals to show her he was listening, but he was not paying any serious attention to her speech anymore; his mind was on a nostalgic trip down memory lane. How much effort the huge team of people had put into this project, making it all possible—what an achievement. All the logistical planning applied, then the construction, and finally, the countdown to the launch. His mind drifted to various people he had worked with for decades; some remained close friends and some had passed on. *What about the heated meeting with Carl Sagan on his proposed idea of getting* Voyagers *to carry the golden disc? We argued whether the additional weight could affect the flight path . . .*

'So well done, Edward. We're now toasting you and your team for all your magnificent efforts'.

The comment jolted Edward from his daydreaming.

'Urh . . . yes, thank you, Mrs President, that was very nice of you to say that'. He looked up at the screen. 'But I have to say that I am accepting your compliments on behalf of our dedicated team'. He sighed. 'It was really because of them. Wherever, whatever, and whoever, they were involved, from the janitors to the flight controllers. We are evermore indebted to them. It is them we should applaud for their commitments to this unique project. What a team I have been privileged to lead!'

The crowd applauded with genuine appreciation.

'Thanks, but hold on'. He lifted his hand, and the crowd went silent. 'But I have to say there is one man to whom I am forever indebted for everything that made the *Voyager* project a success'.

Edward looked intently at the crowd and then gestured towards another woman who appeared on the second screen. She was grey-haired but stood confidently in front of an array of computers and smiled. There were several large monitors emitting some incomprehensible formulae, which were hallmarks of the communication complex with *Voyagers*.

'Hello, Sarah. It is wonderful to have you at JPL. Your dad's years of dedicated and inspired work has been so appreciated by us', Edward said enthusiastically. 'But before you do anything, I'd like an opportunity to explain to the people, here at the convention and through our media friends, also the rest of the world, just where you fit into our team'.

Edward looked at the crowd and pointed towards the woman on the screen in the middle, between the president and the image of *Voyagers*. 'This is Sarah Minovitch, the daughter of the late Dr Michael Minovitch'.

Sarah nodded slowly. 'I feel so privileged just to be here on behalf of my dear dad'.

Edward looked at the press gallery. 'Let me explain briefly who he was'. He paused and then continued, 'Until Michael Minovitch joined us, the received scientific wisdom on interplanetary space flight was grim. Basically, the sums didn't add up. Carrying the rocket fuel necessary to propel a spacecraft to the outer reaches of the solar system would mean unfeasibly huge payloads. The brilliance of Minovitch was in realising a way to avoid taking all that fuel by using the gravitational fields of the major planets as a huge "slingshot". If a craft passed close to a planet, it could steal enough orbital energy to propel it onto another planet and then another. All you needed was the fuel to get you to the first planet. So it was not until 1961 when Michael managed, with the help of a new IBM 7090 computer, the fastest on Earth at the time, to provide a numerical solution to the three-body problem of celestial mechanics'.

'Excuse me, Edward, what in the heck is a three-body?' a reporter shouted.

'Oh sorry, the gravitational effect of three bodies—one being the sun, the second one is the planet, and the third one is, of course—' Edward pointed at the image of a space probe on the large screen. 'The *Voyagers*. This was bold, brilliant stuff. Trouble was, Minovitch was just a lowly UCLA grad student at the time, working at the Jet Propulsion Lab. His scientific street cred was zilch!'

Edward continued with pride.

'It took until 1962 before his theory was taken seriously by the establishment. But the acceptance and subsequent implementation of his ideas changed everything. All the great planetary missions—*Mariner, Pioneer, Voyager, Cassini*—have used Minovitch's slingshot. Without him, there would be no photographs of Jupiter's moons, no fly-by of Saturn's rings, no golden record for aliens to find'.

The audience was spellbound, hanging on to every word.

'The thing was that he had been nominated for a Nobel Prize in 1991 but was not successful. There were others who claimed to have had a hand in gravitational propulsion, which Minovitch strongly refuted. Minovitch, bless him, who passed away in 2020, felt he had not received adequate recognition for his revolutionary theory that eventually made planetary exploration possible.

'Big deal, you might say. A scientist feels his work is unappreciated. Hardly news!' Edward chuckled. 'And yet I'm struck by the poignancy of his quiet protestation. The reputation of his unique and pioneering work is only now becoming recognised, and so in the scientific world, he has created his own golden record.

'So here we are on this very special day, and I thought there's nothing more fitting for us to ask his daughter Sarah but to give it a most fitting gesture and final closure by switching off all the communication equipment that has been our only link to the *Voyager* during its epic pioneering little trip—some trip!'

This little quip lifted the mood of the audience.

Edward looked back at the large screen. 'So in a way, that is his legacy, and for that, we can salute him'.

Edward picked a glass of wine, which had been sitting on a small table next to him, and simultaneously, the crowd lifted theirs; they all raised their glasses and toasted, 'To Michael Minovitch!'

'So, Sarah, we are thankful for your presence in memory of your late father. So please proceed with the honour of switching off the communication channels. I understand, if our calculation is right, the radio transmission from *Voyager* should cease transmitting any time now. The last watt of battery power is calculated as being exhausted as of now'.

In anticipation, Sarah looked down on a large red button sited next to her as he continued, 'That device next to you is a button, kind of symbolic but will switch off all the instruments anyway, again a symbolic gesture to end a nearly 50-year-long project'.

She placed her hand slightly above the button and said, 'First and foremost, I would like to thank you all for being there to witness this ever-memorable event. To be considered for this important milestone in place of my dear dad is a great honour and privilege. I am sure he would not ask for more than that. I'm forever grateful that I am able to continue my dad's legacy . . .' She continued, hovering her hand over it in suspension, 'Here we are. Once I have pushed that button, soon that venerable machine will finally shut down, becoming a dead hunk of '70s technology and decaying plutonium. Only the golden disc on *Voyager* represents a "message in a bottle" out in the cosmic wilderness, linking humanity to any intelligent species that may find it in the future . . .'

She moved her hand slowly and paused for a very short moment; just before she started to commence the shutdown sequence, some irregular signals flared into a series of unfamiliar readings. The data was indecipherable and bore no resemblance to the familiar signals that had been streaming in constantly from *Voyager* for the past ten years.

Edward's eyes narrowed, and he frowned, trying to decipher what was unfolding before him. *HOLD ON!* His mind shouted as the screen went blank. *NO, WAIT!* He wanted to scream but could not get the words out as he was frozen with sheer astonishment. He went pale. *Click!* That was the sound of the button.

The monitors in the conference hall all went blank until the monitor on which Sarah had been on gradually cleared and she reappeared.

Sarah looked at him from the screen.
'What in the holy smoke was that all about?'

She was obviously as puzzled as he was at the event that had just unfolded. Then she looked more closely at the image on her own screen, of the old scientist in his wheelchair. 'You okay?' she asked him. 'You looked as if you'd seen a ghost!'

Edward paused for a few moments while he tried to pull himself together. His mind was reacting as he tried to digest what he and the audience had just witnessed. 'Sorry, Sarah, it's just that my emotions got the better of me! Hard to let go of a 50-year-old project! Forgive me for being a bit sentimental . . .' His voice quavered.

Fortunately, everyone in the audience, including the president watching the whole proceedings from her own screen in the White House, bought it.

He continued, 'Well, I guess that is the end of the show, Mrs President and ladies and gentlemen, and I have to thank you all for your interest in what has been a superb pioneering scientific project. It will take our dedicated team some time to digest all that we have seen. Thank you all for your interest. Bye!'

The crowd gave their thundering applause.

But Edward simply smiled at them and looked down at the people who were all beginning to move away and signalled to one particular man in front of the crowd to come up and join him.

He had known Stevie for a long time, not only as a valued staff member of his team at JPL, but also very much like a son.

Stevie had shared his same puzzlement when he had seen some strange movements on the monitor next to Sarah. He climbed up onto the stage and leant closer to Edward, their heads almost touching together.

'Did you see what I saw?' Stevie whispered.

'Yes', Edward hissed. 'But can you get in touch *now* with Conrad in New Mexico, you know, and get them to save all that last incoming piece of data. They are the last live signals communicated . . . Get my drift?'

Stevie said nothing but nodded as he had a full understanding of what steps to take and moved away from the stage to an adjacent room, which was clearly marked with a sign, 'Authorised Personnel Only'.

One reporter who had viewed the whole situation smelt something was going on and like an experienced sleuth, started to tail Stevie.

Stevie shut the door firmly behind him and held up his wrist, exposing a sophisticated communication control strapped to it, and entered a specific instruction. He held it up close to his mouth and waited for a moment before a response came.

The reporter who had followed Stevie at a discreet distance up to the room appeared to be leaning casually on the wall outside, adjacent to the door. He seemed to have an earpiece in one ear as though he was listening to music.

Up on one of the balconies at the end of the room, there was a towering burly security man, who had been scanning everything with eagle eyes around the conference room. His eyes had been focussed on Stevie, and he immediately picked up the tail, watching every movement the reporter had made. Based on his years of experience, the body language of the reporter was highly suspicious to the security man. He reacted fast. He moved quickly down the stairs and towards Stevie's room and came up behind the reporter.

* * *

'Hello?' A man's voice came through Stevie's earpiece.

He was the man who oversaw the operations of the Very Large Array, one of the world's premier astronomical radio observatories, consisting of 27 radio antennas in a Y-shaped configuration on the Plains of San Agustin, 50 miles west of Socorro, New Mexico. They were the first in long chains of communication, being the first to receive the radio signals from *Voyagers* whenever they were in line directly with Earth.

'Hello. Is that Conrad? Stevie here from JPL'. Stevie spoke with a hushed but firm tone in his voice.

'No, this is Alan, but I'll get him immediately and transfer your call to him. He's here at the control room'.

A few clicks later . . .

'Hey, Stevie, long time no speaking! By the way, how's your family?'

'Conrad, sorry, don't mean to sound rude, but I don't have time for a personal chat. I need your help—top priority, pronto, old buddy!'

Conrad went silent and listened.

* * *

The reporter was trying hard to seem nonchalant while he listened intently, leaning against the wall adjacent to the door. He had his mini recorder pressed against the door, partly hidden by his loosely fitting jacket.

He had heard little so far, but suddenly, his collar was grabbed by the burly security man, and he was yanked away.

'What in the hell do you think you are doing?' growled the security guard.

'I am a National News Association reporter. Look, here is my press identity card', squeaked the man half strangled by the grip that the guard had on his collar while he fumbled to extricate his press ID.

'That room is out of bounds to you and anyone else from the press. So just move your butt outta here. As of now! Bud!' the guard growled. 'That is it—no point trying to reason with me. If you want to go in there, ask the top man in this room'. He nodded in the direction of the man in the wheelchair.

'Oh Christ!' the reporter squeaked and scrambled off in the direction of the stage.

* * *

'Conrad, are your communication instruments with blanket monitoring capabilities of the *Voyagers* still operational?' Stevie said, speaking into his iWatch. 'It must be kept operating at all costs, whether *Voyagers* still transmit or not!'

'Oh gee, I am not sure as I believe it's about to be shut down as part of procedures set in with the response to the . . .' He didn't finish the sentence. 'But hang on, let me dash there and double-check it'. Conrad burst out running.

Stevie walked around in circles while holding his iWatch close to his ear, with his right hand combing his hair back. 'Please, please!' he prayed to himself with an anxious expression on his face.

He stopped walking when Conrad came back on the speaker on his iWatch. He listened for a few moments, but his face remained expressionless. A few seconds later, he rolled his eyes while exhaling slowly. He walked out of the room and looked across the crowd at Edward until their eyes locked. He strolled slowly towards the stage so as not to alarm the crowd and climbed up on the stage towards Edward.

The reporter was already there, standing on the floor next to the stage where Edward was and was trying to engage with Edward. 'Sir, I have a hunch something is not quite right . . .'

But Edward homed in on Stevie who was walking back towards him, giving the appearance of being calm. Stevie looked at the tough guard and pointed at the reporter and winked at him with a flick of head to indicate to him to get the reporter out of the way. The security man got the message and moved towards the reporter. He stopped and bent down to him and whispered, 'I would be most happy to escort you off the premises, sir, as Mr Stone does not feel very well and needs some peace. Do you understand?' He looked down at the journalist, and his eyes locked on the name label clipped to the front pocket and then said with not exactly a threatening but a firm tone, 'Hi, Brett. Let me help you get out of the way'.

Brett looked up at the towering man with some trepidation and walked backwards slowly. 'Erm . . . I'm okay, but . . . but . . .'

'Cool, Brett', the big man cut in with a smile while wrapping his thick arm around the reporter's back and nudged him slowly in a different direction. 'Can you be a sport, buddy, and go to the bar for a drink?'

Brett said nothing but looked thoroughly frustrated while being manoeuvred discreetly on his way. Edward and Stevie watched them moving further out of earshot and then looked at each other. 'Well, did you have any luck?' Edward whispered to Stevie, shifting his eyes to the crowd but still smiling and putting on a bold face.

Stevie bent down to Edward's level and whispered into his ear, 'I got in touch with Conrad, and he's confirmed that the last remaining vital data emitted by *Voyager 1* has been received and safely retrieved onto the hard drive'. He nodded impassively. 'We've got it! We'll have a few more months of analytical hard graft to consider!'

Edward exhaled slowly as he was experiencing sheer relief. He turned around and looked up at the large image of *Voyager* projected on the screen. His eyes narrowed as he gazed at it quizzically. 'Well, well, what's the new angle that you are coming up with now?' he muttered to himself, his shoulders hunched.

He bent forward slightly, his mouth clamped shut, but a smile slowly creased his face. He looked more like his old self, with a bit more colour in his cheeks. His eyes were twinkling, alive with excitement. His mind was calculating hard at what steps would be needed to resuscitate the *Voyager* project, which was now considered dead.

***

A Few Months Later

Chapter 3

21 April 2026

Spring Valley Hospital, Las Vegas

The lavish splendour of the privately funded medical and clinical suites was located on several floors of the hospital and indicated its commitment to providing the best medical care available on the market. Only people with high disposable income or those with medical insurance with the highest premiums could afford its services. The dedication to clinical excellence was well renowned internationally. By providing all the comforts and benefits the patients believed they needed, no matter how extreme they might seem, the obligations were met if there was no likelihood of the patients' health being infringed.

An example could be seen on the seventh floor in a large but well-ventilated room. On the first impression, anyone could have mistaken it for a presidential suite at a five-star hotel, if it were not for the extremely high-tech array of medical equipment standing next to a single bed. This betrayed the primary appearance and function of this room. At this patient's insistence, there were three individual holographic displays positioned at the end of the bed. This was a sophisticated form of videoconferencing.

An old, thin, and fragile man was lying motionless in the bed with a single tube attached to his left arm. The sheets were covering a frame that protected the heavily bandaged stump of his left leg missing from below his knee. His eyes were shut, but a slow but slightly irregular movement of his chest showed his shallow breathing pattern—a life on borrowed time.

A doctor in a white coat stood by the bed, interpreting the various signals his handheld clinical diagnostic reader was displaying. He looked at the patient and shook his head.

'To be frank, I am not comfortable with the idea of you having all these communication devices installed'. He sighed. 'Especially when you've just come out of operation minus half a leg only a couple of days ago. You need absolute rest. You are old enough to know better'.

The old man's eyes flickered and opened slowly in response to the voice. 'Urrmmf', he murmured as if he was trying to find his level of consciousness. He peered, unfocussed, at the ceiling above the bed. Then he remembered instantly where he was. *Oh, the bloody hospital*, he thought. He looked up at the doctor, with his eyebrows furrowed as he was trying to fathom what he was saying. 'Say again?' he whispered, but he surprised himself at his own lack of strength revealed through his weak voice.

'I have to tell you it is my professional opinion that since you have had a major surgery following your deep vein thrombosis, you really must take all the rest you possibly can. I cannot stress my clinical opinions more strongly that you are subjecting yourself to what is highly likely to be terminal stresses!' He pointed at the array of hologram displays. 'These devices have no place anywhere near a patient in intensive care, such as you are!'

'FUCK YOU!' The old man managed to show some depth of feeling in his voice. 'It's my bloody life, and I'll do what I bloody well want. The price may be my life, but that's my choice'.

'I understand that, Edward. But just stop being so focussed on your work. You've lived your last ten years in the wheelchair, which resulted in your getting DVT. So let's focus on you avoiding another DVT in your other leg. I recommend you have some physiotherapy immediately to improve the blood circulation of the other good leg . . .' He was trying to establish a meaningful contact with his world-famous patient. 'Then once you're in much better shape, you can do whatever you like, videoconferencing or any other damn thing that you choose, but if you do not slow down, then you will be a hindrance to your colleagues, and then your work will have been jeopardised by you!'

The doctor moved slowly closer to Edward and spoke in a firm tone. 'I'd like to remind you again you're still not out of the woods yet as there are some strong possibilities there's a clot somewhere in your bloodstream, and so far, you're lucky it hasn't reached your brain or God knows where else. It could be a few hours or months before you will suffer another stroke, and then we would not be able to save you'.

Edward sighed and composed himself slowly as he was trying to find a way of reasoning with his doctor. 'I understand you and respect you for doing your job, and forgive me for my outburst, and that was uncalled for. I apologise for that. Perhaps, with hindsight, I owe it to you, for you to know how imperative it is for me to live out the last remains of the life objectives that I know and fought for all these years'. He gestured towards the array of communication devices. 'These are my very lifeline to something which will be of major historic importance, something so important that it could be classified as a major scientific and international security interest'. Edward moved his clenched hands to his chest and said earnestly, 'I think you need to know something strange and not yet understood occurred to *Voyager 1*, and I must continue to get my team to be on the right track to identifying what it was with utmost urgency! That I need to know *right away* before anything terminal happens to me'.

The doctor said nothing, and he was still looking at the monitor in his hand and comparing it with the permanently coupled monitors by the patient's bed.

Edward's voice was feeble. 'It is vital that I am able to analyse any information to gain a clue as to what the hell happened to the *Voyager 1*. I must know if it has been destroyed by malfunction or some other malign or deliberate influence'. Edward's voice started to gain some strength from his inner life force. 'As we know, time is of the essence, and I don't have the luxury of time available to me. We know I'll probably, or maybe just only possibly, have a few short weeks. I am the one who has the choice to endanger my life for the sake of my understanding the significance or otherwise to mankind. The stress of my work will continue to endanger my life. So be it. For me, acquiring and assessing a new and vital piece of information is called living. I have not yet been able to fully brief my team. That is my priority, not just for me, but also for mankind. I live or die for it'.

A red-haired nurse came bustling into the room, summoned by the remote instruments connected to her alarm system. The sudden increase in blood pressure caused by Edward's outburst had triggered the alarms in her nearby station. The nurse, even though she knew the specialist was with his patient, started carefully scrutinising the life-support equipment readings. Edward and the doctor looked at her briefly and decided to ignore her.

'I see your point. *Voyager* has been your life, and it will be your death.

But maybe with my help, not just yet. But don't tell me I haven't warned you. It is quite exceptional to have these communication devices in your room. They are quite contradictory to our purpose of your health improvement programme, but you made a pretty solid case!'

'Thank you, Doctor Carter'. Edward smiled. 'You are my saviour'.

'You'd better say no more, or I might change my mind! But let me wish you all the best of luck and find out what destroyed the *Voyager 1*'. The doctor started to move out to the door. 'Or not . . .' His voice drifted away but was lost to Edward and the nurse. They didn't hear the last part of the sentence, but it didn't bother Edward at all; his mind was already elsewhere and, above all, focussing on what issues he should need to bring up with his work colleagues who were still sited at the JPL.

The doctor exited the room, leaving Edward with the nurse. She began to fuss with the pillows and tidy the bedding while Edward worked around her, squinting at the information being presented on his array and getting more irritated while his blood pressure monitor showed it.

A small bluish light flickered into life on one of his screens. He repeated the procedures again with various receptors on the tables. Above each box, a ghostly 3D image materialised. The first showed Stevie sitting on a chair behind a large desk. The second and third holograms were of another man and a woman.

Edward looked at the left screen. 'Hi there, Stevie. Nice to see you once again'.

Stevie was leaning back in his chair, head tilted backwards, looking at the ceiling. He was in deep thought. He turned his head abruptly at the sound of a voice. He was a senior systems analyst who had worked tirelessly for the past 20 years at the JPL. He was a key player, ensuring all the essential data transmitted by the *Voyagers* was accurately encrypted and that it could all be retrieved quickly and efficiently. In his earlier days working for Edward, he was very much more like an errand boy doing various mundane tasks, but during the last five years, Edward had started to rely on him heavily for handling all the public relations activities.

'Hello, Eddy! Oh, great balls of fire! I was sitting here just thinking about you! How are you doing? Well, I hope after your op . . . That must have been a tough one, considering the loss of your . . .' He couldn't finish the sentence and was floundering for words when he saw the sheet-covered cage covering the lower half of Edward's bed, displaying the missing limbs. He was clearly shocked.

Edward didn't pay any further attention to him as he moved on to the other two members of his team. 'Hello, Dean and Rachel. I am really glad to be able to contact you all at such short notice. We need to move things along a lot faster following recent major developments. My health hiccups have put a spanner in the works, and we need a major review of where we have got to and what we do next'.

Dean responded, 'Not at all. Like you, we were equally anxious to share our findings with you as soon as possible, but only if you're well enough and up for it'.

His hair was white and unkempt, and he peered myopically through his bifocals. There was a desk label sited in front of him, stating him to be a professor of theoretical and applied physics. He was widely respected for his contribution to deciphering the data transmitted by space probes of all kinds, especially the *Voyagers* when they went through all the space boundaries, such as the heliopause, which is sited at the very edge of the solar system. If there was anyone who could visualise the encoded data and translate it into layman's terms, while conjuring up the pictures so graphically, it had to be this man.

Rachel White was an assistant professor of theoretical astrophysics and was one of the youngest women ever to graduate with a PhD at Harvard. She worked as director of the JPL and was also regarded as the operating brainchild of the organisation. She was one of the few people with a natural flair and understanding of observational astrophysics, which was just a different branch to theoretical astrophysics in practice, and for this reason alone, she was able to run the *Voyager* project at JPL so effectively in the most practical way.

Edward looked at his trusted colleagues quizzically and then got straight to the point by asking if they had analysed all the available data, which would present any new aspects or theories or any new information about the ill-fated *Voyager 1* in its last moments prior to its extinction.

'As you know, I don't have the luxury of time nor the energy to maintain this meeting at length. So in a nutshell, what is your analysis of the readings received from *Voyager 1*? Issue no. 1, can you confirm to me that *Voyager 1* has been destroyed *physically, or has it merely been damaged?* That is, that there are no pieces or debris in the vicinity of the *Voyager 1*'s last reported location?' Edward's exasperation was clearly shown through the tone of his voice, which was higher-pitched than usual.

Clicks and squeaks could be heard in the background. It was the nurse who was trying to read the various diagnostic gauges. She wasn't fully concentrating on what she was doing as she was listening to the conversation being held amongst the four scientists. Unsurprisingly, she found it all riveting.

'Yes, I can confirm some external influence managed to destroy *Voyager 1* completely, but we've checked her sister *Voyager 2*—it's still intact. We don't know if something will do the same thing to it, so we're keeping an eye on it for the time being', Rachel interjected. 'At this stage, we don't really know who, how, or what did it'.

Edward eyed her and asked her slowly and in an extremely measured way, 'Say that again—can you clarify what you mean by *someone*? Someone from this Earth, like China, has managed to terminate *Voyager 1*? How can they do that? Has someone managed to come up with a new technology that we are not aware of?'

Clicks and squeaks manifested again in the brief pause in the dialogue. Edward was becoming more agitated, and he was in no mood for further distractions while trying to focus on conversing with his fellow scientists. He glared at the nurse who was still apparently reading the information from the life-support equipment.

'For god's sake, nurse!' His voice gained strength, rose again, showing his irritation. 'How much longer are you going to keep on fiddling with that bloody apparatus?' His exasperation was clear.

The nurse was startled and took a step back.

'I am very sorry, but your blood pressure is showing a very worrying increase. Edward, I didn't mean to . . .' Her voice was very apologetic. 'Erm . . . I think that should be it?'

Edward raised his voice and almost shouted despite his weakened physical condition.

'Is that important? Can't it wait? I've got much more important matters to deal with!' he fumed. 'It is you mucking around with those infernal gadgets which are raising it!'

'No worry, I can do it afterwards, when you have finished', the nurse said.

She was still standing with her hands clasped in front of her as if she was waiting.

'Then please do me a favour and make yourself useful—GET OUT!' Edward growled at her while his face reddened.

The nurse's eyes widened, and her face flushed in anger. As a highly qualified nurse in the elevated surroundings of the Spring Valley Hospital, she was clearly not used to being shouted at as she was a professional. She took a few steps backwards before she turned around while lifting her arms, absolutely flabbergasted, and she walked quickly out of the room. She was clearly fuming. 'How dare he think he can treat me like that?' she muttered to herself.

Edward moved his eyes slowly back to the holograms while appreciating the silence that was engulfing the room. His face was becoming paler as he calmed down. All three faces were staring at him from the screens in silence.

'Sorry about that. Okay, where are we now?' Edward was trying to recall the last piece of conversation. Then he remembered. 'Okay, Rachel, what you said to someone, do you mean someone like China with new technology that we're not aware of?'

Rachel shuffled a few papers on her desk and looked hard at Edward and decided to ignore his line of questioning.

'I'd better put you straight and cut to the point. Listen to me for a few minutes, and I'll try to explain everything in a nutshell. For a start, we did receive the full readings prior to the end when the transmission ceased. So from there, we were able to scrutinise everything about it, including the strength, timings, and so on, and also did the follow-up tests on our *Voyager 2*'.

'What sort of testing?' Edward chipped in. He was clearly impatient.

Rachel paused briefly and continued to ignore him.

'For the last few months, we've been trying to find evidence to confirm if the *Voyager 1* is still out there as a physical presence. We were able to fire a mixture of short bursts of laser and radio beams directly at the region where we knew the last known position of the *Voyager 1*. We knew the *Voyager 1* was without any reserve of power and not in any position to acknowledge our instructions. However, we felt we could rely on the large antenna dish to reflect our laser beams back to us. I recognised the probability or the possibilities of it being dislocated and that it may not have been pointing directly at us. But we were pretty sure that the reflective surface should be sufficient to bounce back our highly intensified and narrow wavelength beams. We have been able to carry out this testing successfully and can confirm *Voyager 1* is no longer out there in any physical sense. Zero, zilch—that is our definitive verdict. So based on these findings, our conclusion has to be either (a) a rogue meteoric rock has crossed into the *Voyager 1*'s flight path and smashed it into oblivion or (b) something has managed to discharge something artificially at it to blast it out of existence . . .' Rachel paused and looked up at Edward. 'PURPOSELY!' Her voice showed emotion at the end.

Edward stared at her in silence for a moment. 'You still haven't answered my second question—was it still possibly Earth-based destruction, possibly China?'

He seemed to have a preoccupation with China and their abilities and technical objectives. It was universally known that by the year 2025, China had not only managed to surpass America as the world's premier economic powerhouse, but it had also become the largest investor in high-end technology and had gone on to become the world's most highly advanced source in the development of rockets. They had also gone on to create not one, but *two* main spaceports capable of launching interplanetary rockets.

Rachel continued, 'We all know already that to create such an immensely powerful laser gun, having destructive power over huge distances, it would take an enormous and almost unimaginable amount of power to be generated to supply it. We simply don't have this technology at this moment. If China has managed to produce such advanced power systems, have we any evidence yet? If they do, we know they're usually quite hostile to everyone, including us, but they have no reason to be so hostile by destroying the *Voyager 1* as it would serve them no purpose at all. So here, we'll ask Dean to fill us in with his views'.

Rachel put her paper down and looked across to the other hologram on her right. 'Believe me, Dean has some really interesting angles for you to consider!' She was showing some non-professional excitement.

'Thanks, Rachel. Okay, here we go'. Dean took his bifocal glasses off and started to wave them about as if he was using them as a classical music conductor. He exhaled slowly. 'Righto, let's start with the anatomy of the *Voyager*. I don't need to remind you all that we already know very well that one of the sensors still operating was the low-energy charged instrument, and its main function was to measure the differential in particle fluxes and angular distribution of ions, electrons, and the differential in energy ion composition . . .,' Dean continued as if a teacher in a classroom trying to educate the people. 'As we already know, the main purpose of this experiment was to study energy particles in planetary and interplanetary environments'.

'We all already know all that very well', Edward chipped in, irritation showing in his voice. 'We know that the characteristics of ion particles can be found with laser beams, so what, and what is your point?'

Dean gestured with his glasses to Edward.

'Okay, let me ask you, where about on the *Voyager* 1 was it sited?'

'Of course, it was situated behind the sun shield on—'

Edward was about to finish the sentence but was interrupted abruptly by Dean. 'EXACTLY!' he exclaimed excitedly, while he thrust with his glasses as if they were a sword, making a final killing thrust at Edward. 'It was shielded by the sun. Therefore, there is no way in any position to detect any laser beam coming from this end. Therefore, it is safe to say no one on this Earth would have been able to blind it. Let's eliminate all ideas of deliberate malicious intent emanating from our planet, anyone from this Earth'. Dean waved his glasses in a theatrical attitude, making a closing gesture.

Edward stared at him.

'I get it. You are saying that we got our readings from . . . where?'

At first, his eyes narrowed in puzzlement and suddenly opened widely as the penny dropped.

'Are you saying some source of *artificial intelligence* is the source culprit? Please don't tell me it's the extraterrestrials—no way! We need more scientific evidence to back this crazy theory!'

Dean looked back steadfastly at his famous inquisitor.

'I seriously *do* think there's more evidence for this . . .' Dean responded calmly. 'Our speculation is—and you should listen to what I am going to tell you. Brace yourself for this! I'm not really interested in the contents of the readings. It's the *timing* of the readings that intrigues me the most. According to our analysis, there was a burst of four readings at intervals of exactly 3 minutes 33 seconds to the last one-thousandth of a second. The duration of the spike of readings lasted exactly 10 seconds again to the last one-thousandth of a second. The fourth one, we assumed, was with destructive strength. Presumably, it was the last one when the communication link had been severed so abruptly. The timing has to be none other than *artificially* fabricated. Only extraterrestrials or whatever it is with high natural intelligence have the means to create the timing so *artificially*. This is the only conclusion we can come up with'.

Dean threw his glasses down on his desk and triumphantly lifted his hands like a boxer as if he had finally won the bout.

Edward said nothing but stared at the screen in silence. The hairs on his neck started to stand on end, and goose pimples were forming slowly on his arms as he started to ingest the incredible information. *Gee. Stone me. Can't be. Jeez. Extraterrestrials? Wow. What are we going to do about it? How well are we prepared for it? How and how much do we broadcast this theory? Can we dare tell the world about it?* His mind was spinning, and with sheer excitement, his heart started to beat at a higher rate, and he started to lose consciousness.

The life-support machine detected it and started to beep out warning sounds, which shook Edward out of his stupefied state, and he mumbled incomprehensibly for a moment. 'Eddy! Are you okay?' Stevie's voice boomed out, prompting Edward to try to regain his composure once again.

The sound alerts from the monitors had quietened down in response to Edward's heartbeat, which had gradually started to slow.

The doctor burst into the room with a worried expression on his face.

'Edward, what the hell is happening to you?' His voice was calm as he took control of the situation.

'I'm fine!' Edward lifted his hand to him. 'No need to be concerned. As usual, it's just my emotions getting slightly the better of me. How silly to overreact! Honestly, I'm okay now. Just leave me alone as I must continue the conversation with them'. He pointed at the holograms. He looked pleadingly at his doctor.

'Doctor Carter, I understand your concerns and forgive me for being so awkward with you earlier, no excuse for it, but can I implore you to give me a little more time with them? I'm exploring the biggest scientific breakthrough in my life! Not joking!'

Doctor Carter replied very firmly, 'You should have known better. I did warn you to take things really easy and not get so wound up!' He walked to one end of the room and pulled a chair up and dragged it across the room to a spot near the bed but out of Edward's sight. 'I am going to get someone to be with you all the time, just in case'.

Edward sighed. 'Sure, you have my word. I'll do my best'.

'Then go ahead', Doctor Carter said firmly.

'Thanks again, Doc!'

He turned to look at the holograms again and waited for someone to break the silence. It was Stevie's turn with an opening remark.

'Okay, Edward, so now we know what we're faced with, it's a completely new ballgame. I mean this type of information is completely new to us, and now we're in totally uncharted territory with unfamiliar facts, and we're not sure how to deal with it all'.

He started to rock his chair slowly to match his deep thinking and reflective mood. 'Let's start with the possibility that there are either some extraterrestrials out there or something we feel is out there but are not sure what. Then the question is, how and, above all, what are we going to do about it? Only if it ever makes its presence known to us one day, anytime from now up to a few years, maybe it will never actually come anywhere near us, never mind communicating'.

Rachel responded, 'Especially if they are some life forms travelling in a kind of machine with an independent source of propulsion, whatever the type. All of which are completely unknown factors to us at this stage'.

'Yes, we're still not sure about most of these factors, but let's hypothesise. Suppose it does arrive here, then the question remains, how friendly or hostile is it?' Stevie shook his head slowly. 'Remember, years ago, in 2010, Prof Stephen Hawking warned us against contact with aliens. It is biologically feasible that any living species with a superior physique or has a vastly greater intelligence will always triumph over the weaker species simply for the reason of their survival alone. I'm afraid I must agree with him, no matter how ugly the truth may be. He also hypothesised that aliens with superior intelligence might simply raid Earth for resources then move on'.

Stevie stopped rocking his chair and turned to face Edward's image. He was about to continue when the red-haired nurse reappeared. Doctor Carter looked at her and stood up, gesturing to her vacant chair while he remained standing nearby. 'Sophie, please sit here and watch our patient with care and make sure he behaves himself—absolutely no excitement'. He then instructed her about the medical procedures she needed to take in case of emergency.

'Okay, Edward, you're still in safe hands, but sorry I've got to go as I've got another patient to see'. He left in a hurry.

Sophie folded her arms and said nothing. Her eyes were cold, and with a grim face, she was watching Edward, expecting him to apologise to her for his earlier discourtesy. Edward said nothing and ignored her. Sophie's face reddened even more as she was fuming at Edward's lack of response, and she continued to watch him in silence.

'Nope! I don't think the world is ready for that. Can you imagine the massive uproar from around the world that this will provoke in response to this'—Stevie waved his hand—'controversial news as a truly global threat? They will go out flapping around like headless chickens. China may even decide to take its own drastic measures or whatever it will be entirely in its own self-interests, which would be guaranteed to be inimical to anyone else's. Anything is possible. This nightmare will prevail for many months until God knows when'.

'I'm afraid to say from my observations that its intention is simply hostile. What other reason did it have to annihilate the *Voyager 1*?' Dean shook his head.

'Tell me, is your considered professional opinion that whatever is out there is hostile?' muttered Edward but loud enough for others to hear.

He looked so desperately crestfallen. He couldn't fathom why anyone needs to be so hostile to have his favourite toy destroyed for no reason. It served no purpose.

'I don't think we can ever be safe and ready for them, not even with our defensive missile capabilities', said Stevie. 'We simply don't know what type of technology they have up their sleeves'.

'If you said the world is not ready for this, then perhaps it would be best we all said nothing and pray it won't ever . . .,' said Edward, wringing his hands. 'Oh my god, I don't know what to say anymore'. He was dreading to say the words 'THEY arrived here', but the team all understood the implications.

'Look, Edward, I agree with you that it may be best that we say nothing about it. We simply can't afford to have large dollops of egg on our collective faces should we decide to publish our findings to the world, only to find out our conclusion wasn't right! We'll be accused of being scaremongers! It would have a terrible impact on our international reputation—that's my job to preserve and to look after the reputations of you scientists!' Stevie tried to inject some tranquillity into the debate.

'In that case, we'd better keep this sensitive information absolutely secure amongst ourselves until we know a hell of a lot more scientific facts to support our theories and will be in a better position as to when to inform the world', suggested Dean. 'I mean, until we are able to obtain any other contra facts as all we scientists are obliged to do'.

Stevie was carefully watching Sophie out of the corner of his eye. He was wondering what she was making of this highly sensitive debate. Edward remained impassive and composed for a minute before he broke the silence.

'Righto, the way I see it, it's in our best interest to say nothing. Speculation is not science!' He looked at them. 'Unstained facts are speculative. We know our primary job is to keep verifying the information until we reach the stage when our opinions are irrefutable. Can I have your word—nothing has been or will be spoken about all this outside this room?'

Edward looked at each screen in turn.

'No question about it, you have my word', Stevie responded immediately, Dean and Rachel echoing their agreements.

'Let me give you a further bit of warning advice', Stevie said. 'I know from a long-standing friend of mine, Brett Fielding, who is a reporter on the Las Vegas newspapers, that he has a nose on this subject already. He was at the Hilton Hotel and hasn't let go of me, kept pestering me for any further information about the strange incident he saw at the hotel. I've kept putting him off, saying he'll be the first to know when we get any interesting new developments. He's a true journalist who will be just like a dog after a bone if he scents a story. He won't let it go until he gets something he wants. Let me ask you, in the light of our discussions, how can I put him off any further? Your suggestions?'

'Throw him another bone!' Edward chuckled. 'Well, tell him something like the readings from the *Voyager 1* are still incomprehensible and have not been validated. We decided not to proceed with any further research, matter closed. So just tell him to fuck off. But politely, of course!'

'Got it, and I feel you are right, but I know he's really smart, and it won't be easy to fob him off, but I'll do my best. Leave it to me, and I'll deal with him as soon as I can', Stevie said without a great deal of conviction.

Edward was physically wilting and drew the proceedings to a close.

'Okay, let's wrap up now, and we'll all go home and sleep on it or forget about it for the time being'. He shrugged.

He picked up the remote control and pointed at the holograms. 'Sorry, I'm bloody tired, so bye for now. Over and out'.

They waved briefly to him.

All three holograms faded out. Edward sighed with an appreciation of being left in peace once again. As he sank back into his pillows, he sensed there was another person still present. It was Sophie, still sitting impassively in the chair. *Oh hell, how much does she know about all this?* He thought.

'Good, can I take your temperature now?' She moved over to him as if she hadn't noticed anything. She gently pushed an electronic thermometer into Edward's right ear and left it in there momentarily before taking it out to read. She said nothing as the readings had been constantly and instantly transmitted automatically to the computer.

Edward was still eyeing her suspiciously but said nothing as he was not sure of how to deal with her. He was clearly not comfortable in her manner. Her facial expression was far from showing a caring attitude as would have been expected from any of the staff in this highly reputed hospital. *She is so bloody temperamental. Okay, I'll just pretend total fatigue.*

Just then the relief nurse entered his room and nodded to Sophie, who pulled the chair back to its rightful place, saying nothing, and then went to the door and stopped there and turned around looking at Edward. Her head tilted momentarily as if she was trying to induce him to say that something like an apology would be in order. Edward's mouth was still shut tightly and said nothing. Her eyes opened wider, glaring at him, realising he was still not going to say anything. She muttered an inaudible invective under breath and, exasperated, walked out with her head held high in silent fury.

Edward turned his head and tried to snuggle into a more comfortable spot in the pillow. 'Bloody woman!' he sighed.

He closed his eyes to try and sleep, but he couldn't. His mind was still reeling around about the mind-blowing dialogue of that discussion: *Voyager 1*. Extraterrestrials. Hostile. Friendly. Technology differential. Propulsion differential. Time of arrival. Leg missing. In that order.

Finally, he drifted into a deep sleep.

* * *

Some hours later, Sophie walked into the nurses' mess room and sat in one corner, where a screen hung on a wall. She looked around carefully and was satisfied that the room was empty. She waited a moment, trying to compose herself, then used her voice switch. 'Access computer ID Sophie Moore, password Moore-zero-two-four-six'.

The screen flickered into life. *'Access granted',* the computer's synthesised voice responded.

'Computer, search person and phone directory'.

'Acknowledged. Name of contact'.

Sophie paused for a few seconds as she was trying to reflect on what she was doing. Was she doing the right thing? She was not very self-confident when dealing with technical matters beyond medical issues. She felt she could be drawn into a path of confrontation that she wanted to avoid if possible. At the same time, she felt strong and compelled to stand by her principles. *People need to be treated with respect, no matter who they are,* she thought while shaking her head.

She took off her nurse's white cap, and with two hands, she ruffled her red hair, briskly trying to psych herself up. She couldn't bring herself to use her voice to utter the name, not comfortable with it. She pressed a button on the computer control pad, and it projected a hologram of a keyboard on the desk. She inhaled deeply and started to type in details and looked up expectantly at the screen.

'Details recorded', acknowledged the computer. *'Search completed. Person available. Video connection ready for use'.*

She froze. *What the hell am I doing?* She thought. She waited for a full minute, trying to pluck up the courage.

No movement, her eyes were still locked on the screen, reflecting, deeply in thought, and she was still undecided what to do.

'Awaiting response', the computer prompted.

'Oh, fuck it!' She finally decided to press on. 'Connect'. Her voice betrays her anxiety.

A new image came on screen with a background of a large leathery chair next to a large window. The chair swivelled around with a man sitting back in a relaxed manner. His face moved closer to the screen and said, 'Hello. You're reaching *Las Vegas Sun*. I'm Brett Fielding. How can I help you?'

Silence. She was not sure of how to start the conversation.

He shifted his eyes briefly to the side of his screen where the connection detail was displayed. 'I can see you're a nurse calling from Spring Valley Hospital. So how can I help you?'

Silence.

'I know Edward Stone is there at your hospital, having an operation, so I do hope you are not calling me with bad news. I hope he's okay?'

His voice was soothing and encouraging. He was an experienced professional who had years of practice getting witnesses to relax.

'So what's the problem? And I can see the name on your badge is Sophie. Is that right?'

'Yes. I have some interesting information to tell you. It is about the *Voyager 1*'. Now that she had started, she felt her self-confidence rising.

Brett's curiosity immediately rose, and he smiled encouragingly. '*Voyager 1*? I have had a long and close interest in its remarkable saga and will be extremely interested in any new developments. You can be sure that I always maintain extremely tight-lipped confidence about the sources of my information', he said encouragingly. This bolstered her self-confidence enormously, and he could see that she was relaxing.

'No, that's okay. I can understand how difficult and intimidating an experience it can be for anyone like you to talk about something that might be technical or maybe tricky in some other way. Take it easy. How about I meet you somewhere, and we could chat over some lunch in a relaxing environment, and from there, you'll feel more relaxed and be yourself? The pace of our conversation will be only yours to decide. How about that?'

His imaginative fishing rod was out there with the bait on the hook.

She started to have second thoughts divulging something she had sensed was of such enormous importance to Edward and his colleagues.

'I feel so traitorous', her voice quavered.

Brett sensed the fish was swimming away from his bait.

'Sophie, I can see you're a woman of principle, but don't you think the world is entitled to know the facts that may be of vital importance to us all? Maybe if we have a chat, I can help you decide the best track? Two heads are better than one'.

She nodded.

'A benefit to humanity'. The bait was still floating enticingly.

'Oh well'. She warmed up to the idea of being the protector of humanity. 'Okay, I'll meet you tomorrow morning as it's my day off. Say 12 o'clock?'

'Perfect. Do you like coffee? Really good one? How about at my office?'

She nodded.

'I promise you, you won't regret it'. He smiled gleefully.

He gave her the details of his office.

His bait had been taken successfully.

Chapter 4

18 May 2026

Office of *Las Vegas Sun* Newspaper

Brett was rocking in his chair with his feet resting on the edge of his desk. He was looking out of the window but was not paying any attention to any movement going on outside. He was holding the remote control in one hand and a newspaper in the other. He was deep in thought about the meeting he had with the nurse Sophie several weeks before. He shifted his attention back to an obituary column in the day's newspaper and focussed on a large photo of Edward Stone, which was splashed across half a page. It was an old photo of him, looking so much younger in his heydays, when the *Voyagers* were launched from Cape Kennedy in the 1970s. The heading blazed across the page: 'Goodbye, Eddie, But His Legacy Lives On'.

Damn, he thought, *what rotten timing. I was hoping he would recover sufficiently for me to continue my research for my full feature story about the ill-fated* Voyager 1. *It's telling us Edward is now out of the picture, but I've got to deal with Stevie. He's proved to be a tough nut to crack. There must be another source of information that I could use, but where?* He sighed.

'Hal, please reopen the video file dated 22 April 2026, time 10:00 a.m.', he commanded while looking at his large monitor screen positioned on the wall opposite him. He had nicknamed the computer affectionately after the classic film *2001: A Space Odyssey*.

'Noted. Third time today. Length of video is 33 minutes', the synthesised voice responded.

The requested video appeared on the monitor, showing a full view of his office room with a woman sitting upright on a small sofa with her hands clasping her knees tightly. In the same view, Brett could be seen sitting on another chair at the far side of the room opposite her, drinking coffee. Sophie was clearly in an uncomfortable posture and very agitated, her eyes darting all over the place, regarding her surroundings suspiciously.

'Relax, Sophie, and enjoy your coffee. I know you must be feeling very much out of your depth to describe what happened at the hospital, but remember, I'm here to help you every way to give a full and accurate picture. I do share your passion for the truth'. He was desperately trying to rein in his impatience.

'Yes, thanks, Brett, but I am trying to remember . . . erm . . . seems rather vague, and I think it's rather too technical for me to understand and explain what's really happened'.

'That is very understandable, and I can help you out on this, but just take your time, one step at a time. Start from the beginning. Did you manage to hear what they're saying, and . . .?' Brett was trying a soothing counsellor-style approach with her.

'Well, okay, for a start, I know they were talking about the problem with their satellite'.

'For the record, who are these people?' Brett enquired.

Sophie looked at him, clearly rattled. 'Record? I thought this meeting was strictly off the record'. She looked around the room as if she was trying to find a camera.

'Please, let me assure you your anonymity is strictly enforced, and the only people who are following our conversation are the chief editor and me'. Brett pointed at a monitor and then himself. 'It's a lot quicker this way for him to follow our conversation live, without the need for me to repeat it all over again. Remember, you've got the Anonymity Act on your side, which means no one will ever know the source of this information, and that will ensure your identity is not divulged without your personal approval, and above all, your career is safeguarded'.

Brett deliberately kept his manner overtly relaxed and maintained his professional counsellor-style approach.

Sophie sighed. 'Okay, I think it was Prof Dean Carter and Dr Rachel White and the other one . . .' She frowned and tried to recollect the other name.

'Stevie?' Brett prompted her.

'Ah yes, him and, of course, Edward on his bed'. Sophie visibly relaxed as she started to get into her stride.

'That's a great start, Sophie. Please do carry on'.

'I think they were discussing how their satellite had been destroyed and wanted to know who the culprit was . . .'

'Which satellite?'

'I believe it's called *Voyager 1* . . . ?' She looked at him, seeking reassurance.

'I'd be pretty sure that you are absolutely right', he said. 'And you're doing great. Please carry on . . .'

Sophie paused for a fleeting moment to try and collect her thoughts and continued, 'They were concerned that the *Voyager 1* had been destroyed physically . . .'

Brett leant forward in his chair.

'What do you mean *physically*? As if it isn't there anymore?' he questioned her. 'How could it have been destroyed? By what?'

'Yes, that is what they were saying and possibly by someone on Earth and something about a laser beam . . .'

'Hang on, *someone* from this Earth? Like who?'

'Oh, he mentioned China . . .'

'CHINA?' Brett couldn't suppress his bewilderment. 'How could they come to that conclusion?'

'But I didn't stay on longer to hear the rest of the conversation'. Sophie looked down. 'I had to leave the room on Edward's imposition. He was downright rude, and I didn't like it'.

Brett was exasperated, but Sophie failed to detect it.

'But are you sure they said China, not some other country?' Brett groaned mentally, disappointment showing from his hunched shoulders. 'Something so unique that it wouldn't be confined to this Earth . . .,' he offered, but again, Sophie failed to pick up his line of questioning.

She looked up with her face brightening as if she wanted to make it known she was not out of the loop.

'But luckily, I got back into the room sometime later to catch up with their conversation', she spoke a bit more enthusiastically.

Brett reacted as if he was given another lifeline. 'Oh great . . . so well?' he coaxed her.

'Yes, they don't really know how to deal with the whole situation and what steps to take for analysing the threat, if any, and to what extent there is a threat to impact on the world . . .'

'Are you still meaning China?' Inwardly, he was conjecturing, *Why on earth should they intend to do that?*

Mentally, he was debating with himself, *How and what could the Chinese gain? It does not make sense to me . . . especially the power resource and the immense logistical strategy of planning go into it?* Brett's head tilted askance.

Sophie's eyes sparkled a bit. 'Oh yes, I think they believe China may have come up with a new piece of technology that we are not aware of and maybe they wanted to test it out on this piece of junk, knowing we were not going to use it anymore . . . Yes, I do recall them saying something like that'.

Brett said nothing and studied her. He was unsure where to steer her as he felt his confidence in her recall abilities was starting to deteriorate.

He finally shook his head. 'I know China is technically a closed country, but this is quite far-fetched, and if this account is correct, then it would be indeed difficult, or even impossible, for me to make any enquiries with them directly'.

'Why not? Isn't that your job?' Sophie looked at him innocently.

'Oh, come on, Sophie, I can't call them, saying, "From a reliable but confidential source, I believe you were testing a new technology that is capable of destroying a satellite called *Voyager 1* . . .?"' Brett looked at her and waved his hand. 'I need credible evidence to follow up, and it is very unfortunate you left the room in the midst of that crucial conversation', he said.

'It's not my fault! At least I'm doing my best to piece everything together . . .,' Sophie said and stood up.

'Yes, I admire your efforts, but still, there are some pieces of the jigsaw missing', countered Brett.

'Have it your way, I can't help you anymore'. She tossed her head at him and walked towards the door. 'I'll see myself out'.

At this point, Brett clicked his remote control at the monitor, and the video footage froze. He pulled a device from his shirt pocket and spoke into it. It was a voice recorder that he used as a notebook. 'Problem noted here. A window of opportunity missed. When? Need to find another source of info to fill in this gap. Only three people know about it, and they are Prof Dean Winkelman, Dr Rachel White, and Stevie Ford. At this stage, they are still uncooperative with me for some reason. I am not sure why. Probably at Edward's instruction, I suspect. Need something credible to convince them into divulging the full picture'. He paused to consider his options before resuming.

However, the situation of impossibility had prevented him from reaching that option. He continued doggedly in search of a breakthrough on the *Voyager* project. He continued in search of it by pestering Stevie Ford repeatedly and anyone he could contact at JPL.

Unbeknownst to him, it was not until two years later when he was given a breakthrough with a rare once-in-a-lifetime opportunity.

Two Years Later

Chapter 5

Origins Of The Unidentified Starship

The starship was being towed behind two other identical vessels. Of particular interest is the area located inside the outer rim of the secondary cylinder. Structurally, the exterior of floors and walls reflected light with a curious mixture of transparency and opaqueness. Soft colours of varying strengths could be seen permeating through them. The joint ends between the walls and floors were curved and blended as if they were in one piece of material. All data and information were being transmitted and flowed continuously throughout the walls and floors as if encased with thousands of glass-fibre cables using nanotechnology of some kind. Since there was enough light passing through the walls, it removed the need to attach any additional lighting or power outlets. Aesthetically, the initial impression of the inner areas was stark and minimalistic and utterly devoid of any basic trappings and utensils that are taken for granted as part of Earth's human impediment.

There was some observable movement by carbon-based organic creatures that were not related to anything known on Earth. The six individuals were sauntering about, clearly controlling or adjusting the various instruments mounted on pedestals projected from various directions.

Their physical structure was anatomically curious from an earthly perspective. For a start, each had four limbs spreading out evenly on the base and were attached to a form of the abdomen with another anatomical section, presumably a thorax, positioned on top of it with an additional pair of limbs attached symmetrically to it. Such six-limbed insect equivalents on Earth would be known as hexapods. The height of the extraterrestrial bodies was twice that of the average mature human, though whether there were any juveniles on the craft was not observable. The body and limbs were in the form of exoskeletons, somewhat like various insects on Earth. From an evolutionary point of view, insects on land and crustaceans in the sea, apart from dinosaurs, were probably the most successful creatures ever to thrive on Earth. The anatomical physique of the extraterrestrials, therefore, seemed to be broadly similar in concept to insects being the 'six-legged' creatures.

To compensate for the effect of the immensely strong gravity they had created artificially by their cylinder spinning at high speed inside the starship, their exoskeletons were thick and dense of an unknown organic substance. The evolution of their limbs had been required to give extra support to their heavily built physique by spreading their weight out evenly on the flooring. In addition, at the end of each pair of slender but flexible limbs, there were four 'fingers' with two opposable sensitive thumbs. They were very efficient at gripping any object delicately. The defining trait or the hallmark of intelligence that separates man from most of the animals on earth is an opposable thumb. This had enabled their dexterity, guided by an astonishing parallel growth of humankind's intelligence, to create the highly sophisticated technological society on Earth.

The atmosphere inside the starship had to be matched identically to their original planet. It consisted mainly of methane and nitrogen, but small traces of oxygen could be found. On Earth, any creature would find it totally inhospitable to live under such hostile conditions; not to these extraterrestrial creatures, however. They processed methane-eating microbes that lined their 'lungs'. The sole function of these organisms was to convert methane into oxygen, which was consumed by the host for metabolic purposes. Similar conditions could be found with an oxygen-producing bacterium, provisionally named **Methylomirabilis Oxymora**, *which thrived on Earth in a layer of methane-rich but oxygen-poor muds. Instead of retaining some kind of 'breathing' mechanism, as seen almost universally with creatures on Earth, these extraterrestrial creatures did not 'breathe' but had to suck in the gas through several holes located symmetrically along the sides of their thoraxes. The shapes and characteristics of these holes were very much akin to whales' blowholes, especially when they opened to suck in gases and closed at intervals long enough for microbes to 'ferment' the gas into oxygen sufficient for the host's consumption. It was a classic example of symbiosis in practice. Once they had used up the oxygen through metabolism, some traces of carbon dioxide, along with a lesser volume of oxygen, were breathed out in a short puff.*

However, evolution has not been favourable to them in one respect as it has deprived them of the necessity for any sound-creation organs to evolve in conjunction with the breathing mechanism. Like most insects on Earth, they did not process any hearing senses for the obvious reason they lacked any sound-generating organs. The creatures did emit low-pitched hisses as a consequence of the gas inhalation.

However, in compensation for lacking the ability to detect sound, they were graced with two pairs of extremely sensitive compound eyes, which were situated in front and back of a bulbous but movable head on top of their main thorax. Because they were buried and sunken into the head, they couldn't turn on their sockets. To compensate for this, they had a short but very flexible neck and could rotate their heads 180 degrees. Like the huntsman spiders on Earth, they were able to maintain a breathtaking full 360-degree field of view.

Since they were living in a world where the quality of light was vital for unimpeachable communication, their eyes were exceptionally well developed to be sensitive to the broadest spectrum of light. In human eyes, there are only three photoreceptors: red, green, and blue. Colour vision is, therefore, good compared to dogs, which have only two photoreceptors, green and blue, but is nothing compared to many birds that have four photoreceptors: ultraviolet (UV) as well as red, green, and blue. However, compared to these creatures, butterflies had gone further with five photoreceptors, providing them with UV vision and an enhanced ability to distinguish between two similar colours. Only the vision of mantis shrimp, which are the tiny colourful badasses of the sea on Earth, put everything else to shame. These marine crustaceans may be well known for their record-breaking punch, but they also hold the world record for the most complex visual system. They had up to 16 photoreceptors and could see UV, visible and polarised light. In fact, they were the only animals known to detect circularly polarised light, which was when the wave component of light rotates in a circular motion.

However, these extraterrestrials in spaceships possessed no less than 20 unique photoreceptors, which had been evolved specifically to detect light from 300 to 720 nm, which begins in near-infrared, spans our entire visible spectrum, and tapers off in ultraviolet; infrared as the source of radiant heat emitted by any living creatures. Their eyes were darting about and focussing all the images conveyed to them. Their eyes had evolved especially for many biological reasons but for one or two special purposes: communication and possible identification.

The exterior of their anatomy was extraordinarily colourful but varied in subtle shades from individual to individual as a means of identification. In addition to this, there were about a hundred small bulbous spots scattered evenly over the 'chest' part of the anatomy. They were dancing, alive with yellowish green lights caused by a type of chemical reaction called bioluminescence, which is commonly found in fireflies or glow worms back on Earth. Various shades of colour could be exhibited, ranging from pure white to deep reddish, depending on their tone of language and mood to convey. Simultaneously, the spots of intense lights on their chests were flickering and flashing as they were dancing musically alive with bioluminescence operating monotonically, like computer bits in an 'on and off' manner. The continuous sparkle was as though they were dancing continuously and were communicating to one another in some form of light language incomprehensible to humans.

There were only six of the crew in a group that was mobile. They were the skeleton team selected from a thousand colleagues to man the starship. The other thousand colleagues were frozen in liquid nitrogen, which was maintained at a temperature of -200 degrees Celsius, and they occupied a stasis domain deep in the starship. Similar configurations existed on the other two accompanying vessels. Anatomically, they could be compared to mountain stone weta, which can be found in the hills and mountains of New Zealand. This was what made them unique to the fact that when the other species of animals were frozen, the water in their bodies froze and formed ice crystals. These expand and rupture cell walls. This damage to the tissue eventually causes massive internal trauma and death. In the case of the mountain stone weta, the water in their body doesn't crystallise. Insects don't have blood like mammals, but what they do have is a fluid called haemolymph, which acts in a similar way to blood. This is a substance that acts like antifreeze, preventing the ice crystals from forming. When, for example, the weta finds itself encased in ice, it goes into a state of suspended animation, where virtually all its life functions diminish to the extent that life is virtually undetectable and the weta appears to be dead.

Likewise, these extraterrestrials were fortunate enough to be frozen and kept in stasis for many thousands of years, and when they were to be resuscitated or revived, the liquid nitrogen temperature would be raised to the boiling or evaporation point; they miraculously would come back to life and continue their fully functioning lives.

* * *

The aliens formed a circle facing one another while observing an influx of hologram images projected in the middle of the room. Then they paused. One alien coloured mostly in purple flashed some light signals from its chest to a sensor in front and a new 3D hologram of the universe projected into full view that engulfed the room. They looked as if they were floating inside the 3D images. With their eyes in the front and the back of their heads, with little movement of heads possible, they could see everything. They had practically full 360-degree vision. Thousands of stars, in varying strengths, were projected accurately in their positions like a 3D map. Subsequently, the initial image zoomed quickly into another new hologram but slowed abruptly at last few seconds to a final picture developed with magnificent clarity in full view before them. It was the ghostly image of the Voyager 1.

The purplish alien adjusted another device that made the image zoom up again but with mathematical equations and lines being plotted on the trajectory path of the ill-fated space probe before it dematerialised. Another sensor device was bathed in dancing lights emitted by bulbous spots on its 'chest'. They were calculating the trajectory path of the Voyager- 1. An orangish alien extended one of its 'feelers' and waved at the hologram to move it. Simultaneously, the image shifted, and they were shown a new longer trajectory path trailing in a glowing-neon quality image behind the Voyager 1, and the orangish alien waved at it again. A new image zoomed up repeatedly until they were shown a new image of the solar system. They created further magnified pictures of astonishing clarity to reveal a bluish planet with a faint thin ring around it, which would be recognised by humans on Earth as Neptune.

A greenish alien flicked a wave movement to adjust the gravitational effect by Neptune on the Voyager 1, and a new image projected, showing Uranus. They paused and decided to discard it again, and the greenish alien waved it again, with a new picture showing an image of Saturn and a moment later Jupiter, with the image of a trajectory line projected on a curved path around this giant gaseous planet. Several new pictures flared up sequentially until a final image of a pale blue and white planet appeared before their eyes. They were watching it for several seconds while flashing their bioluminescent signals to one another. They were pausing to digest and analyse something. A bluish alien shifted its focus sequentially around slowly to his colleagues to survey the reaction of its crew. But they stood motionless and expressionless. There was no cause for dispute because of the nature of their mindsets, which were in total conformity. They had been trained to rigid codes and practices. With their level of intelligence shared homogeneously amongst the crew, they knew it was utterly pointless to raise any objection if they knew what their goal was to be. In a nutshell, all their motivation had been programmed into one objective—survival. It was with this reason alone that they took a calculated risk of embarking into this unknown region of the universe, named by humans as 'our solar system', but which had not been part of the Gorgass's original destination and plans.

The bluish alien flashed different colour combinations at a device nearby, and suddenly, the room came alive with a new series of different lights, flashing as an indication that some new 'alarming' activities were taking place.

The last starship in tow behind two other identical ships had detached itself and was slowly drifting apart from them. A moment later, the front umbrella had detached itself to create a space between itself and the fuselage of its 'mother' craft. Finally, the main body started to somersault, front over the rear, slowly. Then it started flying backwards but slowly enough to recouple with the umbrella shield. The propulsion unit was now sited behind the umbrella but attached to a very long thin tubular beam already fixed to the latter. There were plenty of space between these two objects, and in addition, the position of the exhaust jet was angled subtly outward so that the propulsion blast would not have any direct impact on the umbrella. The main body of the ship started to vibrate in response to the new motion being created by the power unit.

The bluish alien observer observed the hologram and seemed to be ignoring a new movement the starship was making. It was drifting slowly away from the other two starships, which were still linked together and moving away in a different direction. They had plotted a new flight path for the lone starship to follow. It was moving towards a very small bluish dot located deep in space, known to humankind as Earth.

The chain of events had gone smoothly and according to the plan. However, the group of three ships being towed by the front ship had taken four Earth years of steady acceleration to reach its optimum speed. Therefore, to be consistent with Newton's law of motion, it would take the same amount of force to decelerate the starship to a suitable speed required to orbit a planet. In theory and mathematically, that should take another four Earth years, but since this ship had already detached itself from the other two ships, it was now only a third of the total mass of the three ships, and this would take around 16 months of deceleration. But as it was going on the wrong trajectory, it was flying off course away from the solar system. It had to adjust its path by another four months of extra thrust.

As long as the journey went well according to plan, it was expected to arrive and in sufficient proximity to the target Earth. The year on the planet was going to be 2028. The event was likely to be of some major significance for the Gorgass—and humankind.

Chapter 6

Observatory, Atacama Desert, North Chile

Sitting at a remote spot high up on a mountaintop located in the north of Chile, on the summit of Cerro Chajnantor, an observatory is sited, equipped with a large and hugely expensive 6.5-metre optical-infrared telescope. There were many reasons for the choice of this remote location. The Atacama Desert is one of driest places in the world. It went without saying that a condition with such low water vapour readings permitted a much improved optical viewing of space. This large optical-infrared telescope was sponsored and constructed in 2009 by the Institute of Astronomy of the University of Tokyo. Though it was still the highest altitude observatory in the world, it was well known that it could not compete with telescopes located in outer space in terms of image quality and clarity. However, this observatory had been improved and upgraded constantly as the latest technology was developed and became available. It was in a perfect position and was utilised extensively whenever it was required by various astronomy communities around the world. Its usefulness could not have been better illustrated than when the fabled James Webb Space Telescope (JWST) was launched in 2021.

It was able to complement and extend the discoveries of the Hubble Space Telescope, which had reached the end of its ten-year mission duration and was no longer able to be maintained to operate effectively. It was because of the position of the JWST, which had been placed much further away from Earth and deep in space, that had exposed its vulnerability to the debris and micro-asteroids that bombarded it so relentlessly.

Eventually, the electronic components of the JWST had taken a direct pounding to a point of rendering it obsolete and inoperable. As a result, the operational era of JWST had drastically been cut short in the year 2024, when a large meteoroid struck it squarely. NASA had undertaken a massive new project with colossal funding to try to create a new space-located telescope, as a replacement of JWST. But before they could proceed, there had been ongoing disputes between governments across various countries trying to justify whether it would be worthwhile replacing it, and whether to undertake another huge project with such an astronomical cost on the grounds of its vulnerability status. It was predicted it would not be ready for use until the later part of the 2050s. Hence, there was consequently an exciting opportunity for the core team of ten people consisting of professional elite astrophysicists of international repute. As the major funding contributor was Japan, they also sent technicians to the Chilean project who worked alongside supporting Chilean engineers, all enthusiastically manning the telescopes at the observatory. They knew how to make the best use of their carefully maintained 'baby'. Astro-scientists around the world used the Chilean facilities frequently from a choice based on the extraordinary reputation that the team had built up. They were all in competition with other observatories around the world, including those the Europeans had also sponsored nearby in Chile. There is another newly installed land-based observatory, the Thirty Metres Observatory, located at Mauna Kea, a dormant volcano on the island of Hawaii, but it is sited at a height significantly lower at 4,200 metres.

The Cerro Chajnantor 'scope' had been the acme on the account of its high location and the quality of its work.

Despite the professional rivalry in existence amongst the premier observatories in several countries, it goes without saying that there was indeed a healthy and mutual respect. They breathed and lived their scientific challenges, but while they all strove to be in the forefront of exploration, they exchanged information with great frequency to have their theories validated by their rivals.

There was, however, a big black cloud over the team based at Cerro Chajnantor, something that had affected their ethos and subsequently created great difficulties in operating the observatory as effectively as the professionals wished. This especially limited their freedom to divulge and share their high-quality data with anyone outside their own operational unit. The real hindrance on their progress came from a squad of soldiers commanded by a lieutenant swarming around the building in the most sensitive areas of technical endeavour. They were, however, mostly just engineers and not scientists, and in consequence, their technical capabilities were very shallow. They sat like vultures watching and reporting any aspects of the work being done, which they considered to be of interest to be transmitted to the government in Santiago.

There had been a coup d'état in Chile some two years beforehand. The timing of the coup could not have been more unfortunate. It was led by a three-man junta, all of whom were religious fanatics. The army chief of staff, Field Marshall Vicente Delgadillo, assumed the office of the president. He and his team were committed to eliminating the old centre-left coalition, with its deep aesthetic philosophies and secular politics. The junta suspended parliament, banned political activities, and severely curbed all civil liberties. Under Vicente's blunt dictatorship, it marked the end of Chile's era as one of South America's most stable and prosperous nations.

For the last 20 years, it had led Latin American nations in human social development and economic competitiveness that ensured a substantial improvement in income per capita with an inbuilt degree of economic freedom. However, this all came with a price. Catholics had been severely repressed following the onslaught of people with ever increasingly liberal views of the world. Vicente—following his strict childhood upbringing under Catholic dogma, which had instilled him with intense abhorrence of freedom of sexual choice enjoyed by gay people, including the new secular movement behind the legalisation of abortion introduced a few years before—was dismayed at the slow progress being made on making the government becoming more secular. He believed the people of Chile needed to be re-educated and exposed to much stricter teachings of the church as the natural way forward for fulfilling and enlightening lives.

Under his iron dictatorship, he had interned several thousands of so-called free-spirited people in 'correctional' camps and introduced religious studies in all forms of schools as compulsory. The dreaded religious police were everywhere to ensure absolute piety from the population. Many thousands of people had disappeared without a trace, and the basic freedoms enjoyed by the people at large were being eroded at an alarming rate. All this was being observed by the Human Rights Watch Commission, an international non-governmental organisation based in several cities around the world but which was seemingly powerless to curb the regime.

Many other organisations looked to the Vatican in vain hope it would throw its weight behind the outcry aimed at the excesses in Chile, formerly a typical Catholic country. However, the Vatican had itself been rocked by ever-growing problems that faced it globally. The biggest of these was the continuing decline in active participation in Christian religious life coupled with the diminishing recruitment for the priesthood and monastic life, as well as an alarming drop in attendance at churches. It had been triggered by a major report from the United Nations, in 2014, had denounced the Vatican over its handling of child abuse and demanded nothing but an immediate action against all the clergy who were known or suspected as being child abusers. Ever since then, the Vatican had been trying to find a way to save face and, of course, their credibility. All had proved so far to be futile. Recommendations included a simple idea of handing over the names of suspected clergy embroiled in abusing children to the police proved to be unacceptable to the hierarchy. *After all, God was to be the source of their moral judgement, not the police.*

Nevertheless, although the Vatican was dismayed at the extreme developments taking place in Chile under Vicente Delgadillo's government, it had decided to keep a low profile on this issue. It had a faint hope that the people would prevail and return to the Mother Church without such severe coercion. As predicted in line with a Gallup Poll survey taken in 2015, the trend would indicate that church attendance would drop to about 50% in 2025, with a strong possibility that Catholicism would become a global minority religion by 2050. The church had ever since been trying to find ways of making itself more appealing to the younger generations for them to re-engage with the Mother Church. This had proved to be completely ineffectual so far because scientifically based contrary arguments were so freely available via the Internet and its vast wealth of thought-provoking information was becoming not only accessible but also ingrained into everyone's lives.

Something short of a miracle could save the beloved church. Or Someone? Or so the Vatican and Delgadillo prayed.

* * *

Buried in the observatory, there was a nerve centre where constant monitoring of various space activities was carried out by a small but dedicated team. An Asian man was sitting at a large desk controlling a large array of computer monitors with varying functions. He looked boyish, but a few streaks of grey hair on his temples gave away his actual mid-40s age. Reading glasses rested on the tip of his nose, but he was looking over them at the latest high-tech monitors. These were made of opaque graphene and supported on ultra-thin motherboards in a semicircle around his desk. All the scientific staff used handheld tablets also made of graphene for communication purposes and had become known as GCs.

The scientist spoke quietly to his computer, which used voice recognition and gave synthesised voice replies.

'Computer, display all variable stars that have altered their light intensity between 38 and 100% bracket in the past seven days'.

He spoke in English but with a strong Asian accent, and his voice was soft. All the computers were programmed to function using English as the primary international language, which had been mandated to link all the science branches globally.

'Precise date and time range required', the computer responded with a typical artificial-sounding response.

'Seven days with a date starting on 23 August 2028 at 1200 hours GMT and ends today at 1200 hours GMT'. He sighed with some irritation. *Bloody computers*, he thought, but he admired it for its thorough attention to the detailed protocol. Fair enough, he forgave it.

'Message acknowledged', the computer chirped.

His job was to pinpoint any brightness fluctuations as observed from Earth. These variations might have been caused by a change in emitted light or by something partly blocking the light, so variable stars were classified as (a) stars that periodically became enlarged and then shrink, (b) stars that have an orbiting companion that sometimes eclipsed it, and finally, (c) any object orbiting the Earth that would have blocked or dimmed the luminosity of stars.

A new image displayed showing the positions of stars that had displayed diminished light. He narrowed his eyes in puzzlement. *What the hell is that?* he thought. 'Computer, display and superimpose on this new image all the existing man-made satellites orbiting in the same region. Then configure the trajectories across all the stars that were obscured'.

His voice was gaining intensity as he became more concerned with confirming his initial observation.

'Message acknowledged'.

New images were thrown up in a quick sequence of patterns flashed across the monitors but then transfigured back to the original image.

'Negative. Unable to comply with your instruction'.

'Computer, outline the reason?'

'Cannot meet your request based on existing satellites information supplied. Suspected rogue satellites of either natural or artificial substance. Need new satellite information input for the elimination process'.

He looked across the room to another Japanese compatriot, sitting with another array of screens like his own.

'Hey, Yoshi, how up to date are you with the latest information on asteroids and man-made satellites?'

Miyuki had switched absentmindedly to the Japanese language; his voice was louder than usual as his interest had been heightened.

Yoshi swung his chair around to face him and replied in the same language but in a slightly louder voice.

'About four weeks old, Miyuki'. He shrugged. 'But I can get it updated to the last few hours if you like'.

'Make it so, please, Yoshi', Miyuki called back. 'As soon as possible, old buddy! Thanks'.

'Okay, coming up'. He looked at his colleague questioningly. 'Wha . . . what's the problem?'

'Something is not looking quite right with these stars. I need to start the process of eliminating the foreign bodies that may be blocking our views of them', Miyuki continued in Japanese.

'Hai', Yoshi responded.

He had a rotund physique and a round face. He sported unkempt hair with an oversized pair of glasses resting on his smallish nose, which contrived to give him an air of a professorial owl.

'Hey! You two! Speak in English! You know the rules', a new voice boomed from the far end of the room.

The two Japanese men swivelled their heads simultaneously at the third man. He was a soldier smartly dressed in full military uniform at a small desk, holding a magazine which he had been reading all day. He was bored out of his skull just sitting and doing nothing. He was longing for some new action to spice up his tedious days. He cherished various ideas of bloody-mindedness to inflict on other people as a source of mental stimulation. If he were to be psychoanalysed for his quirky behaviour, it might indicate an inferiority complex. He was having to monitor these Japanese scientists of considerable intellectual superiority. All he wanted was to make himself feel superior to other people, and with that in mind, he had to display his non-technical authority, presence, and personality.

'You know you cannot speak Spanish, and I cannot speak Japanese. Therefore, it's imperative we all speak English! These are the rules', he snarled.

'Yeah, but don't forget this building is being financed and manned by my country and as well as by other countries. All my staff's first language is Japanese', Miyuki spoke with some irritation. *What a prick he is*, he thought.

'There's no need for your harsh tone and high-handed attitude. You must feel how ridiculous it is for you to try to enforce your petty rules'. Yoshi's voice chipped in pleadingly, pointing his outspread hand at the soldier, trying to find the right words. 'Overzealous petty regulation! How can you think our job of fact-finding can be a security threat to you, never mind your country?'

'Tough luck! For a start, you should be grateful we let you operate this observatory under a full licence granted by our government with a mandatory understanding that you cooperate with us and share all the information. End of story!' The soldier stood up, glaring at them.

Miyuki buried his head in his hands. 'For God's sake, okay, just let us focus on doing our job in peace . . .' He sighed.

He ignored the soldier and swung his chair around and faced the computer monitor. Yoshi did the same and started to work on the computer. Their action in ignoring him had irritated the lieutenant even more. He started to walk around in a circle fuming, unsure of what action to take to rebuke them for lack of respect to his authority. None of his soldiers would have ever done the same to him. Never. Then it dawned on him—the problem with the people operating the observatory were just civilians with no military discipline instilled in them. He started to slow down his restless pacing.

Miyuki's computer signalled that it had downloaded a file transferred from Yoshi's machine.

'Computer, use latest satellites information received coded

S-R-zero-eight-two-six and configure it now with the variable stars'. Miyuki squinted at the monitor for a moment and waited for the computer to proceed with his instruction.

'Cannot meet your request based on existing satellites. Need new satellite information input', the computer intoned.

Miyuki rolled his eyes and sighed. He realised there was a new object that had not been charted before. Something new was orbiting the Earth.

'Computer, delete my previous instruction', Miyuki replied. 'I'm giving a new instruction'.

'Affirmative'.

'Computer, please configure the velocity of the main telescope to the timing of these variable stars and then lock on', Miyuki spoke quietly, but his voice had a much more authoritative tone. 'Then magnify to the distance of 20,000 kilometres from the Earth and then capture the image of that unidentified object'.

He paused for a moment. He knew the telescope's internal weakness that it could not focus anything less than the distance he had given. This was the absolute minimum distance for which it was designed to focus. There was a smaller telescope in the next building that could do the job ideally, but it had not been serviced recently for budgetary reasons.

'Once you have done it, then transfer the image to my main filing storage system under code Z-four-three-two'. He paused. 'Alert me once my instructions have been complied with'.

'Please provide your authorisation code', the computer responded.

'Miyuki-zero-six-eight'.

'Code provided and compiled with acknowledgement'.

He waited again.

'Calculating', the synthetic voice chipped in. *'The task will be completed in 20 minutes and 26 seconds, the time window when the object in question will come into focus'*.

Miyuki leant back in his chair and locked his hands behind his head and started to rock his chair. *Come on and hurry up*, he thought.

He could hear in the background the humming sound, which had signalled the motorised movement of the enormous telescope reconfiguring.

He kept looking at his watch, and then he folded his arms. He fiddled with his pen as the response by the telescope began again a few minutes later. Twenty minutes seemed to be forever. He was an impatient man. Then a new image flashed across his large monitor.

He narrowed his eyes, his head tilted. He tilted his head again at a different angle as he tried to fathom the message that the image appearing was imparting.

'Yoshi! Please come here now and tell me what the hell this is'. His voice was higher-pitched with excitement.

Yoshi slid out of his chair and walked over, doubtful and uncertain of what to expect. He leant over Miyuki's shoulder and eyed the monitor. The fuzzy image of an object started to become clearer.

'Computer, sharpen the resolution to the maximum', Miyuki commanded.

'Acknowledged and processing'.

The strange shape of a cylinder with a large shield shaped like an umbrella loomed out of the murk of space. The eyes of the two Japanese scientists focussed on it in total silence. Their jaws started to drop down slowly, their mouths opening wide. They were totally transfixed. The fine hair on the back of Yoshi's neck stood up, and he was covered with goose pimples. Miyuki's cheeks were slowly draining of colour. The new image on the monitor had them mesmerised, and by then, they had failed to notice a third face appearing in line with their faces.

'Holy Jesus! What is that?'

They were startled and looked sideways at him. It was the soldier with his hands on the edge of their desk.

'Can anyone tell me what that is?' It was more of an instruction rather than a question.

They shook their heads in unison.

'We're not sure! It's a new object that has not been identified in our lists of all man-made satellites. Therefore, it's clearly an . . .' Miyuki looked at the short man. 'Unidentified object'.

'UFO?' The soldier chuckled. 'You're having me on, aren't you?' He was laughing but not for long. His laughter was cut short, and he gulped when he looked at the two Japanese men for their response. They were motionless and expressionless to convey the message they were not joking. He started to quieten down, looking sheepish, and started to take a few steps backwards. *Holy jeez!* he thought.

'How, on earth, did we miss it? How can it have travelled here without us detecting it? Has it been travelling in some sort of a stealth mode?'

Miyuki looked at the soldier and replied, 'We don't really know, but I think it's been travelling behind all the planets and moons in our solar system. That is the only way to avoid being detected by us until now. We still don't even know how long it's been orbiting our Earth. We could estimate it is probably two months or less'.

A long silence followed as no one would admit the serious impact their apparent discovery had on them.

'What are we going to do about it now?' Yoshi broke the silence with a question aimed at Miyuki. 'Can we authenticate our sighting with Thirty Metres at Hawaii?'

'Yoshi, that would be a good idea, perhaps get them to verify our opinions and hopefully reach a consensus of how long it's been with us . . .,' he said, his eyes still transfixed on the monitor. 'And arrange a media meeting to announce to the world our discovery of this object which has an appearance of having been created artificially?' They had unwittingly reverted to Japanese.

They were so engrossed in their discussion they failed to see that the soldier was again walking in circles. He was thinking and reflecting deeply on what steps to take for handling this extraordinary situation for his benefit. *What should I do? This is something significant. Who should I report to? I should be able to bypass my captain. Are we the first to see it? Will Chile be the first country to announce it to the world? What information can we tell them? Ah! Maybe I need to restrict the circulation of this fantastic information until a more appropriate time? Is that likely to get me into difficulties, or could I blame these two Japanese boffins?*

Once his mind was made up, he stopped his restless pacing and looked at the monitor with renewed interest.

'That is it!' he shouted, which made all those present jump.

Somehow it had dawned on him it would be the perfect opportunity to elevate his present status from lieutenant to captain, or even lieutenant colonel, his eyes alight with enthusiasm and eagerness at the prospect of the opportunity of a lifetime. More respect. More pay.

'None of you are to divulge any of this information whatsoever to anyone until I say so!' he thundered at them. 'I'm ordering this information to be totally embargoed for the time being!'

He walked over to his desk and typed the commands into his computer, instructing it to shut down all the Internet links with the outside world, except, of course, his own computer console.

'None of you will go out of this place for a few days!' he commanded and looked at them fiercely.

Miyuki and Yoshi looked at each other, astonished at the idea of imposed isolation or censorship.

'But you don't really know if this unidentified object is authentic and factual, and we need to verify it!' Miyuki replied calmly to the soldier.

He knew the cell phones were useless at this observatory because it was so remote that there were no signal masts erected to convey the signals from their cell phones. They were in the 'black spot', and their only lifeline to the world was through the Internet, which could be transmitted to the satellites via the transmitter dish mounted on the building of the observatory. They were very effectively isolated.

'Look, it's a great opportunity for you to make your name known to the world that it was you who authorised the find-of-the-century to become known . . .' Yoshi tried to reason with him but was cut off by the highly agitated officer, his hands waving wildly as he commanded them to shut up.

'Enough! I know what I am doing!' He took no heed of Yoshi's attempt to rationalise. His mind was focussed on one thing, and that was what to say to the minister located at the government building at Santiago.

The Japanese men slumped heavily into their chairs and buried their faces in their hands, knowing that any compromise or cooperation with the nearly hysterical man would prove to be impossible. What a catastrophe it would be, and there was no need for it, they thought. They exhaled and swivelled their chairs around and started to study the new image of the unidentified object.

* * *

The magnificently ornate room, illuminated by two superb chandeliers, showed its original Spanish origin. A plump, heavily built man was sitting in an impressive leather chair behind a large and imposing 19th-century desk. He was wearing a light greyish-brown uniform with many rows of medals pinned on his chest. He had been watching expressionless the large monitor for the past half an hour or so. There was an image of a junior officer on one half of the screen and on the other, a fuzzy image of an unidentified object. He nodded with his sagging chin, wobbling in response.

'Well done, Lieutenant Rafael. You have done the right thing'. He was speaking in Spanish and kept nodding. 'Most impressive'.

'Thank you, Minister. I felt that these images were so important that they should be for your eyes only. You had top priority to know about them before anyone else'.

'Very much so. Say no more and keep all reference to this matter under absolute top security until my further instruction'. He looked across at the picture on the wall facing him. It was a painting of a man in a full military uniform. 'It could be a few days or weeks or even months before you get any further instruction from me or even President Delgadillo. Are you able to hold this whole subject securely locked down until you hear from me personally?'

Rafael's chest expanded with pride, his chin thrust out. 'Yes, sir, as long as you order'.

'Very well, until then. God bless you'. The image on the screen faded.

The minister looked out of the window and paused for a minute as he was trying to visualise how the world would react to this news of great importance. *Unprecedented in the history of mankind*, he thought. Too much for him to handle it.

There were huge political and religious implications. If so, then perhaps it would be better to discuss the whole situation with President Delgadillo to try and find ways to gain maximum advantage for their benefit.

He pressed a button. A few seconds later, a smartly dressed and shapely woman in high heels opened the door and walked in a brisk manner to the side of the large desk. Her high heels were clicking as she walked across the polished wooden floor. She was carrying a GC in her hand. 'Sir?' Her voice was soft and husky.

'I need a two-hour meeting with President Delgadillo. Absolute top priority. Let him know it is most, I repeat, most imperative and urgent that he needs to see me ASAP. I don't care if he's sleeping or praying, just grab his balls to get his attention. Got it?'

He swivelled his chair around to face the window, ignoring the woman who said two words, 'Lo tengo'. It was Spanish for 'got it'.

Chapter 7

13 May 2028

La Moneda Palace, Santiago, Chile

Palacio de la Moneda, or La Moneda, was the seat of the president of the Republic of Chile. Apart from this, he also had several 'safe' houses littered around the country. La Moneda also housed three major government offices: Ministry of Information, General Secretariat of the Government, and Ministry of Economics. The building itself was indeed impressive. It was built in the year 1784 when pure neoclassical Italian-style and Roman Doric influences were at their height.

There was a splendid chapel located at the far end of one of the wings of the palace. It oozed rich history that could be traced back to the early 19th century. In the pew immediately beneath an imposing gold-plated cross, the president of the Republic of Chile was kneeling, praying. He looked up at the cross and breathed out heavily. His attitude was one of extreme devotion. He was clearly troubled as could be seen from his whole drooping demeanour.

'Please, O Lord, can you give me some guidance as to how I should deal with this attack on our beliefs?' he whispered under his breath.

A priest, seated on a pew further back, was observing the supplicant closely. There were no other people in the chapel. It looked as if it was reserved only for the exclusive use of the man at the foot of the altar, who had just come from a meeting that had dragged on for over two frustrating hours.

He sighed and looked around and saw the priest. Their eyes locked together in a moment until the priest spoke in a soft voice. 'How can I help you?'

The president stood up and walked over to where the priest was and sat next to him.

'Would confession be of some solace for you?' the priest asked.

'No, not really, but I'd like to discuss the problem with you about what I heard at the meeting earlier this afternoon'. This indicated the deference the most powerful man in Chile showed to the holy Roman church.

'Of course, Vicente, take your time'. The priest addressed him by his first name; the familiarity showed a depth of rapport between them. 'For you to be displaying such anguish, you must be feeling extremely worried. Take your time so that we will together obtain the Almighty's blessing and obtain his guidance in making the right decisions'.

'Okay. I've had some unbelievable information brought to my attention, so far-fetched that I find it incomprehensible and don't really know where to start. It's not like me to be indecisive, and I don't know if it's God's sign or what'.

The priest frowned in askance.

'I mean, all the efforts I've made to raise this country's religious profile . . .' He looked at the altar where the cross was. 'Whether it is a signal by God to say he's gratified . . .'

'Or disgusted with you?' The priest finished his sentence.

Vicente pondered for a moment and pulled himself together. He gave a concise summary of what transpired at the meeting he had with the minister of information. He started by giving a concise outline of the observatory's operational objectives. Then he gave a precise report of the troublesome images it had recently obtained.

Following all this, he explained his anxieties as to whether the team in question could be trusted, in the accuracy of their report and their ability to keep the information securely within the confines of their domain. 'How should we deal with the unidentified object? Was this the first or the only observatory to identify the object as being unknown in origin?'

He went into deeper details for 20 minutes with the priest listening and hanging on to every word, punctuated with several minor points for clarification.

When the president had finished, he produced his data-transfer device and showed the images to the priest. The priest studied it carefully before questioning him, 'Are you sure it's not a trick or a hoax?'

'We have no idea of when it had arrived in proximity to our planet, from where, and no idea of its intentions. Was it a fluke or chance or deliberate in its intention to make its presence known to us? Or was it by a stroke of luck we found it?' the head of state questioned.

'The most important question I've been asking myself is, are we to treat it as the Lord's portent of major significance that the Day of Judgement has arrived? Or is it an extraterrestrial that has come in the disguise of Satan to inflict war on mankind? Or is it a blessed sign of a reward to be made to Chile as the Almighty has endorsed the progress we have made in following the one true path of Christianity? So what do you think, Father Martin?'

The priest shifted uncomfortably in his seat and looked at the floor. He did not want to meet the president's zealous eyes. This is mad obsession with God. Even though he was still a priest, he was still uncomfortable with the extreme practices of the president's dictatorial rule. Nevertheless, he pulled out an object from his pocket, which was identical to Vicente's. 'May I? I need to study it before I can offer my opinion'. He offered his own DTD.

The specific images and data were transferred in a few seconds from Vicente's to Martin's device. He folded his arms. He was studying it while trying to buy some time and covering the fact he was at a loss for words. There was total silence in the chapel. President Delgadillo was still looking at the gold cross at the altar while Father Martin was studying the DTD. It went on for 10 minutes before the priest broke the silence. 'Most interesting, and I agree with you, it is indeed the most far-fetched news that ever exploded in the face of all our religious beliefs. We just were not prepared for it. I am at a loss as to what to suggest'. He looked at his watch. 'Vicente, can I ask you bluntly—how much time have you got to reach some sort of solution?'

Vicente shrugged. 'I would be happy to stall for a couple of weeks, but the major risk I foresee is that there may be unauthorised leaks. There would be immense international credit accruing to Chile for our scientific capabilities. But in the whole scheme of things, we must handle the broadcast of the information, sketchy as it is, to minimise the impact on all our and even other religious beliefs. This object says quite clearly to me that humans and our world were not the unique creation of the Creator as we have believed for hundreds of years!'

'Then in that case, perhaps we can ask someone with a far greater understanding as to just how we should proceed . . .?'

'I answer to no one but God!' Delgadillo spat out with eyes blazing. His mind was in turmoil.

'I understand, but this matter has a quite extraordinary potential impact on other religions besides the Catholic Church! I really think that . . . you seek advice from . . .,' Martin spoke with his eyes watching Delgadillo carefully from under lowered eyelids as his voice trailed off into silence.

The president had an explosive temper and turned and faced his Father Confessor; there were deep furrows on his brow. 'Vatican?'

Father Martin nodded.

After a momentary pause as he contemplated his options, and as President Delgadillo looked up at the gold cross, it dawned on him. 'So it is a sign from God to be passed to the Vatican?'

'Why not?' the priest said reassuringly.

Delgadillo stood up and walked slowly to the altar and bowed, turned around, and walked purposefully back towards the main doors. Martin watched him in silence. Delgadillo stopped and looked back at him and nodded. Then he exited.

Father Martin shifted his attention to his DTD, a quick check on the time difference with the Vatican and then a few more touches. He looked at his watch and touched the speed dial button. There was an instant response.

'Hello, Martin. This is Marcello speaking from the Vatican'. The voice speaking Spanish had a strong Italian accent.

'How can I help you? Is everything okay at your end?'

Martin checked around again to confirm there was no one else in the chapel.

'Can you spare half an hour with me, and are you sitting comfortably? I've got something really interesting to tell you, so you'd better brace yourself for it'.

The cat was now out of the bag and on the way to the Vatican.

* * *

Back at the observatory, Miyuki and Yoshi were still watching the monitor closely as they had for the last two days. Their eyes were bloodshot and weary. On Lieutenant Rafael's instruction, they were to keep a close eye on the monitor and report to him any new movement or development made by the unidentified object. The job was proving to be very monotonous and fatiguing for them. They managed to snatch few hours of sleep between them during the shifts with other standby teams, but the many hours of concentrated effort were taking their toll. That was when the small lapse occurred; during which time the unidentified object flew out of the telescope range to the other side of Earth.

Rafael, on the other hand, was looking refreshed and well groomed, and there was a spring in his step as he walked around his desk area. He had created the time for himself because he had delegated the duties to his subordinates. His eyes were still glistening at the idea of a big promotion coming in his way. He was still daydreaming since he spoke with the minister of information. He was oblivious to any actions and movements made by any of his staff as they began to lose concentration.

Miyuki had his elbows on his desk and was resting his head in his hands. 'Come on, what are you doing? Make a move! Surprise us with something!' He kept his thoughts to himself but not for long. A few seconds later, the monitor showed a new image.

His eyes widened—a new movement, a faint image of a small roundish object ejected from the main body, the 'mother ship'. It was a very small object, and anyone could have missed it if they had not watched it dutifully. It was like spotting a football ejecting from a moving juggernaut at a distance of a thousand metres away at night-time. It was a stroke of luck for Miyuki that it had happened while it was during his period of duty. He was careful not to display any overt interest to excite Rafael. He made a discreet hand signal to his colleague. Yoshi walked slowly around and appeared to stop almost by accident at Miyuki's side and leant over him and whispered in his ear, 'Are you seeing what I'm seeing? What is it?'

He had seen something similar on his own monitor and wasn't sure if he was seeing the same thing as Miyuki did.

'Don't know, but I assumed it could be a probe of some kind, launched from the mother craft or whatever', he whispered.

Miyuki looked at him and was about to open his mouth and make an announcement to everyone in the same room. But when he looked furtively at the military observer pacing aimlessly about, he hesitated.

'Sod him', he muttered in Japanese under his breath well away from Rafael's hearing.

Nevertheless, something in the scientist's body language piqued Rafael's interest, and he stopped in his tracks.

'What's up?' he demanded in his usual aggressive manner and looked at them with suspicion. 'Have you seen anything new?'

Silence. Miyuki was still deliberating whether to tell him.

'Well?' Rafael persisted.

'Nope', Miyuki said.

'Really? It is strange that it has been out there for so long. We are watching it, and what is betting it is watching our Earth. How long has it been now?'

'Probably less than a month or so, who knows?' Miyuki shrugged and under his breath, said to himself, 'And who damn well cares?'

'And still no movement?'

Miyuki shook his head.

'Well, keep your eyes open then!' He resumed his restless pacing.

Yoshi looked at Miyuki with a puzzled expression on his face. 'Why can't you tell him we saw a possible movement?' he whispered.

'Well, fuck him!' He muttered a profanity in Japanese. 'He'll be the last person to know it if I have anything to do with it! Don't you get it—even with this recent observation, it's pointless to report it to him? What's the purpose of it when it cannot be reported to the world? Sooner or later, other observatories will find this UFO and make their announcement before we do!' He smirked.

'I see your point. Fair enough. Say no more'. Yoshi moved back to his own desk.

Miyuki's eyes were back to the monitor once again and searched for the mysterious object, but it was nowhere to be seen. It had flown out of the viewing range. *Where the hell is it, and what the hell is it?* he thought. *Is it coming down to Earth? If so, where will it land?* He might even find out by plotting the trajectory of where it went, but he decided not to. He was pinning the hope on wherever it went, it would be discovered by other people before that short man, alias the prick, did.

A mental image appeared of the prick losing face when he heard that other people somewhere in another country had been the first to rock the world with the news. He nodded and warmed to it. Sooner or later, the world would turn their attention to his observatory for confirmation. Rafael would be cornered and forced into opening the Internet link. A nice thought, he smiled. And he felt reassuringly good about it. He looked at the monitor and sighed. *Where are you? Come on, show yourself up and rock the world,* he thought.

*　*　*

The object that was first spotted by the Japanese scientists was shaped like an elongated rugby ball 3 metres long and 2 metres wide, like the size of a smallish car, something like a Fiat 500. It had been ejected out of a hole in the mother ship like a pea-shooter, aimed somewhere in the middle of Africa. Once it entered the atmosphere, it became incandescent. A few seconds later, it extended some air-brake lateral fins. As the speed slowed, it started to tumble.

There were not many advanced radar sites being manned in Africa, so no one had the faintest idea that an object was dropping there. Even though there was a brilliant fireball that would normally have been seen, it was happening during the bright African daylight. The sun had camouflaged it well.

It continued to fall until it was about 100 metres off the ground when the fins metamorphosed into new shapes. A hole had evolved in the middle of each fin. There were three fins in total, one on each side of the main body, while the third one positioned at the very back. They had started to suck the air from above through the holes to create reverse thrust created by an engine of an unknown design. The probe braked a few metres off the ground in the middle of a large flat field of long grasses, creating localised small dust storms and minor damage upon the plant life.

This diminished rapidly, and the probe started to move forward slowly and navigated around the large trees and boulders. The sound it emitted was comparatively quiet but at a very high pitch much like a mosquito humming. A single tube emerged from the top of the main body. It could be assumed it was a kind of antenna for communicating purposes with the mother ship. A bulbous protrusion jutted out underneath the main body. At intervals, it beamed lights of low intensity, and the colour fluctuated from red to intense blue. It was scanning, exploring, investigating, but for what was not known. It hovered towards a thick jungle a short distance ahead and stopped dead in its tracks when a four-legged animal moved across its scanning range. It paused as if it was calculating a possible threat or usefulness. Too small and impractical for use, but for what? It ignored the animal and resumed its motion forward into the jungle. The animal ignored it as it could not smell anything strange, and the noise it emitted was very much like mosquitoes that could be heard in the background everywhere.

The probe inched forward into the jungle, but when it came to a large tree, it stopped and then navigated around several large trees and cruised on more slowly, coming across a small troop 0f more than 20 chimpanzees. These were lounging and feeding around a small grassy clearing. On the outskirts of the patch, a large male chimp sat on its vantage point, on a small patch of soft mosses. A large broken branch lay partly embedded in the mossy ground between the group of chimps and the hovering drone. The immense physical presence of this magnificent ape with his battle-scarred face had indicated that he was the alpha male of the troop. He was cherishing some hard-earned peace after re-establishing his leadership once again after having put several young aspiring males in their places.

He first heard faint humming nearby but decided to dismiss it as it was hardly audible even with its acute hearing. However, soon the sound became more intrusive, and that did alert his instincts. It was the leaves and grass fluttering because of the effect of the localised twists of wind caused by the propulsion and downdraught of the flying object. His curiosity was roused, and he turned his head to identify the source of the noise. His eyes widened as he appraised the possible threat. A flying bird? But it didn't have any flapping wings. He couldn't fathom what the new hovering object was and that it had not been seen before. The battle-scarred chimp felt it was another threat to his position, and he did what he always did—charged at the object, screeching with teeth bared menacingly. Then he beat his large and powerful fists on his chest and brandished the nearby sturdy dead branch in a typically dominant male chimpanzee aggressive behaviour. He was highly agitated, threatened by the strange object hovering several feet off the ground, and instead of showing any fear, he had no choice but to act out his duty as the supreme chimp protecting his troop.

All the other chimps had bolted in every direction, seeking shelter in the bushes, deserting the patch of the field altogether. The alpha male screeched at it again and waved his arms around and started to run after it. As soon as he was near enough, he grabbed a metre long solid billet of a dead branch, and using brute strength from his powerful arm, he swung it around until it smashed into the side of the motionless object still hovering in the air. With a solid thud, it impacted on the hovering device, inflicting a minor dent to the side of the enemy.

The vehemence of his strike knocked it sideways, hitting it straight into the trunk of a large tree nearby. As it hit the tree, it rebounded down onto the ground by the root of the tree, motionless. This indicated to the chimp that he was victorious and had removed another threat to his troop. He had won. He tossed the heavy wooden club to one side and stood up on the somewhat bowed rear legs and with his chest swollen up with a massive inhalation of air. He beat his forepaws, which were almost human in their definition, on his chest, making a tremendous drumming noise indicating victory, and screeched in triumph at his fallen enemy. Then he reached for his primitive wooden club again with the full intention of inflicting another mighty blow at the vanquished antagonist. At that very moment, the probe erupted into a new lease of life with violent extra thrust from its propulsion vents shot up abruptly into the air well above the chimp. The suddenness of this manoeuvre had startled the chimp, causing him to fall back while screeching with perplexed rage. He was trying to work out what to do next. His head was cocked on one side as he eyed the foe with perplexity.

The object continued to gain height until it was out of the chimp's striking range and a new device protruded from its underside. This then emitted a highly charged laser beam aimed squarely at the centre of the chimp's chest while he was trying to stand up. At the point of impact, the tissue of the chimp's breast started to sizzle, coupled with a plume of smoke. It was a well-known fact that all chimps species do possess a high degree of tolerance for pain but not to the degree caused by this laser. It was a different type of excruciating pain. The chimp screeched a blood-curdling howl of pain at the torture afflicting his chest. This powerful beast reeled backwards, with his eyes glistening in terror. The skin where the beam was focussed was evaporating with a small flame glowing from the melting tissue. He moved backwards in a vain attempt to get away from the laser beam. This attempted escape proved to be futile as the laser was locked on with pinpoint accuracy to the target area.

He still couldn't shake it off, and the only thing he could do was to scream again. In a desperate move to block it, he moved his right hand in front to cover his chest, only to find the back of his hand was also being burnt. It moved the left hand with the palm outwards in front to stop the agony. Still, the laser burnt whatever obstacle was put in front as a shield, burning another new deep cut. This infuriated the beast into further maddened tantrums. His forearms were also not spared when they were moved across the path of the laser beam. Whenever he moved his protective limbs sideways or edgeways, he would find his chest being exposed once again. The laser was relentless in its ability to generate pain and in its accuracy. Again, more burning. The hole had started to get deeper into his chest, and with that, the pain was increasingly excruciating. It had only been about seconds since he had been waving his limbs about, but the target area deepened persistently. There was no blood oozing since whatever there was, it was already seared and sealed. His forearms were being lasered, leaving a zigzag pattern every time he threw them in front of its chest. Every time there was a small gap between his flailing arms, the laser got through unerringly to the same place.

The ape's eyes were glistening from the relentless excruciating pain. There was no choice but to try and flee away from this place of unrelenting pain. He swung around and started to make a break for it and ran towards an opening in the bush. His eyes widened again as he realised the strange object had marked another target and locked on the middle of his back, next to his heart in parallel to the deep wound inflicted on his chest. He screamed again and ran as fast he could with four limbs, swung over and under several low-lying branches in his path. Unfortunately for the magnificent animal, the probe simply hovered forward, matching its speed, with the laser still locked unfalteringly on his back. No mercy was rendered. He screamed again and tried to run faster but found the pain to be even more excruciating and spread deeper into his back. The cumulative effect of his injuries had slowed his attempts to escape. It had been a mere 10 seconds since he had turned and ran and exposed his back, but this had resulted in the second wound even deeper at a depth of 10 millimetres and was getting closer to the heart.

Finally, the great ape stumbled against a large tree with its massive trunk effectively blocking any further escape. With this realisation, he stopped abruptly and swung around to face the foe, baring his teeth menacingly at it, but found it to be too high up and out of reach in his weakened state. The laser was refocussed on the deep wound on the front of the chimp's chest, damaging the protecting hands even more as the ape instinctively reacted yet again, feebly though, as a last desperate attempt to protect himself, covering the hole in his chest and holding it there for a few moments. But the laser had swiftly enlarged a hole through the badly damaged limb to the main target—the heart. The fatally wounded ape slumped heavily to the ground. The left ventricle, one of the four chambers of the heart, was exposed. In human beings, this part of the heart pumps its greatest volume of blood into the aorta, which then circulates blood into other parts of the body. However, the severe injuries had created huge leakages, and some pressurised blood had found an outlet resulting in blood pulsing out of his chest in an arc of several metres, splashing on nearby bushes. The laser beam had switched off at this instant, and the probe moved away from this chimp, whose life was ebbing away fast. It went on for a minute, the last minute of a lifetime.

The probe ignored the dying chimp and moved over to the plants nearby where the blood splattered, and a new thin glassy tentacle extended from beneath its main body. It was indeed thin, like a man's finger, but a very long and flexible tube, hollow inside. It made contact with a blood-splattered leaf and sucked a drop of blood, which could be seen through the translucent walls of the tendril, travelling up through the tube to the body. The tentacle retracted into the main body. That was it. It was all over in a few minutes. It seemed that time was of the essence, and it had accomplished its mission.

The chimp lost consciousness, head flipping backwards with eyes staring sightlessly, the pupils of its eyes dilated, lifeless.

However, the prolonged use of the extremely high-intensity laser had severely depleted the energy reserves of the probe. There was a markedly different sound from the propulsion unit. It emitted a deeper throaty whine, which signified that it was struggling with inadequate power to maintain its ability to hover. The probe moved sluggishly to a large forked tree branch a short distance away, and when it had hovered over a spot between two thick woody branches, gauging its suitability, it lowered itself into the fork and then apparently became dormant, silence enveloping it. The background noises of the jungle came back to the fore. It was now recharging its depleted power resources, which would take a few days. This period was when there was no apparent activity externally. This was deceptive. Away from sight, a process was taking place deep inside the probe. It was sampling and analysing something of great importance for the future: the blood.

Chapter 8

17 May 2028

The Vatican

Situated in one part of the main administration building in the Vatican, on the second floor, were four large rooms connected to form a long rectangular block collectively known as the Raphael Rooms. They were oozing with deep richness of history, starting with exquisite pictorial decoration, with frescoes executed by none other than Raphael and his school at the height of High Renaissance during the early 16th century. The exquisite antique furniture seen in all these rooms gave out that characteristic musty smell that lingers in all historical buildings. In the centre of one of the four Raphael Rooms stood a large imposing round table made of dark mahogany. There were 12 cardinals sitting around the table, all with red skull caps and wearing black robes with bright red sashes tucked in around their waists.

They sat with their heads bowed in prayer as they sought spiritual guidance in their forthcoming deliberations as was their unfailing ritual in this room.

'Amen', intoned Cardinal Calcagno, the presiding figure, from his beautifully carved and slightly larger chair, and this formally opened the proceedings.

This core of bureaucrats was the Vatican's Secretariat of State. It is the oldest dicastery in the Roman Curia and was the central papal governing bureaucracy of the world Roman Catholic Church.

They looked to be in their late 60s on average, but the chairman, at 85 years old, was the most senior. He was Cardinal Giuseppe Calcagno and was the Holy See's equivalent of a prime minister. His rheumy eyes stared out from his haggard face, and he was obviously fatigued. He had acquired a vast wealth of diplomatic experience, and this made him very highly revered by his fellow cardinals.

With his trembling and arthritic hands, he was having some difficulty in trying to get his fingers to control his personal electronic communicator. These devices had become universally known as PECs over the years since their invention. They were invaluable to a gathering of this nature as they could, amongst many other capabilities, translate to the user's natural language of choice. Though the cardinals were all from different countries, they usually resorted to English, but sometimes their linguistic capabilities were stretched, and the PECs were highly valued.

'Your Eminence, you could try using your verbal instead of your fingers to control your PEC', Cardinal Ricardo Brady suggested, anxious to help his senior colleague to move on with the meeting. He was the secretary of the bureau responsible for public relations.

'Good idea', the chairperson spoke in a soft voice. 'PEC, show me the picture of the new spaceship taken in Chile last week'.

Silence. No response from his PEC. He looked up at the rest of the men in askance. 'Well, why won't it work?' He was looking puzzled.

'Ah, you have not configured it to recognise your voice?' said Brady. 'That is no problem as we have all seen the images on our own PECs when I sent them to everyone yesterday, so shall we proceed, Your Eminence?'

Cardinal Calcagno scanned the faces around the table and took a moment before he continued, 'Then I must thank you all for being able to turn up at very short notice. I am sure you all will understand that I have decided to treat this event as something . . .' He paused and looked at the magnificent paintings on the wall opposite him, as though seeking inspiration. 'Of utmost significance to mankind, and indeed, there are clear implications as to there being a threat to our most cherished beliefs and the future of our Mother Church. We, therefore, need to have a very clear collective opinion as to the counsel that we can collectively give to His Holiness'.

Cardinal Angelo spoke up. 'Yes, you make a good point, but I'd like to ask you if the purpose of this meeting is to create an opportunity to hold a consistory with His Holiness the Pope?'

Cardinal Calcagno said with great firmness, 'Please be patient! All will become clear. First, we need to have a very clear idea as to what the problems are. The implications go far beyond our beloved church and have a major concern to humankind. I have very grave anxieties about all these things, and we have not even discussed or defined what the exact nature of the threats is. So let me begin and set out the scene as I see it, and then we will decide the next course of action'. He scanned their faces for a moment before continuing, 'First, we have had a remarkable image of a device, which appears to be some kind of alien spacecraft. This we received from our very dubious and unofficial source in Chile. We do not know who else on this earth has similar imagery.

'*If*, and it is a huge *if*, it turns out that it is from an extra-celestial object, with some completely unknown life form on it, then we have to seriously question exactly what this means to humankind on this planet.

'The major common ground of all the Earth peoples' religious beliefs is that there is a Godhead of some form or another. We obviously disagree as to our perspectives of how we see it or worship it. But we have all believed that our God created humans and indeed the planet we call Earth.

'If, therefore, there are beings from another world, with an advanced technical capability, are we no longer our Lord's exclusive children? That is what we are here to discuss, and you will now realise that we must have a very deep period of consideration before we can possibly make any recommendations to our Holy Father the Pope. Do I make myself clear?'

There was complete silence for 20 seconds, and then there was complete chaos as everyone tried to speak at once.

The chairman raised an imperious hand, and the meeting quietened down.

'As far as I know, we're probably the first people outside Chile to hear about it, and therefore, I could regard it as a sign of blessing by God. Or was it put in place by Satan to test our faith?

'We are cardinals, alias the princes of the church, and our duty is to discuss the matter and how it should be viewed before we can formulate our opinions. At this stage, we don't really know if the creators of the mysterious object are friendly or hostile. Of course, we do pray the visitation, if that is proved to be what it is, will turn out to be cooperative and beneficial.

'What is our situation to be should there be belligerent intentions? Should it be hostile, then I expect a form of mayhem will reign upon us as punishment for behaving like sheep that have gone astray from the righteous path as mentioned in Isaiah 53:6'.

He paused for a while to let his comments sink into their consciences and to gather his own thoughts, and there were mutterings amongst the cardinals as they began to appreciate the magnitude of the situation.

'"*The public have an insatiable curiosity to know everything, except what is worth knowing*". I am quoting Oscar Wilde', said Cardinal Justin of Vienna in Austria, which was regarded to be one of the most religiously liberal of European countries.

Cardinal Calcagno looked at him, clearly irritated by his abstruse intrusion.

'Ah yes, a nice quote indeed, but what is its relevance, Justin?'

Cardinal Justin, at the age of 62, was the youngest of all the men at the table and the only one sporting dark hair. However, it was because of his youthful exuberance that often put him at odds with the rest of the men at this meeting. His impatience in trying to get things done as quickly as possible frequently set him on a path of confrontation with them. His frustration with their cautious attitudes often arose because of their reluctance to voice their opinions decisively, when they felt that things would be too difficult or complicated, which would then lead to an inevitable postponement in decision-making. *'We'd better leave things to God's will'*.

'Forgive me for interrupting you, I do understand that what you were trying to say to us all is the need to base our decision on whatever information we have before us, here and now', Justin said, fully aware all eyes were watching him. 'However, I'm sure you'll all agree with me that this information is still insufficient and embryonic for us to act on. For a start, we still don't know if the extraterrestrials are even living beings and if they are friendly or not. If they are hostile, then we have a problem on our hands. People would say God is punishing us for whatever problems we have created on Earth. On the other hand, there may be friendly and cooperative intentions to help us with new information that may set us on the righteous path that will benefit the world, maybe morally and environmentally and, dare I suggest, spiritually?'

He paused and looked around at his colleagues.

'Either way, we could say it's still God's plan—a win-win situation for our beloved church'.

A few heads were nodding, and there was some murmuring in agreement.

'However—' He silenced them. 'The essence of the problem as I see it is one of timing. How do we know if it's friendly or not *before* we make our announcement to the world? Above all, how would the other people with different religions treat this astounding event and in what way? To their advantage rather than to ours?

'We cannot say with any certainty at this stage that the craft is manned and if so, by what sort of beings. We may subsequently find out the facts, or we may never know. Or are they hostile and we can end up facing disaster?'

'So what you are saying, it's still technically ambiguous however we play it?' Angelo said.

'Yes, we are actually gambling with the limited information we have at this stage'. Cardinal Justin looked at him and continued, 'It's because of complete lack of facts that is inhibiting us in every way'.

'Then what's your suggestion?' Cardinal Calcagno interrupted. 'I can see the need to acquire more reliable information, is that right?'

'Exactly my point', Justin went on. 'We could wait 'til we get reliable information before we make our announcement, but by then, it could be too late. We cannot sit and wait too long, as sooner or later, the full facts will emerge. We need to maintain our prestige and status as being the first in God's eye to make the necessary declarations to the world. It would give improved credibility to our church, which we've been working towards for the last part of this millennia'.

There was complete silence.

Then Vincent replied, 'Then if we could come up with carefully prepared words, we could say it's a sign from the Almighty that we've been waiting for. Whichever way we play with it, we can still treat it favourably to our case, a means to arrest the worldwide decline of all religious beliefs *anyway*'.

The others reacted warmly to his suggestion, muttering approbations.

'However', Justin pronounced, 'maybe not'. All eyes shifted to him, and the room descended into silence again.

Angelo rolled his eyes. 'Well, why not? Now what's the problem? Are you erring on the side of caution because we don't know how it would benefit other people's beliefs more than ours?'

Justin rubbed his forehead, trying to gauge when to shoot another salvo he knew well that could destroy the atmosphere of the meeting.

'Yes, from *our* point of view'—with strong emphasis made on the word 'our'— 'like we said before, we need to acquire as much information as we can before we can maximise our advantage. The real dilemma we face is that we can only make our recommendations to the Holy Father based on our *assumptions* or *speculation*, and that will play into our hands more favourably than theirs. In other words, we're looking at the whole scenario through rose-tinted Catholic spectacles.

'We also need to learn about the effect on all humankind, including the views of atheists, warts and all. We need to know how they would view the visitation by the supposed extraterrestrials.

'As we already know from our global demographic studies, it's now roughly 50/50 between all the religions and the non-believers. If we can gain pre-knowledge, then we could be in a stronger position to take possible advantages in promoting our Catholic Church'.

'So how do you suggest we talk to them and find out about their views?' Cardinal Calcagno chuckled. 'Seriously, are you having us on? You're making it sound like we're naive about their views! They are simply pathetic with deplorable excuses to belittle our beliefs!'

'If we already know the answers, then why can't we retard their growth?' Justin countered. 'My point is it could be a shift either way in their or our direction. We need to be in a much more robust position to make convincing decisions on how to treat this astounding event in such a way that will favour us rather than them!'

'Okay, I see your point and agree that we should shake the tree to get all the information we need. Yes, indeed, the more information we have, the better we will be able to react. Information is a vital tool of war', Cardinal Calcagno said in an irritated voice. 'And war, not to put too fine a point, is what we have been engaged in for several hundred years!'

He was annoyed with himself for letting Justin take control of the meeting. *He could be useful at times but needed to be kept in check and restrained for all our sakes*, he thought. He looked hard at Justin, scheming on what to say next. Suddenly, his mood changed.

'Look, Justin, as I see it, time is of the essence, and we don't have it. We simply are not able to carry out endless market research with people to glean their viewpoints of the ramifications of something as nebulous and as far-fetched as the supposed extraterrestrials', Cardinal Calcagno said in a slightly mocking voice as he tried to encourage his younger colleague to come up with a more concrete proposal.

'You are correct in your evaluation of the lack of time', Justin said without batting an eye. 'That is precisely the reason I consulted someone with opposing views before I came to this meeting'.

'Justin!' Cardinal Calcagno was clearly more angry than any of his committees had ever seen him. 'How dare you to consult with someone behind my back and without our knowledge! This meeting was scheduled, as you well know, to be absolutely top secret!'

The whole committee burst into irate muttering in support of their usually urbane and mild-mannered chairman. He held up his hand, and silence was immediately restored.

'Justin, please explain yourself, and your reasons need to be profound. Again, may I ask you who this man is?'

Justin looked down at his hands resting on the table. 'Yes, you may not like it, but I did not act without seeking inspiration through prayer, deep prayer, and thorough consideration. It is David Bridgewater'.

'WHAT?'

The meeting descended back into seething unrest again, with the cardinals turning to one another in absolute astonishment. They all knew that David Bridgewater, in the eyes of the world, had been expelled from the Holy Catholic Church in a maelstrom of press and TV coverage for denouncing all religions and promoting atheism.

Cardinal Vincent spluttered in disgust, 'That agnostic traitor!' And obviously, he gained a great deal of support from all around the table. The usually hushed and respectful voices had started to become increasingly vociferous.

Cardinal Calcagno shook his head, and his shoulders slumped in despair. Suddenly, he made an obvious effort to pull himself together. 'Stop! You are behaving like a rabble on a street corner, not what I expect from the highest echelon of our beloved church!'

He leant over the table and looked at Justin with cold eyes. 'Cardinal Justin, I understand you have been trying to use your initiative to bring some extraordinary but possibly relevant inputs to our deliberations, but you should at least have done me the courtesy of telling me first'.

Justin was still looking at his hands as he had for the last 3 minutes.

'Yes, Your Eminence, that is why . . .' Justin paused for a few seconds, knowing too well that the massive implication of what he was about to say next would inflict the mood of the meeting. 'I have asked him to come here, and he is now in the adjacent room and waiting for your summons'.

'You did *what?*' Cardinal Calcagno exhaled in utter disbelief and sank back into his chair as the whole team began muttering again in their disbelief at the youngest member's audacity. He again appealed for silence, and as the mood quietened down, Justin was still looking at his hands and had not moved a muscle.

'I wanted to bring him in so that you can question him in person and get some considered views from a totally different standpoint. Certainly, from your immediate reaction, I do not think it was wrong for me to try and get a different perspective for you all. Certainly, if I had not taken this initiative, you would never have dreamt of even considering even being in the same room with such a reactionary man. Believe me, he has some really lateral views, most controversial and interesting to put to you. Please do give him the opportunity to air his views. Once you have your answers, he can leave this room. End of story', Justin said. 'This way, we will get some way to sort out the issue about the pressures of the lack of time for research'. He ended his comments and shrugged.

All eyes shifted onto the chairperson, waiting for his ruling. He said nothing while he carefully considered the issues raised. He was too wily a statesman to be rushed into a knee-jerk reaction. He realised that Cardinal Justin had acted as he thought to be in the best interests of the committee and was not being obstructive or malicious or seeking personal gain in any way. He eyed Justin in silence for a full minute before he responded with great dignity as befitted his position.

'I believe you have acted in the best interests of this committee. Please ask him to come in. However, I must request all of you to put aside any personal animosities you feel for this gentleman, to behave with courtesy. Remember, he is here of his own free will. Justin, please ask him to come in'.

'One moment, Your Eminence Calcagno, I want you to know I must protest at this idea', Cardinal Marcello stated, his face red with suppressed anger. 'This procedure has never, ever, been followed in the history of this committee'.

'Your protest will be noted in the minutes with thanks. I understand your reservations, but it's God's will, and he will guide us. Have faith in him. Ricardo, please ensure that Marcello's objections are properly recorded'.

Justin tapped his PEC. 'Hello, David, can you please come in now?' As he spoke, he moved out of his chair, and as he did so, he beckoned David Bridgewater to be seated in the vacant chair. All eyes were assessing this rebellious ex-priest.

He wore a simple tweed jacket with a pair of black trousers. His pale blue shirt was open-necked showing a smooth tanned chest. His face was well tanned and shapely toned. But the striking difference about him was the colour of his eyes, which were piercing blue, and his hair was light and very blond.

He moved with confidence to the seat, and if he was nervous, it did not show, even though he must have been very aware as to the extremely hostile atmosphere from the most conservative of priests gathered around the table. He was carrying his own PEC and laid it on the table. All eyes were fixed on him. Some faces were showing their open contempt of him. David folded his arms and said nothing.

The chairperson addressed him, 'Good morning and thank you for coming to meet us in a short time. We understand that you have some views about the apparent extraterrestrials that are in the proximity of this planet. Would you please share these with us, Mr Bridgewater? I presume you have received the images from Cardinal Justin, and if so, can you please give your personal appreciation of what the implications will be? And finally, we need to have your word that our discussions will not be made known outside this room. It is with utmost importance—you need to refrain from divulging anything to any other soul'.

David stood up and slowly let his gaze go round each cardinal in turn. Doing so gave him a psychological advantage. He studied their faces in silence. Then he spoke in a well-modulated voice. 'First of all, thank you for having me in this splendid room, and I can guess how difficult it will be for some of you to receive someone like me, a priest for over ten years before I decide to quit and renege on my holy vows. I have my own personal reasons for all this, and I'll try to refrain from sharing them with you'.

'You'd better not as it wouldn't be appropriate for us to know them, no matter what the ethics may seem to be', said Marcello with some animosity.

'Understood, but still, I'd like to assure you that I do still possess principles, and you have my word I will not divulge any of our discussions to any third party outside this room'.

'A bit unlikely coming from you!' Marcello said, his voice cracking with emotion. 'It is so hypocritical of you to say that! You've already broken your solemn oaths you made when you became a priest!'

'Can you please be cool and just listen to him?' Cardinal Calcagno pleaded.

David nodded. 'Yeah, so ironic, isn't it, that it was because of sheer hypocrisy that I couldn't live with while I was a priest that led to my quitting'. He chuckled.

Cardinal Calcagno indicated that he should continue.

'Anyway, from what I see, through history, you have been going through three major stages of upheaval, which I believe has severely dented the church's reputation and credibility.

'The first stage happened during the early 17th century, when Galileo had endorsed Copernicus's theory of heliocentrism, that the Earth revolves around the sun. Of course, we all already know it had led to the Inquisition's ban on reprinting his works and books. It was not until 1835 when the church had finally ceased all the opposition to heliocentrism, when all his works were dropped from the Index of Prohibited Books.

'Apart from this, Galileo is probably regarded to bear more responsibility for the birth of modern science than anybody else.

'I believe it, whether you like it or not, also goes hand in hand to the creeping erosion of the church's credibility'.

David paused to take a deep breath before he went on. 'Then in the mid-19th century, there was a second stage of a tumultuous upheaval that engulfed the church's reputation. An even bigger threat to the church's dogmas has gathered for over a hundred years, and even now, it's gaining from strength to strength and becoming a way of life. The church had found it impossible to discard'.

'What was it?' a voice cut in.

David simply said one word, 'Evolution'. But it was his piercing blue eyes that added a chilling effect to the credibility of the word.

'But we still hold Creationism dear to our hearts, and there's no way we can dismiss it altogether. It's ingrained into our very existence and teachings, and whether you like it or not, we have plenty of people to believe it nonetheless'. A different voice from another cardinal came up in a challenging manner.

'Yes, that is what I called cognitive dissonance', David cut in.

'What? Can you please define that?' This time it was Angelo.

Cardinal Calcagno exhaled as an indication that he already knew it well but nodded at David to continue.

'It's sort of a medical expression . . . no more of a psychosocial definition', David replied.

'Meaning?'

'When people hold a core belief that is very strong, and then even when they are presented with evidence that works against that belief, the new evidence cannot be accepted. It would create a mental disturbance that is extremely uncomfortable, called . . .' David paused for a moment, and he held his hands apart. 'Cognitive dissonance. Because it is so important to protect the core belief, they will rationalise, ignore, and even deny anything that doesn't fit in with the core belief.

'There you are, that is how religion managed to survive against all the odds. You shouldn't worry too much but be grateful for that. To go with this, hand in hand, you are also likely to rely on *ad Populum*, which means, as all of you are familiar with Latin, if you argue that something must be true simply because most people think it's true, you're presenting a fallacious argument known as *ad Populum*, Latin for "appeal to the people". Or in other words, just because most people believe in God or a universal spirit doesn't mean it's true'.

Cardinal Calcagno said nothing, but he was clearly uncomfortable with the direction the meeting was taking. He already knew the definition of the expression but was hoping it would not be brought up to everyone's attention. But it was too late. He decided to try and shift their attention to another matter to minimise the impact David was making so clearly.

'Did you say there's a third stage?' he said.

David turned his penetrating blue-eyed gaze on him. 'Ah yes, I was just coming to that'.

He looked down at his PEC. 'The third stage . . . I believe that any encounters with extraterrestrials will be another nail in the church's coffin of credibility'.

'Why should it?'

David rolled his eyes, showing that he was becoming exasperated.

'Why can't you simply see the huge potential damage it could inflict on the church's standing? One of the things that I have found rather surprising and a bit depressing is that all of you, the so-called theologians, have given very little thought to this extraterrestrial dimension. You don't want to think about it. It makes you uncomfortable, doesn't it?'

'In what way?'

'Okay, let's try to be the devil's advocate by starting with this', David replied with his arms folded. 'Sorry to use those words in these august surroundings', he quipped with a wry smile. 'I'd like to believe in a creator God. Would such a God have made the universe to bring forth innumerable species of intelligent life? Or would such a God have made human beings on this ordinary planet circling an ordinary star in an ordinary galaxy? To be so absolutely and utterly unique in *his own image*? Some religions teach that what God does right here is supremely and stunningly special. Christianity cannot duck this question: Would intelligent aliens undermine God?'

He paused to gauge the impact of his delivery before he went on. 'Four hundred years ago, Bruno was burnt at the stake for espousing the idea that there's a plurality of inhabited worlds.

'The church thought this was a very dangerous doctrine, and I think the church got it exactly wrong. If the emergence of life and mind are part of the great outworking of the laws of the universe, then we would expect to find that life is widespread. Life would not be just some sort of irrelevant, meaningless, a side issue, but integral to the whole great cosmos'.

He paused and sipped a glass of water from the table. His mouth was dry from the stress he was under.

'This means the fact that, physically, Earth is not at the centre of the universe, and even more so, biologically, human beings are not at the centre of the universe either. We are most likely not at the top of the extensive chain of beings.

'Then my question is, how would Jesus relate to them? The Christian belief is that the eternal Son of God took on human form as Jesus for us. Does the same eternal Son of God then take on the form of ETs to act as their saviour? Do ETs even require a saviour? If so, then does God have multiple personalities for making them and us in *his image*? Think about it!

'Then assuming these ETs are more intelligent or advanced than humans, I think the more interesting question is, does God value them more than he does us? Extraterrestrials might look down on us as being rather primitive just as we look down on apes as rather primitive and slugs as even more primitive. So again, does God pay more attention to them than God does to us? He did that by granting us a lower status of importance than them!'

David paused again and with great deliberation, looked round at each of the cardinals around the table and was satisfied they were still spellbound, and some shifted in their seats, uncomfortable before he went on.

'Then naturally, there will be endless questions to consider. Questioning itself is damaging to the existence of the church. It leads us to question everything for the sake of searching for the answers with which we are comfortable. The church has taught us from the beginning not to question the ethicality of the Bible and just embrace it as the word of God literally.

'Suppose we meet the ETs in person and ask them a simple question: "What do you think of our God?" or "Do you have a God?" or whatever it is, I believe the answer, whatever it is, will be very damaging indeed, so damaging you would wish and pray we hadn't happen to meet them in the first place. It would be a boost and music to the non-believers. I can assure you they would have a field day!

'All this means for the sake of the church is it would be better off not to meet them at all in the first place! Or as history proved it, rather than being shaken to its foundations by the confirmation of life on another planet, the organised religion could embrace the news by adapting and moving on as they did before. That's another strong possibility. But I wouldn't dwell on it.

'There you are, the bottom line is the appearance of ETs will immensely favour the agnostics much more than all the organised religions combined in this world.

'I hope my opinions will help you all with your deliberations, and if I can, I will be glad to answer any questions you may have'.

David turned to the chairman, indicating that he had finished and started to sit down.

'Thank you, David, for your most interesting comments. From what we observe, you must have given the whole subject a huge amount of thought. From the opinions you've given this committee, we believe you were badly advised and led into taking a false path away from our spiritually fulfilling world'. Giuseppe Calcagno was glad their visitor's speech was over and wanted to get him out of the room as soon as possible. He could not tolerate his presence any longer as he felt the atmosphere in the room was already being contaminated by his dangerous views.

'We, and I am sure I speak for all my colleagues, feel so sorry for you and your obvious unhappiness with the state of mankind. You seem to be a lost soul and are seeking to find yourself'. His attitude was serene, but he was seething. To all the men in the room, David was simply an abandoned soul in a lost world with no coherent meaning.

'Who am I? Is that what you mean? I might well best describe myself by referring to Jerry DeWitt's excellent quote: *Skepticism is my nature. Freethought is my methodology. Agnosticism is my conclusion. Atheism is my opinion. Humanitarianism is my motivation*'. David looked around and continued, 'That is why I went back to Mexico City to continue my quest for humanitarianism by lobbying for contraceptives to be available freely to all the poor people in the slum districts of the city. I couldn't live with myself knowing that these poor families could be financially stronger with having fewer children and coupling this with the fact that they had to endure a very high mortality rate of babies not reaching their first birthdays. Why should God punish them with poverty? It doesn't make sense. It is obvious that it is better to sin with contraceptives, and with that, the consequences of having fewer mouths to feed, then the quality of life could be marginally improved. Is that too much to ask?

'It's simply down to the church's unequivocal stance on contraceptives that I began to question my faith. I couldn't live with it. Hence, my view that the way church or God operates through it simply stinks and pathetic! Especially when the Bible is littered with contradictions that it shouldn't be referred as the main source or basis for morality!' David was beginning to lose his steady and calm attitude amid the hostile muttering from around the table.

'Blasphemy! Satan!' Several cardinals were incensed.

'For god's sake, get real! Look at yourselves, you don't know the difference between heads and tails!' retorted David.

'CALM DOWN!' commanded Cardinal Calcagno. 'There is no need for this uncivilised behaviour. It is uncalled for!'

'Thanks, Your Eminence!' David was still glaring back at them. 'I understand your point, but at least, can I say something about my alleged blasphemy? It is so seemingly unfair that atheists are often charged with it, but it is a crime they cannot commit! If you care to think about it, when they examine, denounce, or satirise the gods, they are not referring to people but ideas—not dealing with people but with ideas. An atheist is incapable of insulting God, for he does not admit the existence of such a being. We do not attack people but beliefs—not beings but ideas, not facts but fancies! Think about it again. Blasphemy is indeed a victimless and pointless accusation and is not a crime! Thank you!'

He stood up and said with great sincerity in his voice, 'I think I've caused too much of an upheaval in this room, so I'd better go and leave you in peace to get on with whatever your decision-making process is. From what I can see, it'll probably be more in *your* interest that there should be no contact with these ETs if they do, in fact, materialise. All I can do for you is to thank you for listening to me and wish you good luck'.

He picked up his PEC and started to move out towards the main door.

Cardinal Calcagno exhaled in relief at the sight of David making for the exit. But he held his breath when David paused at the door. He turned his head back slowly, looked at them, and then looked up at the exquisite paintings on the walls and ceiling. He shook his head and said pityingly, 'Look at you. The difference between you and the children who believed in Santa and the Tooth Fairy, they happened to grow up to accept that they are nothing but imaginary friends. But you haven't! It is time for you to *grow up*!'

He spun around on his heel and was out through the door before the cardinals could react.

But this time it didn't come as they were transfixed and shell-shocked and started to shift uncomfortably in their chairs, looking at one another, wondering who would be the first to admit home truths that had been thrown at them so brutally.

Justin moved back into his chair, but he was looking down so sheepishly. All eyes were glaring at him in anger. Cardinal Calcagno growled at him with eyes fuming. 'Look at what you have done, Justin! You have truly put the cat amongst the pigeons!'

'But, but . . . at least', Justin blurted out, 'we know where we stand. I believe it's best we don't try to contact the Ets'. He went quietly to give time to give the atmosphere an opportunity to cool down.

Cardinal Calcagno slumped down and buried his face in his hands and sighed heavily.

'Okay, from what I can see, we don't have much choice, and above all, it is rather inconclusive to know exactly where we go from here. As far as we know, the ET has been orbiting our Earth for probably a month or more. We are not sure, but maybe it's just passing by and watching us for a while before going off to explore other planets. Then great, nobody will become any the wiser'. He shrugged.

'However, if it has decided to contact us, then I'd recommend waiting and seeing what sort of message it brings, be it in friendly or hostile tones. We would then be able to respond with an appropriate protocol. That will be our God's sign, a cue for appropriate action, whatever that might be'. He looked around for any supporting or negative response, but there was none.

He continued, 'So can we all at least agree that we'll draft up two different protocols for optional responses? One, a welcoming note, while the other one, I dread to say, a rebuking note'. At a start, a head nodded. Then there were two heads nodding, then it seemed all were as it was becoming infected as almost everyone caught on.

He seemed to have caught their mood.

'Okay, let's cast our vote on this agreement and have this matter wrapped up for today, so please put up your hands and agree that we'll advise President Delgadillo of Chile to try to do his best on keeping everything about the extraterrestrial issues under wraps for the time being?' All, except him, put their hands up.

'Any objections?'

No hands came up.

'Okay, I'll put in a request to President Delgadillo to see if he can keep the lid on it as long as he can, until further notice'.

He paused for a moment until he was satisfied there was no further reaction from them before announcing, 'The meeting is now closed'.

Then he took a deep breath and said, 'And now we need to pray'.

All heads were bowed in silence only as Cardinal Calcagno muttered the routine prayer seeking the Almighty's blessing on their work and punctuated at the end with a single 'Amen'.

Cardinal Calcagno sank back into his chair and sighed, thinking to himself, *I still do not like the development or the direction all this is taking. It was very much safer to err on the side of caution, and we should have confidence in our beliefs and ourselves. We are entering an abyss, completely unprecedented and uncharted waters.*

His team of the princes of his church all stood and chatted amongst themselves as they left.

Cardinal Marcello walked out by himself, staring fixedly and intensely loathing at the back of Cardinal Justin. His face darkened with fury, and he thought, *We have to do something about that antichrist. We must purge him from our midst and restore the highest levels of holiness and cleanliness of our inner sanctum!'*

He believed it had to be done. Sooner rather than later.

* * *

The following morning, as light crept through the ancient windows of this historic room, it fell upon the hunched and unmoving figure of Cardinal Calcagno still in his wondrously ornate chair.

Chapter 9

22 May 2028

Central Africa

Back and deep in Africa, the space probe that had lodged itself quietly on a forked tree branch for nearly a week, having re-energised its energy cells, stirred back into life. With thrust emitted by its three propulsion fins, it propelled itself well out of the jungle into a new position several hundred metres off the ground and hovered motionlessly. An antenna protruded from the top forward part of its fuselage. A laser was beamed upward to the cloudless sky directly above it and was locked with the passing mother ship orbiting far above. The contact made using its laser lasted for only a few seconds. It was using a form of optical communications, as opposed to conventional, to earthly limited technology S-band radio frequency (RF) communications (or simply 'radio'). Laser-based communications were desirable for three key reasons: massive bandwidth, higher security, and above all, lower output power requirements. In terms of data transference, it had an enormous advantage over RF, allowing for massive data rates of up to 600 megabits per second (a comparison of terahertz worth of data against megahertz in the RF), while also consuming much less power and requiring much smaller antennae. The optical wavelengths were much shorter than S-band radio; therefore, the sending and receiving antennae could also be a lot smaller. All this technology contributed to the superb smaller/lighter spacecraft and highly developed systems that worked in the atmospheric conditions surrounding Earth and also in outer space.

Once it had re-established communications using the 'optical handshake' with the orbiting mother ship, it returned into the jungle and started to hover above the ground in its exploration mode.

However, the new instructions received altered its activities. It was now in hunting mode, going backwards and forwards, quartering the undergrowth. On the mother ship, analysis had resulted in demands for more new information to be transmitted by the probe. The first sample subjected to analysis had been blood.

The probe inched forward through an opening in the jungle with its laser scanning over a broad area, hovered, then appeared to focus on some detail. It emitted a highly charged laser beam at a selected bushy plant, which then vented a small plume of smoke. The probe inched forward and sucked in a minute sample of the vapour. It paused a moment before moving forward to other plants. The same procedure carried on for some considerable time. What it was searching with such apparent diligence would not become evident to humans for some time. The blood sample had set off a chain reaction that would have major implications.

Chapter 10

25 May 2028

Central Africa

Two men were standing underneath a typically huge African dipterocarp tree, and they were craning their heads back to look up through the branches.

'A good job, the ropes are still there where you left them two days ago', Andy murmured with the unmistakable traces of a clipped English accent. 'This tree is a pretty tall specimen, so even with the ropes, it will probably take a good 10 minutes of climbing to reach that branch'.

He was wearing a well-worn and stained khaki safari suit. They were heavily drenched in sweat as it was hot and very humid. Andy took off his wide-brimmed sable-trimmed bush hat and wiped his heavily perspiring black forehead with his forearm. 'Damn the heat, but above all, damn that reclusive frog for luring me all the way here from my cosy home in Cambridge! Anyway, have you got my net with you, James?' he spoke with good humour and a twinkle in his eyes.

'I should hope so, Andy. Otherwise, we would have to go a back to get it!' James retaliated in the same tone with a chuckle and with a soft trace of an Afrikaans accent.

He originally came from Johannesburg and had joined Andy's research team, which was sponsored by the National Geographic Society on the subject of the effect of global warming on the rare tree frogs. These were believed to be exceptionally vulnerable to the effects of global warming.

He was younger and much lighter-skinned by comparison with Andy's. He had a wiry build, medium height, but his clothes seemed to fall off him as they sagged loosely from his perspiring body. He swung his large rucksack off his back, and it landed at his feet.

In his peculiarly unique manner, Andy tiptoed slowly around the gigantic broad-based tree, trying not to disturb any flora or fauna while scanning all the details around the area. He was keen to make sure he was not missing anything that might be of scientific interest and had high hopes of obtaining some unique evidence to support his project. The National Geographic Society sponsorship of his expedition was the result of years of his lobbying and was successful largely because of Andy's years of similar work in this field. He had travelled to this extremely remote and inaccessible rainforest in Africa to document the ecological effect of global warming on the tree-climbing frogs. One species, amongst the rainforest frogs, the Big-Eyed African Tree Frog is extremely sensitive to climate change, and they made a focal point for his studies.

James, although very enthusiastic, was, by comparison, a novice but had been selected by Andy based on an entirely speculative letter written by James, which was full of humour with a strong scientific core.

Andy stopped, squatted down, and carefully pushed a thick bush apart in a casual hope of spotting any elusive frogs so low down. He peeked into the shade underneath the bushes. Still no frog. However, some whitish objects lying near the base of a large tree a short distance further on another side of the bush caught his attention. It was a skeleton. He moved towards it and examined it closely. He was a scientist with a doctorate in the field of zoology, and everything related to living subjects fascinated him.

'Did you see this when you brought the ropes here two days ago?' he called to James, who was still around another side of the tree and out of his sight.

'Heh?' James peered around the tree to get a better view. 'Oh yeah, I saw it but didn't think it was anything interesting. After all, it's a jungle, and we'll come across bones like these everywhere'.

'Yes, I do understand, but from what I can see from the rate of decay, with the help of ants and other bugs doing a grand job of stripping off all the meat off this skeleton, it's probably only a few days old or so and no more than a week tops'.

James looked at him with a blank expression. 'Oh yeah, I can identify it as a chimpanzee or maybe a bonobo'. He scratched the side of his neck.

Andy nodded. 'Rather more like a chimpanzee than a bonobo'.

'How come?'

'You can see from a few broken bones on the toes and a single gash on the skull that all have healed. These are scars of battle from brutal fighting amongst the troop of chimpanzees. It is a brutally fierce way of establishing their male hierarchy'.

'Bonobos, by comparison, are relatively placid . . . ?'

'Correct!' Andy grinned. 'That's very perceptive of you to say that, but anyway, that's not what intrigued me'.

Andy pulled out his pen from his shirt pocket and slid it through a small hole in the middle of the skeleton's sternum. 'I have to say something has kindled my curiosity, James. Can you see there's a small neat hole? And by the look of it, there must be a gunshot wound, quite large calibre, more than 9 millimetres . . . I assume it's probably from an AK507 as favoured by poachers?' theorised Andy, impressing his younger colleague. He carried on.

'No. I know for a fact the calibre of an AK 507 bullet is demonstrably narrower than my biro pen, something I learnt on my treks through other parts of Africa. By the look of this hole, it's definitely a larger-calibre weapon'. He was still sliding his pen in and out of the hole. 'If it were a gunshot wound from that kind of weapon, with very high velocity, it should go right through to its back, and there would be some splintering of the bone'. He lifted the skeleton sideways to examine the spine.

'That's strange, nothing came out of the spine . . .' He stopped speaking as something caught his eye. 'Hang on, there's a small indentation from the outside'. He felt the indentation with his index finger. 'It looks as if someone has been trying to drill partially through the spine from outside'.

'So what? Poachers can be bastards'. James shrugged. 'They're everywhere in Africa, trying to make a living out of slaughtering whatever animals they can find'.

'Still, I don't buy it'. Andy shook his head. 'If they did, why didn't they chop off the head or hands as a souvenir? That's a common practice in Central Africa. But look at it. The skeleton has all hands and skull fully intact. It doesn't make sense'.

He stood up abruptly and looked at James. 'Forget it, we're already wasting our time, let's get a move on. Please pass me the net'.

James rousted around in his pack and after a few moments, exclaimed, 'Oh hell! Sorry. I am really sorry. I forgot to pack it. It's still on the table back at our base camp'. James looked highly embarrassed, having previously made a joke about the long trek back to their camp.

'Oh, James!' Andy exhaled. 'It's a key piece of equipment for catching the bloody frogs up the trees! Do you have your phone with you? Can you call either Vicky or Zach—they are still at the campsite—and have them bring the net here?'

'Sorry, Andy, my phone is broken, and it probably wouldn't work either in this black spot as we're in the middle of valleys'.

'Now what are we going to do about it?'

'No sweat! At least I won't have to walk back to Cambridge! The camp is still only 15 minutes' walk away. I can walk back and then return here with the net within half an hour. Without my rucksack to slow me down, it could be 20 minutes tops'. James took out a ball of nylon string from the rucksack. 'I've got an idea! Why don't you stay here and climb up by yourself? Top-tree work is a one-man operation anyway. Take this string with you?' He tossed it to Andy who caught it and shoved it into a large-sized pocket in his shorts. 'By the time I get back with the net, you'll already be at the top of the big branch where you can throw the string line to me on the ground, and I'll tie the net to the string for you to pull it up. Problem solved! How about that?'

'Okay, good idea, so you'd better dash off now'. Andy pulled the bright orange helmet out of the rucksack and attached the portable video camera onto the front of it. 'I know we're bending the safety regulation, but what the hell, I'll go up on my own, no worry', he muttered while checking the various attachments for the camera.

He switched the camera on and strapped the helmet on his head while watching James jogging off with a spring in his step, despite the heat, and disappearing along the vague trail through the bushes. 'See you real soon!' he yelled.

A typical student with a disorganised mind, he thought. He searched further into the rucksack and found a bottle of extra-strength insect repellent and sprayed it generously over all his exposed skin areas. That should do the trick. 'It would be a nightmare to expose myself to any bug bites while I'm up there', he muttered to himself.

He took a water bottle off the side of the rucksack and drank several gulps of cool water and slid the bottle to another pocket in his shorts. He clipped a metal hook onto the rope and checked the other rope that was anchored securely to a peg which had been hammered deep into the ground. He felt satisfied it was very secure and pulled on a pair of leather gloves and looked up the rope. 'Oh boy', he prayed to himself. 'I hope there will be no bloody biting ants on this tree as they do on over 40% of trees!'

He thrust his left foot into a specially designed stirrup and lifted himself up. Then he put his right foot into a similar loop and alternately walked upwards, moving as if he was practically 'stepping up' the rope. He kept his hands clutching the single rope in front of him, and in 10 minutes, he was at the fork of a large branch after navigating past several smaller branches. *Oh boy, that was much quicker than I expected it to be,* he thought as he took a few breaths and rested. He looked down and felt dizzy from vertigo. *Oh gee, that's quite a long way down from, say, 20-metre drop.*

Quickly, he shook his head and looked upwards across the branch and felt his giddiness subside. 'Okay, let's get me over and crawl along the branch like a caterpillar'.

He double-checked the safety harness he was wearing and was satisfied it was still secured snugly. 'Righto, let's get to that end of the branch and wait there for James'.

He crawled outwards slowly and carefully, pulling the rope behind him. A bug crept alongside his neck and gave him a painful bite. He took a quick swing with his hand and slapped at his neck on the bite, and then there was another one. SLAP! He wiped the bug off his neck and checked to see what it was and recognised it. 'Ah! A bloody tsetse fly!'

He wiped the mangled fly over his shirt sleeve and left it there. He felt a slight breeze blowing on his face, but he ignored it and adjusted his helmet once again. *Man, it is getting quite windy up here,* he thought.

He continued hugging the branch while inching forward. Further along, he noticed the branch was getting thinner, and he then noticed the wind was getting stronger. Perhaps it would be better that way as it could blow the flies away, a blessing in disguise perhaps.

He had failed to sense a new movement lurking behind him. A tubular object loomed into a position just behind him but well out of his vision. It was the probe with the dent on its side. It was making a hushed high-pitched humming with its fins waving slowly to adjust its position accurately. Andy heard the strange noise and was puzzled. 'Have we got a hornet's nest nearby?'

He couldn't identify where the noise was coming from. It was moving slowly towards the base of the branch where his bare legs were. A translucent tentacle dropped down from the 'front chin' of the probe. It started to slither over the naked part of the leg. Andy felt it, and a single word flashed across his mind—SNAKE. 'Fuck me, could be a snake!' he muttered.

His eyes opened wide in horror and squeezed his arms around the branch, trying to keep himself motionless while willing it to go away. The tentacle made a suppressed noise, 'Ppffft!'

It had given him an injection without his realisation. A narrow jet containing a cocktail of chemicals penetrated his skin. Then the probe inched backwards to its former position and remained there motionless. It was as if it had achieved its mission and was waiting for a reaction.

Andy jerked his head backwards in response to the short and sharp pain it had inflicted on his leg. 'Oh, fuck me! Must be a snake bite!' He broke out in a profuse sweat in 5 seconds. 'Not good! I had better look behind to see what type of snake! Gotta recognise what type of snake it was and hope we've got the right antivenom vaccination back at the campsite'.

Ten seconds.

Still bear-hugging the branch, he craned his head slowly around to see what caused the pain.

Fifteen seconds.

The sun shone brightly in his eyes and dazzled him. He had to squint and tilted his head down to take advantage of the helmet peak, which cast a shadow over his eyes. He opened his eyes slowly. The sun reflected off the shining probe, giving it a golden aura. The pupils of his eyes narrowed in response to the brightness. He was astounded to see something hovering next to him. 'What the fuck is that? Could that be one of the new American stealth drones we weren't supposed to know about?'

His mind started to feel groggy. He let go of his right arm and tried to wave at the object.

Twenty seconds.

The exact length of time for the cocktail of chemicals to travel from his leg to his head before it had any effect on his brain—the very reason the probe had set out to have him incapacitated.

His mouth gaped open in a stupefied look. He was losing consciousness very quickly. He had lost the strength of his grip on the branch, and he slipped over it and fell with his limbs spreadeagled. But only for a very short time when his fall was interrupted by a jolt. It was his safety rope that had saved him from falling all the way to the ground. He was hanging and swinging in the mid-air like a rag doll with arms and legs dangling loosely. His eyes were still open, but there was no movement in them. He was comatose. His body was still revolving, but the swing was reduced, eventually to a full stop.

The probe hovered parallel to the motionless body. It emitted an intense laser-based hologram, creating a grid of extremely fine horizontal and vertical lines. These gauged Andy's body and all the possible impediments of all the jutting branches. It then moved slowly down while maintaining the grid to gauge all the possible obstructions of every branch on the way to the ground and then homed in on the dense bush at the base of the tree. It paused momentarily over the bush, and the hologram remained alive while various calculations were being made. It was creating a path for the fall that was about to be created. The hologram grids dispersed abruptly into thin air, and then with a subtle difference of sound made by its propulsion unit, it started to rise to the position immediately next to Andy. It seemed satisfied with the assessments made.

It advanced a short distance towards Andy, and with a device protruding from its chin, it emitted a high-powered bluish white laser beam towards Andy. Instead of penetrating Andy's body as it had with the chimpanzee, it focussed on a new location. This time it was the rope that was attached to his safety harness. In a few sizzling seconds, it cut through the rope like a red-hot knife through butter. Andy started to bounce among the various branches, which slowed his overall rate of fall. This reduced the risks of serious damage to his completely inert body. There was a small error when his head hit a branch at an uncalculated angle, which knocked his safety helmet off and it spun away in a separate trajectory, spinning up into the air and landing on the ground a short distance away.

Finally, like a rag doll, Andy landed squarely on the bush, the very spot where the probe had calculated. The thick bush had broken his fall. His partly crumpled body started to slide off the bush onto the moist ground. His final position showed him to be lying spreadeagle on his front with his eyes still open. His breathing rate was still in regular mode but very shallow, which confirmed he was still alive, barely.

The probe hovered immediately above the mangled body, and its belly started to transform into a new large man-sized bulbous shape. A slit appeared across the belly, and it opened like a military aircraft's bomb bay doors. A single opaque tentacle, with a vice clasp on its end, extended down to Andy's body and gripped the safety harness on his back and started to winch him up. At the same time, an increasingly audible sound was emitted from its power unit. This was a throatier and meatier noise as it compensated for the additional weight of Andy's body. He was being winched up, with his arms and legs still splayed out until he was engulfed in a coffin-sized space inside the probe's belly. The doors started to slide down until they made contact with Andy's arms and legs still spread out. Its sensors picked up the likely obstructions from the limbs to get the doors to shut properly. Given a choice, it could have decided to continue shutting the doors further and having the protruding limbs chopped off. For some reason, it had decided not to.

It paused motionlessly in mid-air as if it were trying to make a calculation on what next action to take. Finally, with a throatier roar emanating from its power unit, it took off steadily into the opening among the trees and shot up into the wide-open sky. It went up several hundred metres before it performed a 180-degree flip over with its belly exposed to the vast blue sky instead of the ground. With this short manoeuvre made, it had to rely on gravity to do its job of absorbing Andy's limbs into the small cavity inside the belly, and in the aftermath of soft dull thuds it had sensed the limbs falling inside, the hatches shut. Soon afterwards, it dived into another roll before it went skywards once again and with a new deep humming roar coming from its fins, propelled it very fast, ever higher. It was making a return to the mother ship, carrying a valuable cargo inside it, like a miniature version of a heavily pregnant whale.

* * *

A few minutes later, James burst into the opening next to the large tree, shouting, 'Hey, Andy, I'm back!' He waved the net around triumphantly and then paused. He looked up and focussed on the branches high above him, expecting to catch a glimpse of Andy. His eyes narrowed, and he waited for any signs of movement. *He's not there.* He looked around and shouted, 'Hey, ANDY! I'm here! Where are you? I'm not in the mood for a game of hide-and-seek!'

Silence.

He was searching around until a bright orange object caught his eye. It was Andy's helmet! He picked it up and saw the video camera was still secure within the structure of the helmet. Another large object on the ground caught his attention— it was the rucksack. He moved towards it while throwing the net away and took a pair of binoculars out of the rucksack. He focussed them on the tree. *Well, he's still not there, but hang* on . . . He paused. *Ah, there's a rope! What had happened to it?* He adjusted his binoculars to gain a sharper vision. *Ah, the rope's been cut!*

He jerked his head around, trying to peek into wilderness and bushes as if he was half expecting a threat from the poachers. He stood motionless for a few minutes, listening.

He detected the usual insect sounds in the background. That was it. No other unnatural sound could be identified.

He was trying to fathom what to do. A sense of panic built up inside him. He started running around in small circles and kept on shouting, 'ANDY!' in a vain, hoping that he might find some signs of him somewhere. After several minutes of frantic search, he realised it was essential that he stopped being irrational and started to think calmly as Andy would behave. He stopped next to the rucksack and hefted it over his shoulder and began running back towards his distant campsite back to the campsite, holding Andy's helmet close to his sweat-drenched chest. 'I've gotta use my laptop and link up with the video clips for any clues!' With this idea firming up in his mind as he ran, he made an extra effort in his running.

* * *

The probe kept flying higher and higher until it reached a few miles up into the deep blue stratosphere. It was starting to wobble unsteadily as it was trying to maintain its height as best as it could. The air was getting thinner and, consequently, was making a huge demand on its propulsion system, which was starting to struggle with its propulsion no longer biting the increasingly rarefied air. It had reached its effective limit and could not ascend further.

It did not have any other more appropriate or supplementary propulsion system that could propel it into outer space. Its antennae had beamed a laser encrypted message upward into deep dark space. The beam was searching around systematically and effectively. Suddenly, the beam stopped its activity—it had found its objective.

It was a retriever probe that was orbiting Earth with the specific task of retrieving the four probes. It had a power system that was designed to manoeuvre in the vacuum of space. It was recovering the first of the Earth probes to have completed its tasks. It was at least ten times larger than its target probes and had four concave recesses around the main fuselage. The recesses were the exact dimensions and mirror shapes of the probes, for which it was designed as the retriever. It hovered into position adjacent to the probe. The laser beams locked the two objects together as if they had an umbilical cord, with data flowing between them continually.

Prior to the moment when the mother ship had dispatched the retriever towards Africa, it had already scattered another three probes of the same design to different areas of Earth. One fell into an outback in Western Australia, while another one fell into a desert in North Africa. The last one fell into the Gobi Desert in Mongolia, the world's least densely populated area. Had these probes been identified by any human agency, it would have become apparent that they were all targeting the least populous areas of mankind. This would have indicated that there had been a considerable degree of prior surveillance to establish this degree of focus.

The retriever homed closer to the struggling and wobbling probe, with their laser beams still locked together. The distance between them was diminishing fast until there was an electronic signal indicating the correct meshing of the two craft had occurred, and the probe had been secured snugly into one of the concave recesses underneath the larger craft.

The propulsion system of the retriever gave out a burst of power, and it started to climb back into dark empty space and went in a different direction into a new orbit away from the mother ship, which was still orbiting the Earth. It would not return to the mother ship until it had completed its mission, which was to retrieve the other three probes as soon as they had completed their tasks. These were scheduled to be completed within a matter of 20 Earth hours, thus reducing the possible damage to the human cargo.

***

James slumped in a canvas chair, his chest heaving and pouring sweat. He had finally returned to the campsite and was met by two colleagues who were overseeing the job of cataloguing the frog species collected by Andy and James.

'What's happening? Where's Andy?' It was the woman assistant who broke the silence. Her voice gave some trace of an unidentifiable European origin. She realised that James was seriously distressed.

'Vicky, I've no idea!' James blurted out after he had recovered some breath and looked at Zach. 'Hi, old buddy, can you please bring the 42-Zero laptop from my briefcase over to me, please?'

Zach picked it up and handed it to James, who took out a shiny but battered laptop and positioned it on the table in front of him. He unhooked the video camera from the helmet and pressed the button to activate the Bluetooth system.

'I sincerely hope we will find some sort of answers to our questions'.

A picture flickered into view on the screen. All three assistants craned their heads close together to get a better look of the video being played out. There were lots of jerky movements as the camera had been panning around a lot, but they could see the hands clasping the rope.

'So he's climbing up the rope!' James commentated.

They waited for a moment before Zach blurted out, 'There, now he's on the branch! He is crawling!'

'Shhh, let us hear it!' James put his hand up.

There was a noticeable high-pitched low volume of sound from the laptop but just audible to them. James touched on the screen and increased the sound volume.

'Hornet nest nearby?' Vicky offered her opinion.

Then they heard the familiar sound of a hand slapping flies followed by Andy's unmistakable voice, swearing, 'Bloody tsetse flies!'

Then the video stopped moving. The assistants froze as they were monitoring the images intently as conveyed by the video. The faint high-pitched sound was becoming louder this time as an indication of the source closing in on Andy. The image jolted backwards accompanied by an unmistakable strangled gasp in Andy's voice. 'Uuurgh!' boomed out, which made all the assistants flinch.

'What the heck caused that?' Vicky's eyebrows raised.

'Shhh!' James put his hand up again to underline the stress he was feeling. He was getting very anxious and irritated. Suddenly, they all heard Andy's voice booming out from the laptop.

'Fuck me, could be a snake!'

The picture slid edgewise slowly to the right, but there was a bright flare from the sun into the camera, which resulted in the images being immediately obscured and preventing any easy identification of what was happening. There followed a lot of confused pictures as the camera faithfully recorded the gyrations of Andy's interrupted fall towards the ground, accompanied by the sounds of his body hitting the branches. Suddenly, all movement ceased as the helmet containing the camera had been knocked off Andy's head and bounced off onto the ground with the dense bushes obstructing the camera view.

'That's where I found the helmet', James said.

'Is that it?' Zach whispered.

'It looks like it'.

James touched the screen control to replay the sequence. The video played back to where the sun glare had dazzled the camera lens. Played. Paused. Played. Paused. James kept tapping his finger at the screen and increased the contrast levels. He replayed the series several more times of play and pauses.

'Stop!' Zach shouted. 'No, go back a little!'

'There!' Vicky shrieked.

The video froze. There were lots of blurred and out-of-focus images of branches covering most of the screen, but tucked in a corner of the where a sharper view of an object could be seen against a dark green background, James touched the screen with his hands and enlarged the image and refocussed the picture. Then with a few more deft touches, the object in question was now filling in the whole screen of the laptop.

'It looked like a drone with belly doors open?' James suggested.

'Could it be some sort of a new American drone that we aren't aware of?'

'I've never seen anything like that anywhere on Earth!'

'But look at the hose or whatever dangling from the belly. Maybe it is a rope, or . . .'

His voice trailed off. James was sitting still as he was hypnotised by the video image. *If it was responsible for the disappearance of Andy, then how should I proceed with what next step to have him rescued?*

'As we know, he's a bloody pom. I think you'd better report his disappearance to the British Embassy', Vicky suggested.

'Vicky's right. We've got a portable satellite dish here that can link us to any embassy in Africa', Zach said.

'That would spark off an international search for him?' James looked at them. 'In the middle of the rainforest, in the middle of Africa, with ruthless poachers swarming around?'

James stood up. 'Look, we don't really know if this drone is being operated by poachers or someone else operating covertly, so we'll need to keep it relatively in low profile until we get a bit of advice from someone as to what to do next and how best to handle this situation. We can't afford to upset the poachers and put Andy's life in peril, do we?'

'Like whom?' Zach asked. 'Someone from the embassy will sort it out for us? Will they contact SEALs or the other one . . . oh, the British SAS?' His initial preference for SEALs rather than SAS, plus a soft nasal accent, had exposed him to be an American.

As James and Zach were discussing what next steps to take, they were unaware that Vicky's eyes were still fixed on the screen.

'Excuse me, I don't want to sound stupid, but didn't one of you say we've not seen anything like this anyway on Earth?' Vicky declared, 'If not from Earth, then . . .' She pointed upward to the sky. 'Space?'

'UFO? Aren't you having me on?' Zach was chuckling. 'Stone me if that is so. We are dealing with a UFO that has abducted Andy! Hell no, I don't want to be part of this incredible theory!'

Still, it did not stop their eyes drifting slowly upward to the sky, except for James, whose eyes were still fixed to the image on the laptop. He was studying it for a moment. Then he announced, 'Nah, I don't think it's possible that way!'

'Why not?'

'Look, Vicky, I've also got a passion in aviation engineering, so all I can see the drone has only got a sucking air propulsion system in its fins. That means it can only operate in an air environment using air as a means of hovering. Therefore, it won't work in the vacuum of space! It's as simple as that. It doesn't have the technical facility to travel into space'.

'Any other possibilities?'

James shook his head. 'Vicky, don't be paranoid! Let's be pragmatic'. He gave her a disdainful look. 'Can we try the first step of contacting someone and report Andy as a missing person?'

Zach was already at a small locker on a table where he unlocked and took out the burgundy-coloured passport. He tapped a few buttons on a tablet already mounted on the same table. 'Every minute wasted may not be helpful, so I'm making a move', he announced.

He looked through the list and touched one. It was the video contact for the British Embassy based in Kinshasa, the Democratic Republic of the Congo. A grainy picture of a woman loomed into view on the screen. 'Hello. You're reaching the British Embassy. My name is Rachel. How can I help you?' Her accent was unmistakably English.

'I'd like to report a missing person'.

'Oh right, can I ask who's missing? And please confirm that he or she is a United Kingdom citizen . . .'

'Yes, I've got his passport, and his name is Dr Andrew John Nelson, passport number is . . .'

The manhunt for Andy had started.

Chapter 11

26 May 2026

Observatory, Atacama Desert, North Chile

Miyuki had been sitting quietly in his chair, apparently with his eyes focussed intently on his array of monitors displaying the images of the alien spaceship. This was quite a deliberate impression he wanted to give, as if he was studying and monitoring it, trying to digest some useful patterns of information—far from it. He was primarily observing people's behaviour out of the corners of his eyes. He had been intrigued by the activities of various people in his large operating room. More specifically, it was Lieutenant Rafael that Miyuki found to be fascinating. It's been several days since another person came onto the scene without any prior notification and took the charge of the observatory. As it was to the Japanese team, this seemed to be as big a surprise to Lieutenant Rafael and very much to his dismay. The new staff member in question was Major Diego. He easily outranked Rafael, and he had been installed by the Ministry of Information at the site to oversee the censorship being enforced rigorously.

Rafael had always thought he had the blessing of the powers within the government for him to be the sole controller of the observatory until Diego walked in unannounced. His face darkened with fury as he felt the rug had been pulled out from under his feet. He felt so frustrated that the prospects of his promotion had dwindled rapidly. Diego had been making his presence acutely felt by all the personnel at the site. 'What have I done to deserve this?' he muttered to himself. 'I did everything by the book and even got the full attention of the minister himself. And now why this?'

Anatomically, the difference between these two soldiers couldn't be more markedly different. For a start, Major Diego was strikingly handsome, and his body frame was much taller than Rafael's, standing well over 6 feet tall. His body was much slimmer and more muscular than Rafael's. To make the matter worse for Rafael's credibility, whenever Diego walked around the room, he completely disregarded Rafael's presence—utterly. Only when he wanted something specific from Rafael, he would address him by his rank as though on a parade ground and granted an audience with him briefly. But the way he demanded responses from him was made in a blunt and tactless manner. He went out of his way to demean Rafael whenever possible. Diego had made it known he would prefer to give orders rather than discuss matters whenever possible.

Diego was aware of Rafael's feeling towards himself, but for some reason, he privately cherished it and would do anything to inflame and deliberately discredit Rafael. He had been doing it already for a few days since his unannounced arrival publicised by his declaration.

'I'm here on the specific order of the esteemed minister of information, and my job is to oversee all the administrative procedures at this site and to ensure that the strictest censorship is in place until further notice. No one is allowed to travel outside these premises or make connections, verbal, written, or electronically transmitted, with anyone outside these four walls . . .' He looked around the room. 'Have I made myself clear?' His command of English was excellent, but it was heavily accented with Spanish.

His iron military discipline had gained him rapid promotion, and he was quite certain of his own abilities to impose such discipline on this bunch of civilians, including Rafael. He realised Rafael had stayed at the site for longer than six months, and therefore, he knew the dynamics of the site well. This was something where he had an advantage over Diego. It was with this reason alone Diego saw him as a threat to be dealt with.

Diego, upon his arrival, had questioned everyone on the site, and he wanted to know everything as to how the observatory operated. On the first day, he marched around the entire site to gain an impression of the overall layout. He was invariably accompanied by a small entourage of fawning technicians and administrators. Often he would stop and point at various devices, barking several questions in quick succession to keep everyone on their toes and to leave no one in doubt as to who was the chief.

When Diego reached the Observatory Operations Control Centre, Miyuki, alongside Rafael following him sheepishly wherever he went, answered him dutifully. Diego listened and nodded in silence at every answer uttered by the scientists until Rafael tried to cut in by mentioning something useful. He would often brush him off in a very off-handed manner, reinforced by occasional remarks, such as 'Shut up, I didn't ask you to say anything unless being specifically addressed to you!' or 'You are a soldier, not a bloody scientist, so just shut up until I want you to comment in which case I will ask you specifically'.

Every time Miyuki looked at Rafael, he could not help noticing the impassive expression on his face; he was clearly fuming under his breath, with eyes glaring in fury at Diego. Miyuki would not have wished to be in his shoes but somehow admired and was in awe of Rafael for being able to maintain such a non-responsive veneer and refrained from retaliating. If looked at closely, it was easy to see that he was like a dormant volcano in imminent danger of blowing its head off at any time.

Finally, they came to the main and large operating room, where a vast array of computer screens could be seen everywhere.

Diego stopped in the middle of the room and scanned the whole scene slowly and methodically until he locked his eyes on one corner and asked, 'What's that? Is that what I believe it to be, a console for operating the Internet mainframe?'

'Yes, it is indeed', replied Miyuki.

'Who is manning it?' Diego asked.

'Erm, I believe it's Rafael's job'. It was another scientist who replied.

Diego's head turned around and aimed his question directly at Rafael. 'Then why don't you stay there then? How can you leave it unmanned, and it's obvious that anyone could have access to it and gain access to the outside world!'

'Fear not, Major Diego, no one can access it without my password!' Rafael replied with a trace of a smirk in his voice. 'I don't share my password with anyone, not even you! So it is secure'.

Diego detected it but wasn't rattled by it and decided to keep the pressure on him. 'I need to remind you that my status outranks you. Therefore, you will have to tell me your password anyway!'

'I can't do that!'

Diego took a few steps up to Rafael until he was towering over him and said with a threatening tone, 'Are you implying you will not follow orders from an officer of senior rank? That is what I believe is blatant mutiny, and based on that, I could have you court-martialled and have you put in the military prison'.

'Errrm, no, Major. I can see your point exactly, but I was only implying how secure the Internet mainframe is'. Rafael's response was slow, but he was trying to think fast on how to regather his composure. 'Minister of Information Hugo De Guzman, personally gave me instructions that I was not to share the codeword with anyone, except him, and I believe he outranks everyone in the army, including you, I presume?'

'Then do you have this in writing?' Diego kept up his pressure.

'Oh no, not exactly, but we have the mutual understanding—'

'Not good enough! Hugo has already instructed me to take over this place, with his orders that everyone be made answerable to my command, unless you want me to take it up with the minister?' His face was threateningly close to the lieutenant's.

He was calling the bluff of Rafael, who took it unwittingly with an immediate response. 'No need for that, and I accept your direction, but I need to remind you that once I handed the password to you, then you are fully accountable for any problems we may encounter with the Internet mainframe in operating?'

'Yes, of course, but I don't need you to remind me of my responsibilities! It is not your job to do so!'

Rafael clenched his fists behind his back as he visualised the idea of taking a punch at the objectionable Diego's face.

Miyuki could see the situation becoming dangerously ugly and decided to interrupt them. 'Excuse me, but can I please remind you that there are still other astronomers operating in this same room, so can I suggest we all go back to our stations and resume our duties? I believe we have absolute and overriding authority to ensure that our observations of the alien spaceship must be continued without interruption. Surely this must have the highest priority?'

Diego's head pivoted slowly to line up his eyes with Miyuki's. 'I agree with you, and I respect your request'. He turned his attention back to

Rafael and pointed his finger at the console. 'You'd better go back there and stay manning it until my next order'.

Rafael unclenched his fists and said, 'Yes, sir, give me a few minutes ...' He turned around and walked towards his console. When he got there, he ripped out a piece of paper and grabbed a pen from his desk. He scribbled something on it and walked back to Diego handing it to him. 'There you are, my password for the Internet mainframe, and now you're fully accountable for it, sir'.

'Fine, but I am still not happy with your attitude'. He took the paper and folded it. 'You are now a marked man. I will be watching you closely from now onwards'. He inserted the folded paper into his breast pocket.

Diego looked at the small group of people. 'Go back to your stations and carry as you were before. I'm going to another site. Report to me as soon as you notice any new movement on this spaceship'. His orders were snarled in an unmistakably threatening manner.

He walked off without any indication of where he was going and left the group of people moving off to their station in silence.

Miyuki walked to his own console and sat in his chair, contemplating what to do. That interlude had taken place two days ago, and since then, Miyuki had been surveying other personnel around the room, but there was one person who was of particular interest to him. Rafael, whose behaviour was becoming visibly exasperated and had displayed much more than his usual behavioural quirkiness, kept walking in circles, deep in thought, and muttering angrily to himself. He was clearly fuming.

Miyuki tilted his head and looked at the image of the alien spaceship, which had remained unchanged in its position and continued orbiting the Earth in a regular pattern just as it had over the last few weeks.

He started to smile and looked across the room at Yoshi until their eyes locked together. He flicked his head imperceptibly as an indication that he wanted him to come over. Yoshi looked back at him and nodded. He stood up and strolled slowly over, checking with Rafael to confirm he was not drawing any unwarranted attention.

Yoshi looked at Miyuki's screen as he was in the business of examining it but whispered in Japanese to Miyuki, 'What are you trying to achieve? But I couldn't help noticing you are grinning. I've been watching you watching Rafael, so tell me, what's going on in your head? Care to share it with me?'

Miyuki nodded. 'I think I've got an idea—I'm going to make use of Rafael's situation and exploit it to our advantage'. His voice was barely audible, not to alert Rafael's attention. 'An opportunity not to be missed!'

'How so?' Yoshi's eyes looked at him imploringly.

'Leave it to me. Go back and forget it for a while. Just carry on with your work as usual, as if nothing's happening before'.

Yoshi walked back slowly and sat in his chair, displaying no emotion nor any interest on the screens he was watching. Miyuki had thrown his full attention at one screen and with a finger; he swiped and touched an application. He was opening a new e-mail window. He looked at Rafael to check if he was still walking in a circle, and he was. He started to type slowly and paused at times to gather his thoughts. His e-mail started to materialise:

To: Hugo De Guzman
cc: Rafael Costilla
From: Miyuki Kagawa
Subject: Progress Report of the Alien Spaceship
Attachment: image#06.26MK

For the attention of Honourable Maestro Hugo De Guzman:

Since Major Diego is not here in presence at the observatory site, I am under the order of Lt Rafael Costilla to deliver you immediately the latest progress report of the above object in question. He has personally authorised me a rare window of opportunity to gain brief access to the Internet for a few seconds to deliver you the latest report, which, we believe, is of significant interest to you.

It has come to our attention that there is a small round opening formed at the edge of the cylinder-shaped body. It materialised about an hour ago, but nothing came out of it nor any further movement in connection with this opening. Based on our initial observation, we have no inkling of what it is for. However, we will continue keeping it under close observation. I have attached the image file for your perusal.

I share Rafael's vision and belief of keeping you fully updated of any changes made to the appearance of the said object. It has continued circling our Earth for the last few weeks at the outer high-Earth orbit distance of 19,690 kilometres at the direction of southwest to northeast with an inclination of 63.4 degrees.

I would like to make it known to you that, thanks to Rafael's jurisdiction, despite us being kept here against our will, all the staff and personnel at this site were treated relatively well and have high morale. We are grateful for it. We will endeavour to cooperate with Rafael with all our ability, as it would benefit us to do so, given all the difficulties and unknown factors we are facing with this alien object.

We will wait in earnest for your further instruction.

Kind regards,

Dr Miyuki Kagawa

Miyuki opened the image file and saved it again to another format, with the original a week-old date changed to the current time. He scanned the image to check if there was any indication of time and date being displayed. He was satisfied there was none.

Miyuki leant back in his chair, checking his e-mail for a moment before turning around, and looked at Rafael who was still walking in circles. He waited for a moment as he was trying to find his courage of starting the chain of reaction that was about to materialise. He found it, and he took a long inhaled breath and called out, 'Rafael, I believe you'd want to know immediately if something has changed to the appearance of the alien spaceship. I didn't notice it until I made the comparison between the first picture of when we first encountered it and the latest one that was taken about 30 minutes ago'.

Rafael stopped walking in his tracks and flashed a look at him. He then searched around the room to check if Diego was there in the presence and was satisfied he was nowhere to be seen. He walked slowly towards Miyuki and said to him, 'Well, show me what you have seen'.

With a few touches on the screen, Miyuki quickly hid the e-mail, and in place of it, he brought up a picture of the alien ship and immediately came up another near-identical picture next to it. 'There, you can compare it now'. He pointed his finger at a very small opening. 'I didn't notice it until I zoomed it up'.

With a slight movement of fingers, the picture enlarged rapidly until the opening filled across the screen. Rafael looked at it with his mouth open in amazement. There was a bead of sweat trickling down the side of his forehead. He felt unsure of what next step to take as he was grappling with the turbulent train of thoughts being formed in his mind. He was at loss for words.

Sweat broke out on Miyuki's forehead as he was trying to say something that was so contrary to his nature. He was completely lying through his teeth. *Shit, come on, pull yourself together and keep calm. You know you can do it,* he thought it to himself.

He knew the opening was actually made about a few days ago but declined to report it in vain hope someone on Earth would be alerted to the space probe ejected from this opening. Nothing had happened since then. He wasn't sure what's happening out there; he had no access to the Internet. If something had happened, Rafael, through Hugo, should have known it by now. He wanted to rock the world to the presence of the alien ship but never felt so powerless about it until now. Now the time is ripe for action. A golden opportunity to rock the world was now within his grasp.

'Forgive me, I took the liberty of creating this e-mail on your behalf, not Diego's, but just you'. Miyuki's mouth was dry, but his voice was normal. 'I believe you should earn the credit due, not Diego. You were with us from the beginning'.

He called up the e-mail on the screen, and Rafael studied it for a moment. Rafael's eyes widened. 'Interesting and nice e-mail you've written, but why should I permit you to write on my behalf? You know full well I can't permit you to access the Internet. Diego had made it plain that we're to report him as soon as we notice any new movement on this spaceship'.

Miyuki responded, 'Yes, I'm aware of it, but can you contact him now by mobile? You know our mobiles are inoperable at this remote site anyway'.

'Errr, no . . .'

'Then wouldn't it be in Hugo's interest to know it immediately? Why wait for Diego? Time is of the essence, and Hugo would appreciate being informed at once'.

'I can see you've got a point, but . . .' There were some doubts about Rafael's eyes.

'I want Hugo to be fully aware that you have a significant part in running this operation and retain full control on this site, and with this in mind, you are and have been actually delegating the tasks to us, not Diego'. Miyuki was trying to appeal to Rafael's egos.

He looked at Miyuki and looked sideways at him as he noticed the beads of sweat trickling down his cheeks. 'Thanks, but why are you perspiring and flushed? Is something bothering you?'

'Oh, I'm so excited at the new discovery and, of course, am equally nervous at the implication of what this opening may bring us'. Miyuki was raking his mind furiously for a plausible answer to offset the fact he was sweating because he was not comfortable with lying. 'But that's not the point. I believe you deserve the credit due to you rather than Diego, and you can see on the e-mail it will be addressed to solely Hugo and you. It will show you are in control of this room rather than Diego. Just grant me a few seconds of Internet opening, and once I send it away, you can close it down immediately. No one, especially Diego, would be any wiser. He would think twice before coming at you when you have Hugo on your side and probably be grateful for your thoroughness and effective control'.

Rafael looked at him and said nothing. Miyuki noticed it and kept up the flattery. 'Letting you know, the staff in this room felt we have more rapport with you rather than Diego and wanted to help you any way we can'. His mouth was getting drier, and his voice was starting to rasp. 'This is an opportunity for you to complement Diego's position by emphasising Hugo's management skills by his delegation to his creation of teamwork?'

Rafael was still watching him and looked at the e-mail. He felt a small stirring of emotion and a sense of pride. Miyuki had been trying hard to stoke him up by appealing to his pride, which he knew would be his Achilles heel. But still, Rafael hesitated as he looked around and realised Diego had left the building. Miyuki sensed there was a trace of nervousness about him, and he kept up the pressure. 'I can see you're worried about Diego, but he's not here in this building as I believe he's gone out to another town several hundred kilometres away and won't be back for another day or an hour if he dashed here by helicopter.

'But we have no means of reaching him anyway. I don't think Hugo would cherish the idea of us sitting on our asses wasting away the time waiting for Diego to come here', Miyuki continued with his voice getting coarser.

He stopped and grabbed a glass of water and gulped a mouthful of water. He paused and felt better with his mouth lubricated before continuing, 'So you can see my point, as I was trying to say, it's a good opportunity for you to redeem your control in his absence. You are the next and most senior person to oversee this building according to the Army regulations'.

Rafael stood up swiftly and said, 'Okay, you've sold me, but I want you to move your hands away from the keyboard, and I'll go and get the Internet back online for 10 seconds. Once you've sent it away, I'll switch it off. Got it?'

'Got it', Miyuki said, putting his hands up in the air.

Miyuki waited for him to move off to the Internet console before he acted quickly. The moment was exactly when Rafael's focus had turned onto his own Internet console while he walked towards it. Miyuki quickly pressed a point at the screen and a small new window of e-mail address next to 'Bcc:' materialised, and he blindly punched one letter immediately above the spacebar. The letter was 'B' to summon up and match the surname alphabetically, and the name 'Bond' appeared in the address box. It was Katie Bond. *Oh okay, I don't recall her, but I don't give a damn who it would be as long as someone gets it*, he thought. He quickly turned his face to Rafael who simultaneously turned his head around and looked at him and noticed he was still holding his hands up. He missed nothing. Perfect timing.

'Okay, I'll put the Internet online now, but I'm letting you know I'm still watching you and all other staff, including Yoshi'. He surveyed around the room until he was satisfied all were not near their consoles. He punched several buttons on his keyboard and finally hit the final button 'enter'.

'Okay, Miyuki, you can send the e-mail out now'.

Miyuki waved his hands and pressed one button. 'That is it, thanks, Rafael'. The e-mail vanished from his screen.

Rafael glanced briefly at the e-mail that appeared simultaneously on his screen. He checked the address it had been sent, and he was satisfied there were only two parties: Hugo and, of course, himself. He typed again at his keyboard, and the Internet was offline in a few seconds.

'Great! Now I want you to keep your eyes strictly focussed on this bloody alien ship, especially watch that new opening, and report to me immediately if you see any new movements!' he shouted at everyone in the room, but he was feeling nevertheless happier as he thought he had something that Diego hadn't. He had won the respect of scientific colleagues at the site. He believed he had it in spades from them, and he, Hugo, would soon be the man at the top.

Miyuki swivelled his chair around slowly and locked his hands together behind his head and looked at his screens. He was feeling so smug. 'I can't believe I've done it right under his nose', he congratulated himself.

Yoshi had been watching Miyuki like a hawk for the last 10 minutes, and a grin spread slowly on his face. He knew something was happening but said nothing. Suddenly, his mouth gaped open as if the world had been exposed to this e-mail, and they would turn their attention on us and unintentionally put us in an even more delicate situation. Yoshi was alarmed at the notion of falling into further problems, especially because he was uncertain of what would hold for them later. He walked over and whispered to Miyuki in Japanese, 'What have you done? Don't you think what you have done could have put us in an even more difficult situation? You're practically inviting the authorities for further confrontation with us or even landing us in hot water!'

'No need to be alarmed, I believe I've got everything covered. Go back and leave me to do the job of worrying about it'. He replied, trying to shoo him away.

Yoshi was unmoved. He was still not buying it. Miyuki rolled his eyes. 'Look, I was careful with the content I typed on my e-mail, and I made sure to mention we are more of a "hostage situation"'.

'If anyone sees it, they'll know what to do. I do have faith in their sense of perception of our situation'.

'You'd better do it', Yoshi said. 'Otherwise, I'll never forgive you . . .' His last sentence trailed off as he pivoted around and walked off.

Miyuki leant back again and exhaled out slowly. He was still smiling and congratulating himself with the feat he had just pulled off. He thought, *Oh boy, here comes. I hope this time the world will be alerted to the alien ship and remove our credibility of keeping it under classified wraps any longer. I don't care about it. They're more than welcome to it.* But the question he asked himself, 'How soon will the world become rattled with the unprecedented news?'

Once it was out, then Rafael would have no choice but be forced to put the Internet back online. He warmed up to this idea. Then he chuckled when he realised Hugo would probably be the true clown ending up with a huge loss of face. How fittingly his title being the minister of information, whose job was to oversee the media and information, ensuring all forms and flows of information being maintained selectively to bring it in line with the government policies.

It would only be a matter of time before he would be sidetracked politically by the power of the Internet alone. He was paying the price for underestimating the power of technology.

'Come on, Katie, whoever you are, please do us a favour, just ignite the bloody fireworks!' Miyuki whispered to himself.

* * *

Chapter 12

27 May 2028

Office of *Las Vegas Sun* Newspaper

Brett walked into his office, carrying a cup of coffee he picked up at a nearby diner. He threw his electronic tablet onto his desk and walked up to the window and looked out at the scenery of the city. He was clearly tired and irritable. He had just come back from Northern California, where he had to cover the news of a shooting at a local high school. The shooter had not only managed to slip past the sophisticated security scanning devices, but he had also accessed their metal workshop, where he managed to create and assemble a crude but effective automatic rifle, and with it, he opened fire on students in a cafeteria, killing 16 of them.

Brett did not like writing this sort of report, knowing it was a highly sensitive situation, and it was so difficult to gauge how the public would react to his style of presentation. He was normally happier covering scientific subjects. Would it allay or inflame attitudes towards the sensitive issues about gun law, which had still not been resolved after so many years, one way or another? Above all, he felt he was wasting his talents and creativity on producing a report covering such a sad event and illustrated the skewed society hell-bent on its right to own guns, regardless of the circumstances it had inflicted. What irritated him even more was the fact that this incident was the third in a space of eight weeks. 'This is the worst aspect of my job. I hate these situations!' he moaned to himself. 'Three times in two months! Come on, what's happening to society?'

He was sipping his coffee and lost in thought when his computer beeped, signalling he was getting a video call from his editor-in-chief. *What does she want this time?* He sighed as he walked over and decided to remain to stand and voice-activated one of his screens to the video connection. His boss, looking like the ultra-smart businesswoman she undoubtedly was, appeared on the screen.

'Morning, Brett, I can see you're back in the office. I guessed you've been to the school massacre'.

'Yup, Helen, so what's new about it, eh?' His face was grim, his voice gritty with fatigue.

She went on, without giving him time to answer, 'I want you to drop everything and get ancient hound dog nose out for what I smell is a really deep story. I want you to write a story that may make or break this business of ours as we are getting absolutely hammered by our competition, and our revenues are so far down that you and I will be looking for jobs unless we can crack a real news-blaster exclusive!'

Brett sipped his coffee again and still said nothing. The frown on his forehead started to smooth out. Helen noticed it and continued, 'I've decided to reallocate your massacre story to our new cub reporter Sarah as quickly as you can brief her, as I have a real humdinger for you!'

'Okay, boss! Make my day?!'

'Well, you'd better sit down and brace yourself for something that I'm about to deliver to you!' The editor-in-chief smiled. 'The real news bombshell that you've wanted for a long time!' She paused for a while. She had decided not to divulge further information as she wanted to play cat and mouse with his emotions. He finally sat down.

'I'm giving you five days from this morning, and I've already booked live TV space and the "net-maggy" for your input'. It was a slang term she used for an Internet magazine.

'Five days! That's tight. Aren't you pushing it?'

'Either that or . . .' Helen didn't finish her sentence, but Brett completed it for her. 'Or this becomes a shooting case'.

'That's my boy!' Helen smiled. 'Send your shooting unedited story across to Sarah. I assume you've already collected some roughs and news views and photos on which she could work?'

He lifted his tablet. 'Yep, it's all there ready', he said. 'Now what's the angle on the news that you want me to cover?' He was clearly intrigued and could not wait to know what it was for him.

'Someone has got in touch with me recently asking for you'. She looked closely at him. 'Only specifically you, above other news journalist'. She grinned. 'God knows why!'

'Huh? Okay, who is it?'

'Stevie Ford', she said simply.

'Are you having me on?' Brett's eyes widened. He knew the name very well but had been out of touch for the past two years. 'I thought I'm the very last person he'll want to get in touch with!'

'Well, he's taken the time to explain his reasoning for contacting you'. Helen's eyebrows raised. 'He wants to remake contact with you. So hear him out, will you?'

'So . . .' He could not believe his luck. 'When can I see him?'

'Well, brace yourself—he's actually here in my office!'

Brett said nothing. He was simply gobsmacked and not sure what to say. He saw Stevie appearing alongside Helen on her screen. He was waving and smiling.

'Hello there! If it's okay, can I come around and make my apologies to you in person?'

'Oh . . . well . . .' He was at a loss for words. He was flabbergasted and did not know what to say, but he quickly composed himself. 'Erm . . . okay . . . come right over! Know where my office is?'

'Sure, give me a few minutes, I'll be there'.

The screen went blank. Brett stared at it with knitted eyebrows. *Why now? Something serious must have surfaced that must have prompted him to contact me. Yes, I know I've been after that* Voyager *story for a long time, if, indeed, it is a story. But—*

A soft knock on his door jolted him from his deep thinking. 'Yes, come in!'

The door opened slowly, and Stevie's face peered around it. He looked very apologetic. As he came into the office, he kept one arm behind his back, clearly hiding something.

'I still cannot believe you'd contact me, never mind setting your foot in here! Especially after you blocked me out at the Hilton Hotel two years ago! What's changed this time?'

'I know, I know!' Stevie nodded. 'Please give me a break, and I'll explain my story, and in good time, you'll know my reasons, and hopefully, you'll accept my peace offering!'

He pulled out his hand from behind his back, clasping a bottle of Glenfiddich single-malt whisky. 'Well, here's my olive branch. How does that go down with you?'

'Oh, my favourite! How did you know?'

'You should thank your boss as she's the one who tipped me off!'

He put it on his desk and looked at the empty chair in the corner.

'May I?'

He sat on it without waiting for approval. He looked at Brett and sighed.

'Okay, can you spare 30 minutes?'

'What choice do I have after such a magnificent bribery?!' said Brett, still admiring the bottle.

'Okay, here we go'. He cast a dreamy look out of the window. 'Let's go back to the Hilton Hotel, okay?'

'How could I forget that!' Brett turned his attention reluctantly from the bottle back to Stevie.

'Yeah, forgive me for the heavy-handed treatment you had from the security guy'. He put his hands up. 'That was uncalled for'.

'I've always thought journalists like me are just the undesirables you'll take all the measures to avoid . . .'

'Yes, naturally!' Stevie chuckled. 'But it was your persistence that actually won me over!'

'I had to! I knew there was something fishy about your story that didn't add up!'

Stevie pointed his index finger at him. 'Mmmm, it was probably down to your reporter's nose for the smell of a story that did not fail to impress me!'

'Maybe! Maybe not!' Brett folded his arms. 'Okay, let's start from the beginning, and what have you got for me this time?'

'Fine, just bear with me, I'll try to explain everything starting from that event at the hotel'. He took a deep breath. 'Okay, here we go . . .'

'Hang on!' Brett took out his Unicom and pressed the recording button. 'Gotta record it, hope you don't mind. Please continue . . .'

'I'm cool with that'.

Stevie started to explain at his own unhurried pace, starting with how the signal interruption from the *Voyager 1* had set him and his team off the quest for a reliable source of data that would explain the short burst of quirky and unintelligible signals transmitted by *Voyager 1* in its last spasm of life.

'And don't tell me you've got there?' Brett interrupted quickly. He could not contain himself as he sensed this was where the real story was going to begin.

'Please be patient!' Stevie threw his hands up. 'It's important that you need to get the full picture first!'

It had taken him more than 20 minutes as he spelt out the background with a scientist's deliberate and organised precision before he came to its conclusion. 'There you are'. He looked straight at Brett. 'Now can you see the reason for my reluctance to share our discovery with the world until we are 100% sure of the authentication of our translation of the *Voyager*'s irregular signals?'

'Then what have you concluded?' Brett could not hold his excitement.

'Well, I'm not sure of the final outcome, but I get several possible clues'.

'Well?'

'Can we use your monitor screen?'

'Sure, where do you want me to start?'

'Can you please display all the latest internationally relevant news bites over the last few days?'

'Sure!'

Brett pivoted his seat round to face another large screen. He gave the relevant instructions to the computer to display the news items. Rows and columns of various news bulletins, all could be seen at the same time. They were clips of major news being streamed in from local, national, and international sources.

'Display the international news only. African only, if you can'.

'Computer, display the African news only'.

'Displaying'.

Rows and columns of various news bulletins, all could be seen at the same time. Brett looked at Stevie. 'What are we looking for?'

'Anything to do with the disappearance of an Englishman in the Congo Republic?'

It did not take him long to find it. He touched the screen to link up the source of the news.

The screen showed a large grainy picture of a drone with a caption flashed underneath, *'Englishman missing. To whom does this mystery drone belong? Where did it come from?'*

'That is, I believe, a clue that I need to follow up', Stevie announced.

'Clue for what?'

'My gut feeling tells me that the drone is not from this Earth but probably from space'.

Brett shot an are-you-having-me-on look at Stevie to see if he was joking. The seriousness of his face showed clearly he was not. 'But what has *Voyager* got to do with that?'

'Good question, but the timing of *Voyager*'s terminal signal 'til now and the discovery of this strange drone is around two years, so that's provided us with a calculation we can use for the distance an object could travel'.

Brett frowned. 'I still don't get it. What object are you looking for? What are we expecting to see?'

'That is just what we did not know. That is why recently I have requested my old friends at Thirty Metres Observatory located at Mauna Kea in Hawaii to recalibrate their telescope to search for something abnormal in outer space. It needed to consider the starting base precisely where *Voyager 1* was at the time of its last signals'.

'Abnormal? As in what? What are they expected to look for?' Brett interjected.

'Something unexpected or unusual', Stevie continued. 'A potential source for the drone to originate from'. He studied the news for a moment and continued again, 'Possibly, I could be wrong, but what I am doing is a matter of an elimination process that I needed to start with the observatory at Hawaii'.

'How soon will they let us know?' Brett was already starting to consider himself as a part of Stevie's team.

'Could be anytime now or a few days or weeks or even months! We cannot even know that we will get a definitive answer'. Stevie scratched his head. 'They've got a tight budget, so they only have a small window of opportunity to search for something outside their usual scientific objectives'.

'If they ever found it, would they report it only to you?'

'Yup'.

'Do you have that level of authority?'

'Something like that. I can alert the White House directly'.

'Will you share it with me as an exclusive?'

'Possibly, if you want it that badly'. Stevie looked at Brett. He was baiting him. 'It depends on what sort of news you are looking for'.

'Give me the details first, then I'll be the judge and see where we can go from there...'

Brett's speech was interrupted by his office door being pushed open, and Sarah burst in with 'Hi, honey! Oh, oh, I didn't realise...so sorry...I just wanted...er...to have a quick word about your story on the shooting. I'll come back later'.

She stopped, red-faced, and glanced at the screen and saw Stevie smiling at her. 'Oh, hello there', she said. Her inquisitive nature got the better of her and looked at Brett and then again at Stevie.

'Does he have anything to do with the school disaster this morning?' she asked, her eyes lighting up.

She was hoping Brett would introduce him to her, but he was rattled by her interruption and snapped at her. 'Nope! Nothing to do with the shooting at all!' His manner was unusually brusque.

She sucked in her breath and whispered, 'Okay, that's fine, but no need to snap my head off!' As she walked away back through the door, she looked back at Stevie. 'Thanks anyway. Have fun with whatever you are doing! I'll come back later for your inputs'. She blew Brett a kiss and waved at Stevie.

Stevie's personal phone beeped. He looked at it. 'Speak of the devil! I can't believe it's Katie Bond!'

He lifted his phone to his ear and muttered quietly into it. Brett ignored him and shifted his eyes to the screen. For the first few minutes, Stevie listened in silence and then mumbled, 'Huh? Yeah...really? Yeah? What? Really! Seriously?' He covered his phone mouthpiece and looked at Brett. 'Do you mind if I divert her call to your screen?'

'Of course, feel free to use my call centre!'

'Katie, can you please hang up and call me again via Brett Fielding at the *Las Vegas Sun* newspaper office? I'm here in his office, and I want to receive your call and possibly share it with Brett. Do you mind? Huh? Yeah? Thanks! You're a gem!' He ended his call with Katie. 'Perfect timing! She's got something really interesting to show us!'

He repositioned his chair closer to the live screen. 'Can you move a bit?' He was indicating to Brett to give him a better view of it.

'You have a video call from Katie Bond, Hawaii', the computer chirped.

'Accept call', instructed Brett.

The screen flickered into life, showing three people sitting in a tight group. There was a blond woman sitting in the middle of two men. Stevie recognised her and said enthusiastically, 'Hi there, Katie, thanks for calling me again. It's good to be in touch. I believe you have something to tell me?'

On the screen, it could be seen she was whispering something to the man on her right, and he nodded. She looked at Stevie, and she jerked her thumb at both men and said, 'Well, I think I'd better introduce these guys to you first. On my right, it's Dr David Wright, director of operations of Thirty Metres Observatory, located here at Mauna Kea in Hawaii. On my left, it's Adrian Wright, same surname but they are not related'. She smiled. 'But nevertheless, he is the senior and head of PR of the same observatory'.

Stevie nodded to them. 'Greetings to you all, but I should just let you know I'm here in this room with Brett and our communications with you are secure'.

He was thinking to himself, *Holy Jehossophat! People as important in their world as these three means something of major significance is cooking.*

Adrian said, 'Before we start, I'd better let you know that we're finding that we are in deep water with no experience in communicating really major news to the world, and we need someone who is completely trustworthy and will act with absolute discretion. Our news, we believe, has massive international significance'.

Katie chimed in and said, 'That is exactly why I suggested you to my two colleagues. After all, it was you who warned me to expect something startling and abnormal'.

'What have you found?' Stevie asked with some asperity, his pulse quickening.

'Not quite so fast. We did not find it', David spoke up in measured tones. 'On the contrary, someone else is ahead of the game'. He looked at his colleagues and then at him. 'You'd better brace yourselves for it . . .'

'Stop the fudging and tell me who found what?'

There was a trace of irritation in Stevie's voice based on the apparent laid-back response by the Hawaiian's team.

Adrian broke the silence. 'Well, it's about an e-mail we received yesterday, and we'll forward it to you now. Take a close look at it, and come back with your suggestions on how we should deal with it. It's from the observatory based in Chile. We got it early yesterday morning, and since then, we've been arguing on how we should react. That's why we've decided to come to you and see if you know anyone who may deal with it constructively and responsibly without causing an international panic. To be fair, you're the one who alerted us along the lines of what we might expect. We felt it right to come back to you to seek your valuable and balanced input. Looking at it, as you might say, from our end of the telescope, it seems you were expecting our call?'

'Ho, ho, very funny. Please forward the info you have as we are just beating around the bush without having anything concrete to talk about'.

Katie looked down and typed something and looked at Stevie. 'It's been forwarded. Take your time, Stevie'.

The computer on the other screen gave an audio beep, signalling an incoming message. Stevie and Brett started to read it for a few minutes. They frowned in unison and then clicked the file attachment. Loomed up, filling the whole screen was an image of a strange object, a dark massive unnatural creation.

The colour drained from their faces, and it was Stevie who could not help blurting out with a deep exhalation, 'Jeeez, is this for real?' He could not contain himself.

Brett said nothing. He was simply rooted to the spot.

'We have confirmed the authenticity of this e-mail. It hasn't taken us that long to reposition our telescope and locate this alien object', Katie said. 'It's there at this very moment, no question about it, but we were still amazed to know how it got there without being detected by other observatories around the world. Now can you understand how monumentally important this information is?'

Stevie sat motionless for a good 5 minutes as he was rereading the e-mail and studying the picture several times over, again and again, trying to ingest it and deciding what next steps to take. Finally, he regained his composure and looked at the three people who were still watching him.

'I agree with you, it is very big news indeed!' said Stevie. 'I completely understand your concerns on how we should deal with it in an entirely secure manner. The way I read the e-mail, I believe it's in all ours and your interest that you, not the people in Chile, should take the credit of 'finding' what appears to be an alien space vehicle of some kind. You want this news broadcast through me and announced to the world, through my wide press contacts?'

Stevie looked at Brett.

'Starting with you?'

'Why should we?' asked David. 'We didn't find it in the first place?'

'If you read the Chilean e-mail carefully, I believe this man, Miyuki, is trying to tell us between lines that his observatory is under government's jurisdiction and that there is some kind of censorship being imposed'. Stevie was speaking in an authoritative manner. 'The way I see it, we have no way of knowing how much danger their lives could be in. The best way is to take the heat off them and play it safely by indicating that it was your observatory in Hawaii that had spotted the spaceship—you, not them'.

'Sounds fair enough. Okay we'll follow that line of reasoning', said Adrian, nodding. 'You've got a valid point. I agree with you that it's our duty to help out these people who may be stuck in such a delicate situation'.

Stevie continued, 'I think the best way is for me to reach someone I know at the White House. He has immediate and direct access to Pres Rachel Wallace at all times'. He looked up thoughtfully. 'Yes, leave it to me. From there, I'll be able to advise you when to make the announcement or whatever future security clampdown may be required'.

'Agreed!' Katie smiled.

'Done!' Stevie looked sideways at Brett who was still sitting motionless. 'I would like to make a special request to you all, the people at your observatory, if you could authorise Brett to come over and meet you all, with a view to producing the news exclusively. He deserves it as he's been badgering me for the last two years for the right to a piece of exclusive news! So okay with you all?'

The Hawaiian team looked at one another, and then Katie nodded to Stevie.

'Can you hold on for a few moments while I just have a word with my team? I'm going to switch off the mics'.

Katie turned to her colleagues and discussed with them for several minutes in total silence. Finally, she turned around and faced Stevie and Brett, switching the microphone back on.

'Okay, once the news is broken, we can grant Brett some exclusive interviews with us, and our cover story will be that we found the alien spaceship on our own. We need to move fast, and for that reason alone, you, Brett, had better be ready to fly out here to Hawaii ASAP? All agreed?' Katie looked at Brett.

David and Adrian looked at each other then turned to Katie and nodded their agreement. 'Apart from anything else, we will need all the guidance from Brett. We have never had to face the world media, and with a story like this, it would be quite an ordeal for us'. It was Adrian who spoke.

'Right! That's settled, Steve and Brett. We are agreed, and we will want your assistance in the world media feeding frenzy that is certain to follow', David cut in.

'Katie, can I have that in writing?' said Brett without thinking. He was dazed with the idea of landing a once-in-a-lifetime exclusive scoop.

'Aye, e-mailing you our approval in a few minutes. And you, Steve, to put us in contact with the White House sooner or later. Are we all in agreement?'

Brett's heart was beating so hard, and he felt beads of sweat trickling down his neck; he was trying to say something, but all he could manage to utter were 'Yup, absolutely' in a weak voice.

'In the meantime, we'll keep on standby for our constant communication. We will continue keeping in touch with you and will help with the press release. Bye then'.

'Understand. Bye then'.

The screen went blank. Stevie looked at Brett. He was still sitting with his hands holding the edge of the desk for several seconds before he started to jump up and down with his clenched fist punching the air. 'I'VE GOT AN EXCLUSIVE! WHAT A SCOOP!' he hollered. Stevie laughed at his reaction.

Then he fell back and slumped into his chair and remained there motionless for several minutes as he wanted to savour the moment when he had achieved the unthinkable, when he clinched such an extraordinary deal with these people. It was, indeed, beyond his wildest dream. He looked at Stevie. 'How can I thank you? What have I done to deserve this?'

Stevie shrugged. 'Why not? Make the most of it while you can!'

Both turned around slowly and took another look at the e-mail with the image still visible on the screen. Brett muttered to himself, 'Oh hell, what am I going to do now?' *Shall I bring it up with Helen and get her to authorise my flight to Hawaii?* he thought.

He looked at Stevie Ford. 'Were you really expecting something like this to happen? If so, when?'

'Oh, about two years ago, at the Hilton Hotel, and since then, I've been dreading something like this would happen'.

'How come?'

'Well, through the process of elimination, Edward Stone and I concluded that something had destroyed our *Voyager 1* artificially rather than by nature-like comets or meteors. We decided to sit it out and sort of wait in hope to see if it was just a false alarm'. He looked at Brett. 'Unfortunately, it doesn't look like that now'.

Brett looked at other news screens. 'I see what you mean, and it looks like the timing of the disappearance of an Englishman in Africa does tie up with the appearance of this mystery drone and the ETs spaceship!' He pointed at what appeared to be a somewhat fuzzy outline of some kind of portal on the side of the spaceship.

'Is that an opening? We cannot be sure and will have to do some calculations to assess the relative sizes of the drone and the portal, but it would be a logical explanation of where the drone came from in the first place!'

'Sure thing', Ford said. 'I have a million questions to ask about this drone and the extraterrestrial spaceship, especially as to whether its mission is peaceful or hostile. Those must be my main concerns'.

He was contemplating what the next steps should be. He realised Brett was not the person he had previously thought to be, a cold and calculating journalist. He had underestimated him grossly. Time to put his disparaging views behind.

'We need to work together and try to handle the whole event in a constructive manner without causing international panic', Stevie said. 'Perhaps starting with a warning to the United Nations to look out for any more strange-looking drones? Hopefully, sooner or later, we'll know what to expect of their mission'.

Brett nodded. 'Let's work together and achieve a positive outcome!'

Here commences a new era of a mutual working relationship between the two men. They have a new mission on how to deliver the news without causing total panic—*if* their surmises proved correct. The countdown had started for the media to have a total meltdown.

Politicians were going to have to become adults all of a sudden.

Chapter 13

28 May 2028

Somewhere in the Western Australia Outback

A large six-wheeled white camper van was cruising along a barren and desolate road with dust billowing in its wake. There was a large company logo emblazoned on both sides of the van, and it read, 'LINKSPAN Ltd.' With a small subheading beneath, which read, 'Civil & Structural Engineering Consultants'.

On closer inspection, there was no one sitting in the front seats, which confirmed the van was under cruise control, navigated automatically by the GPS coupled through built-in sensors located on large bull bars mounted at the front. It had been driving on its own for the last five hours since the early morning of that day.

Inside the air-conditioned van sat three people, two men and a woman sitting around a compact square desk in the middle with one edge welded to the side wall of the van. They were all concentrating on the large relay screen mounted on the wall against the desk. Each had their own identical keyboards and sensor mats emitting infrared holographic images onto their personal GCs. The senior man in his late 40s had a dark, tanned, and weather-beaten face. He was sitting between the woman and the younger man. He wore an open-necked short-sleeved shirt with the company logo stitched on one side of the breast pocket. He threw a glance at the woman and muttered to her, 'Emma'.

She didn't respond immediately. Her focus on her screen was intense, which showed her level of commitment to her job.

She had wavy hair, dark auburn, hanging down just above the nape of her neck. She had petite features, which accentuated the size of her soft hazel-coloured eyes. She also possessed faintly noticeable freckles on her nose and cheeks, giving an air of a 'neighbourly prettiness' look about her. She had a tall, slim build. Her short khaki trousers and tailored short-sleeved safari shirt showed off her nicely tanned arms and legs. She was very much an outdoor type of girl.

She had a strange habit: Whenever she was concentrating deeply, she twitched her nose. The older man noticed it and smiled. He knew the reason for her lack of response when she still hadn't answered him. He understood the situation. He moved his left hand towards the woman's GC to try and catch her attention. It did the trick. She threw him a quizzical look. Her eyes were bright with curiosity, but this masked her quality of fierce intelligence.

'Oh sorry, Nigel, what did you say?'

Her speech had a slight lisp, but there was a lovely underlying timbre to her voice.

'Emma, how did you get on with the stress analysis of the rigid frame for the inclined legs? Can you please confirm your calculation of the stress you've made on the support legs, bearing in mind we may need to opt for the long single span bridge as indicated in our choice of bridge code number 10c?'

'I think I partly understand you, but let me double-check what you were actually saying . . .'

She quickly glanced at her GC but more particularly on the supplementary screen attached to it. She was the only person in the mobile office who had the unusual-looking device which she also had on the table. These appeared to be two V-configured pen-like tubes, some 6 centimetres long, mounted on a small black computer cube with a built-in microphone. There were tiny pulsating blue LEDs on the tops of both tubes. These were projecting and illuminating a translation of recent speech onto a flat white screen erected in place immediately next to her GC. Like her colleagues, she had been concentrating on the GC screen in front of her but occasionally glanced sideways at the text appearing on her flat screen.

Whenever the other two men spoke, the dialogue was instantly translated into text. When needed, she would respond to them verbally. However, her speech had a distinct sound. The sole reason for this was she was profoundly deaf and had one electronic cochlear implant fitted into the right side of her head just above her ear. Her wavy hair concealed it well, and any strangers who met her wouldn't have had any suspicion of her deafness. This invisible disability had made her social life very challenging. The twin tube device was an old model and had been superseded by more recent technology, but she found it extremely useful as her own personal translator, which enabled her to function well with hearing society at any given time. It was a tremendous help to her ability and to her self-esteem.

'Ah yes, Nigel, my calculation for the stress analysis confirmed that we need to use that type of material'. She looked at him, flashing her dainty smile. 'Mixture of concrete and steel code 28b. But we need to make sure the single supporting span is no longer than 30 metres long'.

'Brilliant, that should reinforce our recommendation to go for that type of bridge for the creek at Yellowdine Nature Reserve that we've surveyed yesterday', he responded. 'I believe there's a strong chance we'll be able to replicate this same type of bridge where we are going. It will make more economic sense to repeat the same design'.

He looked at the younger man on his left. His dark skin and facial features gave away his origin as being Indian.

'Duleep, I know you've only been with us for two days, and you're new to us, but the job you did yesterday at Yellowdine was excellent. Based on the mapping inputs of the landscape you've provided by using the drone, we were able to carry on with our tasks very accurately'.

'Thanks, Nigel, it's nice to know my work is appreciated'.

He was still watching Emma; he was mightily impressed. He had found out by accident early that same morning about the nature of her deafness when Nigel reminded him to try and face her when speaking to her, as it would help her lip-read him better. The sound she received with her cochlear implant was far from perfect, as the quality was very robotic and metallic. She had to learn over her lifetime to compensate for this by getting her brain to attune the inferior sound she received through a microphone attached to her speech processor. This was in the form of a hearing aid positioned above her ear. It then transmitted signals to a magnetic transmitter, a relay device, and converted the signals into electrical impulses that were picked up by 22 electrodes. These electrodes acted as a stimulator and sent the impulses to different regions of the auditory nerves. Contrary to many people's expectations, an implant did not restore her normal hearing. The standard of hearing received through cochlear implant was of a very crude quality. However, it did give her a useful representation of sounds in the environment and helped her understand speech to some extent.

'It would be great if you can repeat your results with the survey drone at Mount Manning Nature Reserve where we are going now . . .' Nigel looked at his watch. 'We should be there in about 15 minutes, give or take'.

'Great, I can assure you that you can rely on me'. His eyes were still on Emma.

'From what I can see using the satellite-based images, it still cannot compute accurately for the depth and width of a large creek or riverbed. I intend to amplify our survey inputs accurately with the new drone we've purchased. It's got new measurement sensors built in to give it enhanced 3D mapping abilities', Duleep said, remaining looking at Emma.

'Cool, but I do still need Emma to walk to the other side of the large creek to verify by eyeballing any possible openings where a potential new link road could be sited', Nigel said. 'They believe it will cut several hours off their usual route between Perth and the new town in the process of being built'.

Emma was still watching her translator flashing the translations. She was acutely aware of the interest in her that Duleep was showing. She said nothing.

'Emma, don't you mind if I could ask you some personal questions?' The caption flashed, which Emma had read, prompting her to look at Duleep.

'Sure, what is it?' From her life experience, she knew what to expect from his line of questioning.

'How much better can you hear with your cochlear implant? I kept hearing stories as to how wonderful and marvellous this technology is and the benefits it brings to your deaf people. I really do not understand the whole scenario'.

She sighed, knowing she had to repeat a greatly condensed description for umpteen times when encountering new people with their insatiable levels of curiosity on how deaf people lead their lives. She shrugged. 'Not particularly that well as people expect it to be. It's very synthetic and has a robotic-like quality. It's okay in some cases, and its results vary enormously among different people'. Her voice had little variation in tonal pitch. 'Sometimes I do wonder if it is all rather overrated'.

'Then why do you have it?'

'I didn't ask for it. I was fitted with it when I was only a year old as it was the expectation of the hearing society with their customary view to "help us", believing it would provide social benefits by allowing us to integrate with the hearing community'. She looked him straight in the eye. 'But it doesn't take away my true identity as a culturally deaf person with a capital D'.

'Culturally deaf?' Duleep furrowed his eyebrows. 'What does that mean?'

'If I take off my hearing aid, I am indeed totally a deaf person and cannot hear anything at all. But it doesn't stop me from socialising well with other deaf people using our sign language'. She put her hands up in the air and smiled. 'My other language is called Australian Sign Language or AUSLAN for short. I love the vibrancy of deaf people community. I'm proud to be part of it'.

'You can sign!' Duleep gaped at her. 'Does that mean you can talk with any deaf people in the world?'

Emma rolled her eyes. 'Not really. Lots of different countries have their own form of national sign language, and they do differ quite a lot from one another. I would have some difficulties understanding the deaf American using their own American Sign Language, even though they do share English as the common language with us Australian people.

'Deaf people in England using their distinctive BSL—sorry, I mean, it's short for British Sign Language—they would have difficulties in corresponding with other deaf people in Europe in their own native sign languages'. Emma continued glancing at her translator captions to check the level of accuracy of her statement and was satisfied with the result that was being delivered. 'However, we can resort to another mutual language, which is called International Sign Language, which can be used alternatively to obtain some degree of understanding—' She didn't finish her sentence as a sudden impact jolted the van and high-pitched alarms sounded.

'*EMERGENCY!*' A series of flashing signs and an artificial voice indicated, '*Impact detected on the front left side of the vehicle*'.

The huge van screeched to a halt as the brakes were automatically applied, and the rigs' tyres spewed dust around. The engine and onboard systems were automatically switched off.

All three people looked up and undid their safety belts and searched out of the windows to see what they had hit. It was Nigel who first spotted a lifeless body some 10 ten metres down on the road behind them.

'Oh, a bloody roo!' he muttered to himself.

Emma followed the direction of Nigel's eyes, and soon she spotted the reddish furry heap. 'Oh dear, I believe that must be a red kangaroo'.

'Gotta check if it's dead or not', Nigel said as he stood up to reach a locked compartment located above Emma's head. 'Excuse me, Emma, I need that rifle . . .'

He pressed his thumb on a small button sensor, which scanned and confirmed the authenticity of his thumbprint. The door clicked, opened wide, and he lifted out a Remington semiauto high-powered rifle with a large telescopic sight mounted on it. He checked the magazine and confirmed that it was full. He reached for his wide-brimmed Stetson and pulled the side door open and stepped down into the blistering heat outside. He looked back at them and said, 'Gotta check it, and I may have to put it out of its misery for mercy's sake'.

'Oh gee, I didn't realise it's that hot outside', Emma uttered in response to the heat building up inside the van.

Nigel smiled at her while slinging the rifle over his shoulder and started to stroll towards the lifeless body. He scanned the shrub around him and noticed there were many other kangaroos hopping in all directions. *What had spooked them?* he wondered.

He stopped and knelt next to the large kangaroo. Its eyes were still wide open, but there was no movement in them. He touched them briefly to gauge any flicker of life—none. Then he put his hand under the forepaw, on to its chest, to feel for any heartbeat—still none. 'You lucky bitch', he said, feeling satisfied that there was no need for him to take further action.

He stood up and surveyed the barren landscape. There were a few stunted trees, boulders, and dried shrubs littered around and lots of uneven ground with depressed hollows. He had noticed the general directions to where the other kangaroos bolted and narrowed his scrutiny when something caught his attention in one particular spot. He could see blurred movement some 200 metres away. He couldn't fathom out what it was, so he raised his rifle and peered through the telescopic sight. He could see two small clouds of dust swirling around but couldn't see any further because they were partly obscured by the uneven ground.

'Bloody hell, it's only a devil's wind created through a vortex of hot air', he said to himself while shaking his head. 'Is that what had spooked the roos? What a bloody bunch of jumpy creatures they are!'

With his right eye still locked on the eyepiece of the telescopic sight, he moved his rifle slowly sideways to the left and then to the right until something caught his attention—a rabbit. It was hopping away in the other direction from the dust cloud until it stopped on a small mound of earth. He moved his left foot forward and leant forward slightly. He lowered himself into a proper hunting position. He clicked the safety catch off and squeezed the trigger slowly. A loud crack rang out, and the rabbit flipped up backwards, and by the time it landed squarely on its back, it was already dead—a clean shot through its heart. There was nothing more he could do, and he slung the rifle across his shoulders and knelt to pick up the tail of the kangaroo and dragged it behind him further out from the roadside and strolled back to the van.

He found Emma and Duleep still watching him intently.

'What the hell happened?' Emma asked him.

'Oh, the roo is dead, that's for sure'.

'No, I mean I saw you watching something, and then why did you have to shoot a rabbit?'

'Well, I thought I saw something, but it was only devil clouds, a small tornado caused by hot weather', Nigel said, looking at her. 'And the rabbit? What's the problem? It's only a feral pest that needs to be put down, some target practice for me'. He shrugged and chuckled.

He lifted his rifle above Emma's head and clipped it back into its brackets in the locker and slammed it shut. He settled into the driver's seat, switched the engine back on, and the auto control systems turned the air-conditioning back into life with a low-pitched hum.

'We're already wasting our time on this bloody roo, so let's get moving on, and the sooner we get there, the better', he said, looking at his watch.

'Resuming the journey', acknowledged the computer. *'Distance to the rendezvous will be 12 minutes'*.

The van accelerated smoothly forward and started to gather speed along the road. The team resumed their positions and clipped on their safety belts, turning their attention back to their computer screens, oblivious to some new movement at the site near the dead rabbit.

* * *

The drone, identical to the one in Africa, was still hovering stationary inches above the hollow, with its propulsion system throwing up a small cloud of dust. The deep impression in the hollow had helped obscure its body from Nigel's field of vision. But it was not blind to Nigel's movement and recorded everything that transpired. The recent data it had received had identified the long metal tube held by the alien creature was analysed to be a weapon. A recognition of the threat it posed was immediately transmitted to the parent probe.

The drone inched upward and then forward over the top, throwing up more dust clouds in its wake, and soon came to the dead rabbit. A flexible tentacle descended from it and systematically moved over the lifeless furry form until it found the bullet hole in its chest and exited out through its back. The tip of the tentacle moved delicately into the wound and sucked a few drops of blood. It withdrew the tentacle back into its body. It continued to move on towards the larger lifeless form, and when it got there, it remained in a fixed spot for a minute or so. Its perception of the lifeless substance confirmed there was no tear nor a punctured hole through the skin, which means there was no blood externally. For some reason, it lost interest in it, and quickly, it made a new move forward to the road where the van had parked. It remained there while testing and analysing the air in the vicinity. A minuscule trace of human odour had been detected. It started to advance along the road in the same direction where the van went. It was obvious that it was now after a new prize: the occupants in the van.

**

'Rendezvous reached', the GPS announced.

The van braked gently to a full stop. Nigel peered out of the side window and noticed there was a dirt track adjacent to the main highway where they had stopped.

'Okay, it's an uncharted road, so I'll have to take over the van and drive it manually to another spot'.

He shifted into the driving seat and switched into manual drive. He made a U-turn and manoeuvred the van onto the unpaved road and drove on for another 20 minutes until he saw a new scene, a deep and wide gorge dead ahead. As it was at the height of the dry season, it was bone dry. Nigel carefully examined the upper and lower parts of the gorge as far as his eyes could see. There were no apparent endings to the ravine in either direction.

'Right-ho, here's the spot where they want to build a new bridge'.

He turned to look at the other two occupants in the back as he spoke. He knew he had to for Emma's convenience when he was speaking. It would aid her lip-reading skills. It was the fact that only 40% of speech could be read while 60% was based on pure guesswork. Emma was fortunate to have worked with Nigel after a long period of several years and was already familiar with his lip movements.

'Got it. This is where you had it in mind for me to go and brave the elements!'

Nigel smiled. 'Okay, no problem, let's get this wrapped up quickly, and then we'll get back home in good time', and then he looked at the desk space. 'Can we clear up our desks before we go?'

Emma pressed a button, and the misted glass cube slid down until the top part was flush with the desktop. She grabbed her translator components and decided to shove them into her pockets. She joined the others walking to the back of the vehicle. Duleep opened the tail door, which displayed several shelves, each section organised for various tools and parts. All were neatly clipped into their allocated locations. In a separate compartment was a folded table and a surveyor drone clamped neatly next to it.

Emma pulled out a bright orange construction site safety hard hat from one shelf and put it on, but the plastic strapping inside the helmet had proved to be an obstruction to her cochlear implant transmitter. She found it uncomfortable to wear, so she took the transmitter off and inserted it in her breast pocket. Duleep noticed it and looked at her. 'Without it, are you really deaf now?' he asked. 'If so, then why do you need to put on your hard hat?' He pointed at his own ear to indicate what he was talking about.

She understood him and shrugged. 'Yeah, so what, Duleep?' She looked at him. 'Bloody company regulations', she said. 'It is mandatory with all work environments'.

Then she smiled. 'If you need to communicate with me, just alert me through text on my mobile'. She took out a small old smartphone and waved at him. 'I can feel the vibration when the ringing tone is switched to silent mode'.

She pressed a button on the side of her helmet, and a clear visor dropped into the place in front of her eyes, and she pointed at it. 'Or you can transmit the text or any images onto my head-up display visor', she said.

'Ah, got it'. Duleep nodded.

She took out a bright fluorescent orange belt with brace straps and slid it over her body and clicked it snugly around her waist. In several randomised places around the belt and straps, there were several bulging pockets containing several state-of-art measurement gadgets. She also went to the onboard refrigerator and clipped two bottles of water to her belt. 'It is too dangerous out there if you get dehydrated!' she said to Duleep.

Nigel and Emma walked up to the edge of the steep cliff of the ravine.

She surveyed the contour of the creek. 'It looks about 20 metres deep and roughly 150 metres wide', she said and tightened the chin strap to make her hard hat fitted snugly.

Both looked across the creek. They could see there were several large boulders and gum trees on the other side of the creek, but they were trying to figure out the whereabouts of a suitable opening.

'I am not convinced of precisely where the opening should be, but nevertheless, once you've found the more likely ones, guide the drone to the position . . .' He pointed his finger at a gap between two boulders. 'I hope that's the place . . .' But he didn't finish his sentence as he got interrupted by Duleep.

'Excuse me, Nigel!' he shouted. 'I think we've got a malfunction on one of the six propulsion fans on the drone!'

'Oh right-ho. Can you replace it with a spare one?' Nigel shouted back.

'Aye, I'm doing that now and shouldn't be long, 5 or 10 minutes tops'.

There was a puzzled look on Emma's face as she wasn't sure what was going on until Nigel turned around to face her and explained diligently to her what the real problem was. He put his hands up and spread his fingers, and he said, 'Ten minutes'. She nodded in acknowledgement.

'Okay, no worry, just take your time, and take care as it looks really rugged down there. I'm going back into the van for a cold beer'.

This time she didn't understand him but guessed his intention anyway. She walked gingerly over the edge and found a few footings down the slopes and disappeared from Nigel's view.

Nigel strode back and sat in the driver's seat and shut the door quickly. He switched on the standby systems, and the auxiliary engine started up to power the electrical systems and the air conditioner. He could hear the humming noise, which indicated the auxiliary air-conditioner was kicking in. He pulled out a bottle from the refrigerator. Then he switched on the small television mounted on the dashboard and selected the news channel. It was putting out the news and results of the cricket being played between England and Australia. Relaxing with a beer in his hand, his mind drifted away to the next day's job. What a busy week it was, and even more so when the company had been trying to cut down the number of hours the employees were required to work following the introduction of more robotics.

He was jolted from his daydreaming state when Duleep opened the passenger door and climbed in with a laptop and sat next to him.

'Got the drone fixed. It's now up in the air', he said, his eyes focussed on the screen of the laptop.

A bird's eye view of the van could be seen on it. He was very dexterous with his fingertip control of a small joystick with one hand and the other was flying around the keyboard.

'Hold on Duleep'. Nigel looked at him. 'Keep it in the air until we get the signal from Emma. We need to give her some space'.

'Fine, I'll have that beer . . .'

'Sorry to break in with a news flash', the TV on the dashboard announced unexpectedly. *'There's been a report of the Englishman named Dr Andrew Nelson who had disappeared from . . .'*

Nigel looked at the TV, but Duleep wasn't as he took a beer and then refocussed his attention on his own screen. The TV continued prattling on. *'It was believed he's been kidnapped by a mystery drone, which no one has claimed to own . . .'*

Duleep's ear picked up the word 'drone', and he shifted his attention on to the TV screen on the dashboard, and it went on in many fragmented sentences. *'The CIA in America had vehemently denied it had anything to do with this drone . . .'*

A picture of the bulbous drone flashed across the TV screen.

'There may be strong possibilities that it's operating on its own somewhere in the world. It's imperative that no one must approach this mystery drone—it is believed to be extremely dangerous. If anyone has seen it, then it must be reported to your local police . . .'

Something in the corner of Nigel's eye had caught his attention. It was a new movement made several hundred metres ahead of the van. A metallic white object was steadily hovering across the barren landscape, and yet he couldn't make out the shape of it. Nigel grabbed a large pair of binoculars from under his seat and peered through them. He pressed a button on the side of the binocular to activate a built-in Bluetooth.

'Duleep, can you connect the Bluetooth from my binoculars?' Nigel asked, not taking his eyes from his glasses. 'Are you seeing what I'm seeing . . . ?'

A new image flashed up on the screen of Duleep's GC. 'Aye, got it', he said. 'And I'm recording it'.

Nigel cradled his binoculars while resting his elbows on top of the steering wheel and locked his view on the floating object. After a few moments, the object vaulted over the edge of the creek and disappeared.

Both looked at the laptop and moved their eyes simultaneously back to the TV screen.

'Gee, isn't that the same one?' Duleep asked.

Simultaneously, they shifted their eyes slowly up to the featureless landscape and paused. There was no further movement to be seen.

'EMMA!' they shouted out at the same time.

'We've got to get her before that object does!' shouted Nigel. 'I believe it is after her!'

They bolted out of the van, and Nigel ran around to the side of the vehicle and jolted the door slide open. Duleep was walking around erratically in a circle, holding the laptop as he was not sure what action to take. 'What am I going to do?' he shouted. 'Where is she? How can I find her . . . ?' He was clearly in a state of panic.

Nigel paused for a few seconds, trying to contemplate the best option available for him to use. Suddenly, he had a brainwave. He looked at the drone still flying above the van and gestured at it. 'Duleep, I've got an idea—why don't you stay here and use the survey drone to use the homing signal from Emma's helmet to locate her? I will follow and use the drone to guide me to her, got it?' He was still shouting at him, 'I'll be using my mobile to watch the camera images live'.

'Oh right-ho! Got it, got it, got it . . .,' Duleep said, trying to find his composure. 'But what are you going to do when you get her?'

'I'm going to try and shoot at it with my rifle, with the intention of disabling it'.

'Oh great, got it, great idea . . .'

Duleep focussed his attention on the laptop screen and moved the scrambled around in a different direction and manoeuvred around several dried bushes before coming into an opening. Her mobile vibrated out in her breast pocket, and she paused to take it out. She peeked at it and twitched her nose in puzzlement.

'*Danger! Don't go near that flying object!*' the text on the mobile readout. *GET BACK to the van NOW!*'

She shook her head. 'What the hell he was talking about?' she quizzed herself. 'What was the big deal about the surveying drone? Why was it dangerous? In what way? Was he trying to play a practical joke on me to flush me out of my hiding?' Again, she shook her head in resignation that it did not make any sense to her. She typed out the text on her mobile, '*WHAT? What are you talking about? Are you saying your drone will fall on me?*' and pressed send.

At this very moment, she sensed the soft wind billowing around her legs. 'Oh yeah, he had found me this time, so what?'

She continued to ignore the wind effect on her, and she pressed the button on the front of her hard hat to drop down the visor to give herself some extra protection against the wind blowing into her face.

She started to lift her head slowly to check out the source of the wind. Her eyes widened, and her mouth hung open at the same time. Right in front of her, about 3 metres away, she could see a large bulbous object hovering almost motionless at her head height. Without her hearing aid, she was in a completely silent world and failed to detect any noise. She was clearly astonished at the sight and sheer size of it.

What the fuck is that?

She looked down on her mobile and read it again. '*Danger!*' And she glanced up at it. A train of questions flashed through her mind. *What on earth is it? What is it doing here? What does it want?*

She slowly put her mobile into her pocket and buttoned it securely. At this very moment, the object dropped a tentacle from underneath, which spooked her to take drastic action. She realised she had to run for her life.

She leapt over the bush and sidestepped another before sprinting out into the opening ahead. She was naturally athletic, and after a few strides, she looked back over her shoulder to see if she had shaken it off. She was alarmed to see it was still following her closely. She put an extra effort into her running and jumping over a few small boulders in her pathway. Finally, she came to a small cliff that blocked her path, and she braked hard and joystick. The drone whirled out of its stationary position an[d] the creek. The hunt for Emma was on.

Nigel climbed inside the van and pressed his thumb [against the] scanner button and waited for the assuring familiar sound [of the locker] to click open—nothing. 'What the hell was happening?' h[e asked] himself.

He pressed his thumb at it again and realised there w[as] condensation building up on the button, rendering it unable [to recognise the] fingerprint—the classic hallmark problem of condensation w[hen] air touches the cold object. Someone left the door open too l[ong and] hot air had crept inside and touched the ice-cold locker. 'F[uck!' he] cursed himself.

He shoved his hand inside his pocket and pulled out a h[anky] and wiped off the condensation off the button. He pressed [down] on it, and this time the gratifying click indicated the locker [opened] successfully. Still, a few seconds wasted. He grabbed the rifl[e from the] rack and ran out, taking a few steps as he rechecked the mag[azine, as an] experienced hunter always did.

He ran towards the creek while sliding a fresh bullet into t[he chamber] of the rifle and looked up, trying to search out the drone. He f[ound it and] started to clamber down the slope of the creek, stumbling a fe[w times on] the way but managed to pick himself up and continued walking[. Then] he suddenly stopped and turned around and shouted at Dulee[p who was] out of his view. 'Hey, Duleep! Perhaps it would be best if you ca[n reach her] through her mobile, telling her to watch out for the strange obj[ect.']

'I hear you! Yep! Sure! Will do so!' came the reply. 'But am [trying] to find her!'

Nigel resumed his fast walk towards the drone, which was [flying] in a zigzag path, which was a typical technique of surveying mo[vement. 'Come] on, come on. Where are you?' he muttered to himself.

* * *

Emma had stopped as she nearly reached the bottom of the [gorge. She] sat down for a brief rest while she studied the next track to try. S[he stood] up and could see the surveying drone flying erratically. She foun[d herself] at a dead end with huge boulders blocking her way. They towe[red over] her and obscured the sight of the drone for a couple of minutes [while] swerved sideways into a new direction. She grabbed a quick glance behind. *Fuck me! It's still there!*

She was panting and sweating hard because of the additional cumbersome weight of equipment she had around her braces and belt.

She saw several trees ahead and thought the trees could be useful in giving her some extra protection. Or so she thought. It gave her some extra stamina she hadn't thought she had before, and she burst out running in a new direction towards the clusters of stunted trees ahead. While she was running hard and focussing forward, she failed to notice the hovering machine had a new device projecting from underneath, and it emitted a highly charged laser beam squarely at the centre of the tree trunk ahead and just in front of Emma. *Purpht!* A small intense plume of smoke started to smoulder before bursting into flame. She was shocked to see a flame spurting out from a tree on her left, and she changed her direction to the right. *Purpht!* There was another one spurting out on another large tree on her right. *Was the object really shooting at me?*

She turned her direction to the left again, only to find another tree emitting a small localised flame. She turned to her right. There again, *purpht*, another flame on another tree in her pathway. Then it dawned on her that the object was simply shooting intentionally at several selected trees in succession as a means of herding and cornering her into place. She stopped and pivoted herself around quickly to face the object. It was still very close, which showed her that she had failed to shake it off. She sidestepped to the left, and immediately, there was another flame erupted on a tree branch. She stopped and stepped back in the other direction, this time to her right. *Purpht!* Same result with another localised flame erupting on a large shrub.

She looked at it with her eyes blazing. *What do you want?!* She signed at it.

She realised she was practically cornered. The flames had started to increase in strength on several trees and shrubs. They were tinder dry, and it did not take much to ignite them quickly. She was horrified to realise that they were getting bigger and about to engulf her. *I'm not going to get burnt! Please help me, Nigel!* She was about to scream but saw the object was moving backwards to create a space for her to move away from the burning trees. *A break for me!*

She burst out in front, heading towards the object, and slid under it and saw another opening ahead. *I'm going to make it!* She thought, and a new spark of hope exploded inside her.

She took a few more strides before her right foot got jammed in a rabbit hole, which sent her plummeting spreadeagled into the loose earth covered with rabbit droppings. She realised she was immediately underneath the hovering object. She jolted herself over into a new position. She was now lying on her back and looked directly upward at the object. *Now what?* She signed furiously at it.

***

Duleep was still fumbling with the joystick on his control unit and manoeuvring the drone's camera and propulsion systems. 'For god's sake, where are you?' he kept muttering. 'Why did you have to switch off your homing signal?'

He continued to keep the video camera on the drone moving in every direction. The drone went higher in vain hope it would give him a wider angled view of the surroundings. 'There! What's that? Don't tell me it's smoke!' he asked himself when he spotted a plume of dirty white smoke in one corner of the screen. 'Let's go there now'.

The drone moved sideways into a new direction. Directly underneath it on the ground, Nigel was already panting hard and sweating profusely with all the effort of running he had made following the drone. He knew it would be futile to shout Emma's name as it would not make any difference, with her transmitter hearing aid removed. He looked up and saw the drone moving in a different direction; his heart sank. *Oh, fuck me, where it's going this time? Has it found her?*

He saw the drone wobbling as if it was trying to wave at him in acknowledgement that it had found something. He waved at it as a sign that he was trying to get over very rough ground towards it. He took a deep breath and made renewed efforts to run after it. It was not long before he smelt the burning. 'What's happening there?' he asked himself.

***

The torpedo-shaped object was still hovering directly over Emma for a short moment before it lowered itself to several feet above her. The shadow of it had increased steadily until it engulfed her from head to foot completely. She froze with fear and felt she could not do anything, except watch the event unfolding before her eyes. It was much bigger than any drone she had seen in her life. A tentacle dropped down and started to slide over her lower leg like a slithering snake. It continued sinuously further up her leg towards her body. It stopped when it found a spot. It was the upper part of her naked thigh. The tip of the tentacle injected a high-pressure narrow jet into her skin. It inflicted a severe sting. Her head jerked violently with the reaction, and she screamed, 'Ouch, that hurt!'

Nigel heard the familiar voice screaming and started to sprint even harder, bouncing between rocks and shrubs as he made desperate efforts to reach the source.

She turned over and started to crawl on her knees and elbows in vain attempt to move away from the dominating presence of the alien drone. She didn't get far as the chemical cocktail injected into her had started to reach her head. All it took was 20 seconds before she collapsed and became immobilised. With her head keeling over, she lost consciousness. The belly of the large probe had started to transform into a new bigger bulging shape. Just like its sister probe had done in Congo. It was shaping itself into a new and larger size with a gaping opening appearing across its belly. Out of it, a single larger tentacle with a large claw on its end was descending to Emma's body. It gripped her fluorescent orange belt with its straps and was about to start winching her up.

Out of the thick swirling smoke, a stone's throw away staggered Nigel. He was holding the mobile in one hand and his rifle in the other. He was panting and coughing from the smoke and unaccustomed effort, with sweat pouring down his face. His eyes were watering as the effect of the smoke, but he caught sight of the large shining drone making contact with the inert body on the ground. He threw his mobile aside and knelt with one knee on the ground, lifted the rifle to his shoulder, and took aim.

The propulsion fins of the probe emitted a throatier sound as it was compensating the additional weight of the human cargo. Then the probe sensed there was a human figure behind it. It spun around and was now facing head on to the kneeling figure. The inputs it was receiving had signalled that it was getting a new threat from a human figure holding the long metal rod in its hand.

Nigel could clearly see Emma being winched up, and he crooked his finger through the trigger guard and lined up the cross hairs of the sight on the main body. He was still panting hard and racking his mind whether to shoot, but at what? He was trying to determine the balance between the safety of Emma and damaging the drone, which had no obviously vulnerable target. He quickly realised there could be a strong danger of bullets ricocheting off the drone and inflicting harm on Emma dangling in mid-air beneath it. He paused, and his finger froze on the trigger. *Forget the main body! Now what?* He was desperately trying to assess which part of the drone to shoot at to disable it. *How about the propulsion fins?* He shifted his rifle slightly towards the tail end fin. *No, if I disabled that fin, it could cause it to crash on top of Emma! That's not a good idea!*

He paused again as he was wrestling with what decision to make. He opened his left eye, which was not using the telescope, to gain himself a better view of the drone in the vain hope it would aid him with his decision-making. The delays he made in being decisive proved to be a gross error in judgement he would be regretting for the rest of his life.

The probe, with its enhanced scanning mechanism, sensed a small window of opportunity and took action on it. It emitted a highly charged narrow laser beam— a fraction of a second in duration. This was much faster than the speed of a blinking human eyelid. It was the pinpoint accuracy of the beam aimed at Nigel's exposed eye and seared the retina at the back of his eye, and that caused him to jolt his head back, screaming in agony. Even though he had blinked in a reflex reaction, it was too slow compared with the infinitely superior speed of the laser beam. That was all that was needed by the probe to blind him with the intention of disabling him. He threw his left hand to cover his left eye and dropped the rifle. It was agonisingly painful and he staggered clumsily backwards and fell on his back.

The probe sensed there was no longer a threat posed from the human who was still writhing on the ground in pain, and it resumed the winching. It was repeating the same manoeuvre as its sister probe did with another male human in Africa.

Nigel, with his left hand still covering his left eye, shifted his head around slowly to focus his right eye. He was nervous and unsure if the drone would inflict the same injury on his good eye. He managed to grab a glimpse of the event unfolding before him, and with it, he heard a throatier roar emanating from its propulsion fins as the probe took off steadily into the opening among the boulders and accelerated out and up into the wide-open sky. He could see Emma's arms and legs dangling down under the drone, and it was not long before he glimpsed it making a rollover in the mid-air. It had absorbed Emma's body and limbs completely.

He looked up and scanned around as he heard his own drone hovered into view, out of the smoke swirling around it. He lifted his right hand and waved to it frantically. He shook his head in disbelief, with his shoulders hunched. 'Emma?' It was the only word that he could utter.

He was in total despair.

Chapter 14

Date: Unknown

Place: Arnhem Land

Emma opened her eyes and found herself lying spreadeagled, face down. She lifted her head slowly and carefully and scanned the surroundings trying to figure out the habitat she was in. *Where the hell am I?*

The landscape was featureless and barren with few shrubs and odd trees. She glanced at a tree at some 50 metres further up and recognised it instantly as a eucalyptus tree, with which she was so familiar. The fog in her mind started to clear a bit. *So I'm still in Australia, but exactly where?*

She sensed some whirling and dusty air billowing about behind her, and she looked around to see where the wind was coming from. Her eyes widened. *That drone!*

With its unmistakably recognisable shape and prominent probe that she had been trying to shake off a few moments ago, it was still there but hovering motionless a few metres up in the air above her. She slowly rolled over and positioned herself on her back with her elbows resting on the ground. *What the devil does it want?*

She continued scanning the landscape until she caught sight of a billabong obscured by rocky outcrops several hundred metres down to her right. *Water? Would that give me some protection against the probe's laser?*

She continued surveying, but her mind was racing as she worked out her options.

She manoeuvred herself slowly to a sitting position and shifted her focus to the probe. It remained hovering motionless in the same place. Slowly, she shifted into a kneeling position. Still, no further movement could be detected from the drone. *So far, so good*, she thought.

She realised she was still wearing her hard hat and fluorescent orange utility brace and belt. They were cumbersome and restricted her movement, so she took them off slowly and furtively and laid them on the ground beside her, all done with her eyes locked on the drone. Again, it made no new movement and remained hovering exactly in the same spot. She was trying to analyse its design for any inkling of its origins. It gave away nothing. 'Where are you from? What do you want from me?' she questioned herself and sighed. *Should I wait for it to make the first move? Then what?*

Then she remembered its hostility. It had been shooting at her with its laser probe. She slowly lifted her hand and sheltered her eyes and looked up at the position of the sun. *Must be around midday. Was it the same day? Does it matter really to know which day is it?*

She started to stand up very slowly, watching carefully for any reaction from the threatening object and glanced sideways. She was able to make a better calculation of the distance to the water's edge and found it was much shorter than she had anticipated. *It's only about 200 metres away!*

She looked back at the drone, which remained motionless. She reassessed the risks. She took a few deep breaths, trying to brace herself. Suddenly, she started to try and sprint towards the lake but found that her legs were wobbling and unresponsive. *Perhaps it's because of the injection?*

But after a few moments, the circulation in her legs improved, and with every step she took, they were getting stronger. She felt the breeze against her face coming off the water and felt much more invigorated. She focussed even more closely on the billabong as she neared it. She continued running hard until she stopped suddenly at the cliff edge a few metres above the water. At first glance, the water was murky and coppery in colour, but she could not make out its depth, and she was unsure whether it was safe to dive in. She quickly looked around and was horrified to see the drone was gaining on her. *Crikey! Seems it won't give up!*

She panted and tried to find her composure. Then she took a deep breath and jumped off the cliff and made a big splash as she hit the water surface with her feet first. She was relieved to find that it was several metres deep and was able to stay below the surface. She kicked her legs furiously and swam hard, trying to keep herself submerged. She was thankful that the water was hindering the ability of the drone to track her progress.

She continued swimming slightly deeper. She could make out the terrain of the bottom and continued swimming and pulling herself along, using a few rocks sticking up from the bottom, to propel herself faster. She could not hold her breath any longer. She started to swim up slowly until her head broke the surface without making a splash that could give her presence away. She saw the drone was still hovering just above the water but going further away from where she was. *Great! It's not able to detect me while I'm under the water!*

She took a few more deep breaths and sank slowly into the murk caused in the wake of her swimming. She continued swimming for another 20 metres until it became shallower and decided that she could try to haul herself out of the water and hope to find shelter somewhere. She swam a few metres further and realised that her swimming was creating a muddy wake in the shallower water. Her left hand grabbed something in the water, and her right hand found another one. It was some kind of root. *Could it be the roots of a mangrove tree?*

She eased herself further up until her head broke the surface of the water. She could see the tree hanging over the water and providing shade. *Great, that should give me some better cover!*

She rolled over with only her face showing just above the level of water and then started to crawl to a shallow sandy bank next to the cluster of roots. She could see the drone was still hovering further away from her, in the distance, some 100 metres away. *Perhaps I should wait here until it goes away for good!* She relaxed a bit but found herself still breathing hard. *Should I wait here, but for how long?*

The drone skipped across the surface of the water and stopped abruptly and took a turn back towards the direction where Emma was located. She watched it in bewilderment. *Oh shit, has it found me?* She took a quick breath and sank slowly into the water. *Gotta keep me in the water!*

Unbeknownst to Emma, the probe skipped across the water for several metres until it came to an abrupt stop some 50 metres from her, where it had sensed a small ripple. Something swam just beneath the water, and with the drone's limited analytical and programmable capabilities aboard its internal computer, it could not analyse that there was another living object, a small fish, had caused the ripples. The probe hovered at the exact spot for a few minutes before it started to move into a new direction. This time it was moving away from where Emma was and flew to the far side of the lake.

Emma couldn't hold her breath any further and was resigned to the idea the probe would find her as soon she came up. Her head broke the water surface and was amazed to see the probe flying away even further from her. *Oh, thank goodness!*

She started to crawl slowly onto the sandy bank and laid herself on her back with her body partly submerged in the water. *Let's try to keep still and wait before it goes out of my sight.* She was delighted to see the drone getting even further away.

Something, a small movement a few metres away, caught her eye. A brownish-coloured object was drifting towards her. She blinked and tried to focus on it. At first sight, it looked like a small log. Then as it came nearer, she could see a pair of cold calculating green eyes. *Oh shit, a crocodile!*

Despite her love for outdoor activities, one of her weaknesses was her deep-rooted abhorrence of reptiles, such as snakes and lizards. She was totally transfixed by the sight of it, and she was immobilised like a rabbit caught in the headlights. *What should I do? Should I stab it with a stick?*

Thousands of questions flooded her brain, but she remained transfixed to the spot. The crocodile drifted closer to her until it paused a few metres away. Then without warning, it launched itself at her, and as Emma's reflex reaction of self-protection was to put her leg up as a shield, it grabbed it. Much to her horror, the monstrous jaws caught her leg, enveloping her lower limb up to her knee with its teeth puncturing her skin. She shrieked and instinctively grabbed a low-lying branch with her right hand while making slashes at it with her left hand. The crocodile's response was to tighten its bite further and started to drag her back into the water. *No!*

She knew once it had dragged her underneath, there was no chance of survival. Crocodiles could stay underwater for much longer than humans could, so the only hope of survival if attacked in this manner is to fight back and get away. Simply struggling and trying to pull free was usually futile and would induce the inevitable underwater death roll, during which an arm or leg stuck in the crocodile's jaws would be likely to be ripped off. She knew this, and it had become her utmost priority in her fight not to be pulled underwater.

Emma looked back at the branch she was holding and realised it was sturdy enough to hold her weight. She grabbed it, making an unyielding vice-like grip with her left hand. She was threshing like mad with her other leg. For her, it had become a war of survival. The crocodile was much bigger and heavier than Emma, and it was in its natural element. The beast was winning as Emma tired, and she found it getting harder to maintain her grip on the branch. *What now?*

She was racking her brain quickly to see whether there were any other tactics that could get the crocodile to let her go. *Go for the eyes!* She knew they are supposed to be the most vulnerable part of a crocodile's body. *Try to hit or poke the eyes with something!* But she realised she could not afford to let go of her grip on the branch that was becoming a lifeline to her survival. *How about the vulnerability of the palatal valve?*

All crocodilians have a flap of tissue behind the tongue that shuts their throats when they submerge in water. This flap prevents water from flowing into their throats when their mouths are opened underwater. If an arm or leg is in a crocodile's mouth, it has been possible to prise this valve open. Water would then flow into the crocodile's throat, and the reptile would instinctively let its prey go. For a very moment, Emma contemplated this option and tried to wriggle her left foot to see if it could reach the back of the crocodile's throat. She quickly realised the crocodile's snout was much longer than her left leg, and she was not able to reach the palatal valve. The whole of her lower leg was firmly enclosed in its jaws. She continued to flail about in the water with her free right leg and was focussing so hard to keep herself from being pulled underwater, that she failed to see another new object appear above the crocodile. It was the drone. When she paused momentarily in her violent struggle, she suddenly saw it.

I have a double dose of horror! She couldn't make her mind up which terrified her the most.

She wondered if the splashes she created had attracted its attention. The crocodile was already getting deeper underwater with Emma's upper body slowly sinking with it. *Perhaps it's come to rescue me!*

She screamed at the drone trying to beckon it to help her. It moved slowly towards her, and without warning, the laser beneath its body started to emit a bluish-coloured laser beam at the branch just above Emma's handheld. The laser was making a sizzling sound as it was cutting slowly across the branch. She saw what it was doing and realised it was trying to cut the branch away. 'Oh wait! What are you doing?!' Emma screamed at it, saying it in sheer panic. 'Why can't you just shoot at that bloody thing?'

She realised the crocodile was already submerged, and the thought flashed through her tired mind that perhaps it had no way of getting the laser to penetrate the water.

Suddenly, the branch snapped off as the crocodile increased its pressure, and with her hands still holding it, she started to sink deeper into the water. She screamed, 'NO! NO!'

Her voice cut off abruptly when her head slid under the water. She was taking a piece of the branch with her and getting deeper into the darkness as she neared the bottom. Her mind screamed, *OH MY GOD! NO! NO! NOOO... NOOO...*

As she entered a void of blackness and emptiness, a sense of futility enveloped her, and she ceased struggling and accepted her fate. She tried to scream *NO* once more, but she couldn't. Her mind was exploding with soundless and desperate shrieks of

Noooooo . . .

Chapter 15

Date: Unknown

Place: Spatial Corroboree

OOOOOOH!

Nno . . . nno . . . nuph . . . nuumph . . . Emma started to sputter as she fought and clawed her mind out of the void of blackness. She couldn't fathom the blackness that was engulfing her and what she was fighting against. *NOOoo!* She spluttered and sucked in air. She exhaled and screamed. She startled herself. A scream of hope and life. She opened her eyes; the pupils were pulsing, dilating, and contracting. She saw glimmering lights above her. *What?!*

Her foggy mind started to clear little by little. This time she sensed she was lying on her back. She realised she was still breathing hard. She bolted herself into a sitting position and immediately buried her face into her hands. Beads of perspiration were breaking out on her forehead and neck.

She spread her fingers apart and wide enough for her to peep through. *Where am I?*

She then remembered the drone and then the dreaded crocodile. She snapped off her hands from her face and looked down on her legs. *They're still there!* She caressed her hands on her legs and found there was no disfiguration of any kind on both legs. She exhaled out a sensation of immense relief. She studied her legs again and saw a purplish mark on her right thigh. *Where did I get that bruise from? The crocodile!*

Her mind cleared further, and suddenly, she remembered the sting by the drone. *That tentacle with a sting!*

She shook her head and marvelled at how authentic her dream was. *My god, that was a hell of a dream!* She believed that the drone was real and the crocodile was not the real thing. How glad she felt to still be alive. But her sense of exhilaration was cut down at this very point when she started to survey the surroundings. Where on earth was she?

She decided it was indeed a room. What kind of room, she could not make out, as she had not seen anything like it before in her life. The walls were pulsing with some softly glowing light, metamorphosing into a wide range of colours. She realised there were four rounded corners. *Gotta a square room of some kind.*

She looked up at the ceiling and realised something was obstructing her field of view. It was the peak of her hard hat that she was still wearing that limited her view. She unclipped the chin strap and took the helmet off and laid it carefully on the floor next to her. Then she did the same thing with her fluorescent orange utility brace and belt. *That's funny. I thought I had taken it off at the billabong?*

This was all done while she was still surveying the walls and ceiling. There was no light coming out from the ceiling. It would seem to have a soft and matt grey surface, but nothing protruded from it, nor were there any inkling of construction lines or joints. Everything was completely smooth and flat. She looked down on the floor—same thing; same colour, no lights. Only the walls seemed to have millions of tiny pinpricks of iridescence that were flowing and swaying like colourful seas.

She stood up and walked towards the wall and caressed it with her hands. She felt the texture with her nails, and it seemed to be some kind of hard rubber. The colours changed as though it had been energised by her touch. Quickly, she took her hands away as she was unsure if it was harmful or not—nothing happened. She hesitated but touched the wall again and continued caressing the wall slowly until she came to the second wall. Light danced around her fingers. She realised there was no indication of gap lines of any kind at all. Immediately, she gauged the other walls—no door, no window, no ventilation grills of any kind. *How did I get here in the first place?*

Suddenly, she realised and sensed the temperature of the air in the room. It was not only hot and sticky, but it was also sweltering and suffocating. *It is just like the last time I was outside the camper van, and am I still in the same place in Australia?*

She looked around again at the walls in the hope that there would be openings, but none were to be found. A sense of claustrophobia started to swell up inside her, but she shook her head. *Get a grip of yourself!* She steeled herself. *Focus on something and continue with your inspection!*

Her years of training with civil engineering had conditioned her mind to scrutinise many types of unknown structures and materials and challenged herself to think logically and apply her critical thinking to formulate answers. She took a deep breath and exhaled slowly. *Right, let's start with the texture of the wall.*

She put her face close to the wall, and she realised they seemed semi-transparent but could not see further than a few millimetres deep. The myriad of lights blocked her ability to see further.

Her nose twitched habitually while she was in deep thought. She licked her lips and realised her mouth was dry. She looked at her utility brace and belt, and there were two thermally insulated bottles of water still attached to it. How glad she was. She picked one bottle, unscrewed it, and took several gulps of cool water. *Oh boy, how thirsty I am!* She sighed, feeling good.

She went back to the same spot and knocked hard at it to gauge the thickness of the wall. Lack of vibration had indicated that these walls were solid and thick. *Oh, my cochlear implant!*

She slid her hand into her pocket and took out the hearing aid and positioned it behind her right ear and switched it on. She called out, 'Hello'—nothing.

She clapped her hands—still nothing. She took the aid out and inspected it. The orange indicator was flashing. *Oh crikey, the battery's flat! Can't be that!* She sighed. *It's supposed to last 14 hours on one charge!*

Her spare battery and charger were at the camper van. She was now in a totally silent world. She scanned the walls and ceiling. No video camera or microphone or speaker of any kind could be detected. She screamed at top of her voice while jumping up and down, 'HEEYYY! I'M HERE! WHAT DO YOU WANT? CAN YOU SHOW YOURSELF?'

She paused and waited for a few minutes—nothing. Then she repeated her erratic behaviour once more. Then she waited for another 10 minutes—still no response of any kind. The walls continued pulsing and rippling with the colourful sea of lights as consistently as ever.

She sighed and leant against the wall for support, and her nose twitched. *Yes, my mobile! Perhaps it will tell me the time and date!*

She poked her hand into her breast pocket, dropping her hearing aid back in, and in exchange, she took out the hand-sized glass tablet. She touched it with her index finger, and it came alive. Her eyes widened at the word flashed across the screen: No Service. *Can't be! No signal strength!*

She touched it a few more times in desperation and was dismayed to see it confirmed there was no signal. She tapped it again a few more times, and the message flashed: Last data movement has been confirmed it is 21.15 hours since last used. *Don't you tell me I've been unconscious for over 21 hours!* Then she felt some rumbling in her stomach. *Yes, that explains why I'm hungry!* She looked at the water bottle and took a few more sips. *Better conserve it*, she thought. *Perhaps I'm at a black spot where there are no signals? Or I'm deep underground where the signals couldn't reach?* She sat down and sighed. *Am I a prisoner?*

She bent her knees up and embraced them, resting her chin on them. She started to rock herself slowly as if she was comforting herself. She glanced sideways and rested her cheek on her knees. Her eyes narrowed as she focussed on the far corner of the floor and wall. *Hello, what's that? How come I haven't seen that before?* There was a small hole with some items stacked neatly next to it.

She started to crawl towards it and peeked into the gaping hole. Even though the room was illuminated softly by the four walls, the hole was intensely black, and at first glance, the depth of the hole was unfathomable. The size of the hole was around 6 cm in diameter. *Is that possibly a type of ventilation duct?*

She spread her hands over it and then lowered her face above it to see if she could feel a breeze on her face. No indication of air movement. Slowly, she plunged her hand into it, and she could feel the wall of the hole was sloping and angling out horizontally, but she continued inserting her arm deeper until the hole went up to her armpit, which prevented her groping further. She pulled out her arm and glanced at the items placed immediately next to the hole. One was a cylindrical shape in a metallic grey colour but with a soft covering on top. Then there were another three round pieces stacked on top of one another, each was brown, olive, and reddish orange in colour. *They remind me of rice cakes!* But no plate could be seen, and she was not sure of their purpose.

She picked the cup up and shook it briefly. She could feel some fluid movement inside it and poked one finger through the lid top. Her eyes widened. It dissolved apart to pave way for her finger to slide through and dipped in. She pulled it out and tasted it—no flavour. *If that is water or at least some sort of liquid, then the 'rice cakes' must be food?*

She picked up the top brown 'rice cake' and nibbled it. She could taste something but could not place it as the texture was confusing. It was hard and crispy. She took another bite, and this time the taste was becoming more detectable. *Mmmm, doesn't it taste like pork, or was it chicken?* She could not make her mind up which type of meat it was, but she did not care as she was hungry. *Oh boy, I am ravenous!*

She started to munch hungrily, stopping between each bite only to sip the cup of fluid to lubricate her mouth. Then she stopped and grabbed an olive-coloured 'rice cake'. She took a small bite and chewed slowly to see what flavour it was this time. *Does it taste like some type of leaves? Must it be greenery?*

She put it down and picked up the orange biscuit and took a nibble. Bitter and acidic flavour came through. *Whoa, that must be a citrus fruit of some type!*

She swallowed a few more mouthfuls of the cool liquid, and she stopped. She felt that her stomach had started to feel bloated and sat with her face bowed between her legs. *Whoa, I think the water has swollen the food!* She burped loudly and sighed feeling better. *I'd better stop now and leave them for another time!* She put all the half-eaten items back to where they were before. She conjectured that if someone had provided food and drink, *That someone would want to look after my welfare!*

She stood up and walked to the centre of the room. She tried to touch the ceiling and could only just reach it when she stood on tiptoes. *Must be 3 metres high?*

Then she remembered her utility belt. She knelt and rummaged through the pockets and took out several devices and laid them out in a neat row on the floor. She selected one. It was a typical measuring and echolocation device that used infrared light to gauge distance as used by estate agents when measuring rooms. She positioned it against one wall and pressed the reading. Then she did it again with other adjoining walls. She scanned the reading—same calculation of 3.2 metres wide in both directions. Then she did the same again with the floor-to-ceiling measurement. She looked at it and exhaled a small breath. *Same reading! Very much a cube-shaped room!* She stood up and eyed the hole in the corner. *If that was not ventilation, then what is it for?* She cocked her head. *Maybe drainage?* She looked at the cup and food. *If that's drainage, could it be a kind of plumbing for my bodily waste?* She walked up to the wall and sat down with her back pressing firmly to the wall.

She examined the joints between the walls and floor. *Hang on! Something's not quite right!* She pressed her cheek on the floor and peeked sideways. *Huh, can't it be? Floor must be curved!* She realised the curve of the floor was very subtle and not very noticeable but curved nonetheless. She looked at the hole. *Wondering if the floor was designed to channel the fluid into the hole?*

She wanted to make sure her eyes were not deceiving her. She looked around and picked up another level measuring device from her utility belt. She positioned it and pressed a button that emitted an infrared light that was supposed to illuminate the floor. It only covered it partly. She slowly adjusted the device until the infrared light hit the far side of the floor but with no light line seen in the middle of the floor. *So that's confirmed my suspicion that the floor is indeed curved! But why?*

She repeated her action but this time at right angles to the first measurement. The device showed the infrared line illuminated right across the floor. *Are you telling me the floor is shaped something like a cylinder?*

She grabbed the bottle and was about to take another swig but stopped halfway through. She looked at the bottle and then the floor. She decided that perhaps it would be a great way to create a small experiment to see if the floor was shaped to channel the fluid to the hole. She walked to the wall furthest from the hole and poured a few drops of water onto the floor. They remained there motionless without any indication of water rolling down the floor. She frowned and repeated the test with a few more splashes of water but this time in the middle of the room and again next to the hole. They all remained exactly as they fell. *Stone me, how come they don't roll down and slide to that hole?*

She exhaled and sat down. She then looked up at the ceiling and decided to repeat her investigation with the infrared levelling device. She stood up on her toes, holding the device high up and close to one end of the ceiling, and pressed the button. She realised that this time the ceiling was indeed curved but mirroring the floor's curve. *The floor's concave while the ceiling's convex!* She sat down again and rested her chin on her knees, with her nose twitching, which showed her mind was calculating hard.

She simply uttered only one word, 'Why?'

She looked at the droplets of water on the floor and cocked her head.

How come gravity is spread so uniformly across the floor? She jolted her head back in a reaction as though her head had been hit by a lightning bolt.

I am in some sort of high-tech world where there is an artificial gravity system!

She racked her brains, and a vague memory came back to her about the trip she made to the funfair where she amused herself with attempts made to stand on the inner periphery of a giant wheel, which was spinning at high speed. She leant back against the wall and surveyed the room once again.

'I've never seen a drone of that kind anywhere on this world, and . . .,' she said to herself, pausing halfway as something had dawned on her. 'If it's not from this world, and the construction of this room is equally so *alien* to me, therefore, it's gotta be from outer space!'

Her heartbeat quickened for a moment, and she held her breath, trying to regain her composure. *How can I confirm if I'm in outer space?*

She eyed her hard helmet lying on the floor and remembered that part of building construction industry's zealous safety health-conscious regulations required all hard hats to be always worn and that they were always recording with integral video cameras. The reason for this was the insatiable health and safety regulations imposed by the insurance companies. All accident claims were authenticated and backed up with evidence from micro-memory systems.

She crawled quickly towards her helmet and slipped it back on her head. She slid a retracted visor into position in front of her eyes. It served a dual purpose: safety protection for eyes and as head-up displays (HUD) as commonly used by pilots flying combat aircraft. She switched it on, and it illuminated a menu across the transparent visor. She tapped it again a few times and found what she was looking for—the video library. She slid her finger on her visor once more again and found a specific video file. One more tap, a video projected on her visor, and she started playing it from the beginning. She could see some jerky images of the ravine, which confirmed her walking movement. With another adjustment made, she got it to fast-forward. The video movement quickened until she touched it to stop and played it again. This time she could see some fire and smoke coming in from every direction, more jerky movements, then she could see the drone positioning itself above her with a tentacle swinging and homing to her right leg. A picture of bright blue sky flashed across her visor, indicating the shock she had to endure from the sting in her leg that caused her head to flip back. Then she could see the slow movement of the ground. *Must be me crawling?* Then she could see the ground closing and hitting the helmet and blocking the built-in camera lens. *Was that how I got comatose?*

The vision of the ground started to get smaller as if she was being winched up in the air, more movement. She was puzzled at the upside-down view. *Oh yes, I must be hanging vertically up in the air with my head down!*

She took off the hard hat and held it upside down and continued watching it. She could see herself swinging around slowly. *Ah there, that's Nigel!* She could see another man in the distance. *What was he doing?* She could see him kneeling and aiming his rifle at her. *Why was he trying to shoot me?* She focussed hard at the video images and realised the angle of the rifle barrel was slightly out of line. *No, maybe he was shooting at the drone!* She was aghast to see Nigel throwing the rifle aside in a violent reaction as he covered his left eye. *Oh no, it must be that deadly laser! Was he blinded?*

Then she could see herself flying ever higher with the vision of ground receding quickly. A few moments later, she could see herself being loaded into a very small space inside the earthbound drone, but the images were very jumbled, and then everything went black.

She waited as she could see the timing of the stopwatch being replayed steadily—nothing happened, and there were no images at all. She decided to play the video forward at high speed. The stopwatch numbers blurred and flashed by. She waited for a few minutes until, suddenly, a new image flashed up. She touched it quickly to pause the replay. The stopwatch displayed 20:16 hours. She touched it again and got it to play again. She could see herself being lowered into the room. The very same room she was now in. The video showed the drone was hovering high up in the void behind the ceiling, and then the doors slid shut. She looked up at the ceiling and searched for any telltale opening lines—found nothing. *I assume that the ceiling is the only way in and out?*

She looked back at the inverted hard hat she was holding and whispered to herself, 'I hope Nigel's okay, but that showed me one thing: the drone or someone or something holding me should be treated as possibly hostile and would need to be treated with very great circumspection'.

She played the video again and waited until a new movement, which revealed her waking up in the room where she was now. The stopwatch read 21:06 hours. She walked around the room slowly with her head bowed in deep thought. *Jeez, 21 hours? Would that be enough to fly me out to outer space? Maybe.*

She stopped and stared at the clutter of devices on the floor next to the utility belt. She selected the infrared levelling device and positioned it on the wall next to the floor. The sharp infrared light beamed across the wall, and from here, she could clearly see how much difference there was in the curve of the floor. The middle of the floor was about 20 cm lower than the ends. She took out her glass tablet and switched it on. She was now using it as a calculator. Her years of civil engineering training and experience had conditioned her mind to gauge the dimensions of sites very efficiently and quickly. Her fingers flew across the numbers furiously, and a moment later, she held up her tablet and looked at the numbers. She was awestruck.

'Wow, if the floor continues through the hidden adjoining rooms, and if my calculation is correct, then the overall size of this supposed cylinder is really big!' she said. 'Something like a diameter of 500 m!'

She continued walking in a circle and she was so engrossed in her deep thought that she was oblivious to changes occurring on the walls. The pattern of lights had changed. Slowly it morphed with more brilliance. That failed to attract her attention as she was focussing on the floor.

She looked up and was startled to see new patterns of light appearing on the wall opposite her; thousands of pinpoint lights dancing erratically across one wall. She looked around the room, and the other three remaining walls were not repeating the same pattern as the one in front of her. 'Why that wall only?' she questioned herself.

Some irregular lights flicker and made changes to the usual pace of colours, which quickened and slowed down. She waited for a few minutes, hoping something would reveal itself—nothing. The wall in question kept emitting lots of new lights all in different patterns. She gave up and turned around facing another wall.

Suddenly, this time the wall started to come alive with lights, repeating the same pattern of colour as the previous wall. The previous wall died down and resumed its former usual sea of lighting patterns. She turned her body around again and this time facing the former wall. It resumed the dance of lights. *I think it's trying to catch my attention! What does it want from me?*

She folded her arms and resigned to stand waiting for many more minutes. Finally, thousands of lights started to accumulate together into as yet unrecognisable shapes. It was like the wall had transformed into a super large TV screen. Then it slowly metamorphosed into letters. She held her breath, and it continued firming up further until new words appeared in glowing red:

CHILD
THAT
MIND

Then another new word came up in the same font: *STOP*. The style of the font was thick, bold, and condensed.

'What are you trying to tell me?' she said, and she was clearly puzzled.

She cocked her head. 'Isn't that what the warning marks on the road look like?' she said.

Then new words came up: *GIVE AWAY*.

'Unless . . . unless . . . they can only be seen from a bird's eye view?' she said with her eyes widened.

'Are you trying to test me if I understand these words?' she asked the wall.

She mumbled as if she was talking to herself, 'That confirms my suspicion that I am indeed inside an alien spaceship, looking down at Earth, and somehow it had copied and was projecting these road markings!

'Jeez, I can't believe I'm in outer space in somebody's bloody spaceship! Not only that, but they are also actually trying to communicate with me!'

Her mouth sagged open.

She took several deep breaths as she tried to compose herself. She calmed down a bit. She nodded slowly and held out her hands as if she was praying at the wall and inducing it to provide her with more answers. Silence. 'I get it, but how can I communicate with you?' she said. 'You noticed I cannot hear without my cochlear implant processor? Right?'

'Can you please show yourself? WHO ARE YOU?' she yelled—still total silence.

She wasn't sure if they had made any noise because she had not been able to use her hearing aid, but there was no specific visual response. Then it started to show her more road markings like the speed limit numbers. Then it went back to CHILD THAT MIND again. The wall kept rotating the same words all over, again and again. *Was it inviting me to clarify the meaning of these words and symbols?*

She still focussed intently on the wall. So far, she could see no evidence of a loudspeaker or microphone built into the walls, but all the images on the walls only conveyed information using lights as the sole source of communication. *Perhaps it was acknowledging that the best way is to communicate visually rather than by sound?*

'Okay'. She sighed. 'I need to get a start on communicating with them, but how?'

She looked again at the clutter of devices on the floor. She was racking her brain to find a way of utilising her resources. *Need a computer with a screen for translation!* She realised her helmet had some basic operating systems built into it, but it was designed for video operations primarily. *Not much use here. I wish I had that translator pen. That would be ideal . . .* Her eyes widened suddenly. *Hang on! Didn't I take it with me when I left the camper?!*

Her right hand was trembling as she carefully felt in a side pocket. She pulled out a slim leather wallet containing a kit of two silver pens and a small black triangularly shaped holder with two small holes in it. The triangle acted as a base holder for the pens but also has a built-in microphone plus a miniature computer located inside it. It was an old piece and a limited edition of technology built in the early 2020s but had stood the test of time well.

She took a deep breath and said, 'Oh great, I can do something about this!'

She kissed it and looked at the wall. Her mind was working furiously trying to find the best way of using her translator pens. She realised there was an elaborate operating system built inside the triangular holder. Not only that, but there was also a huge storage capacity of dictionaries in several major languages to aid with verbal translation. *Oh yes! It should work!* She thought.

Her mood suddenly perked up, and she went to the wall and sat down with her legs crossed. She positioned the holder on the floor a few feet away from the wall base and inserted the two pens into the sockets. She clicked the small button on the pen holder to switch on, and one of the pens emitted a brightly illuminated in form of hologram keyboard onto the floor while the other pen projected a TV-size screen directly onto the wall at her eye-level height. *Yes, I know it's an old piece of technology, but it has served me and has been invaluable to so many deaf people over the years.*

'Now what? How and where can I start?' she muttered to herself, her nose twitching. 'What language should I use that could be more likely to be understood universally?'

She looked at the neon-lit qwerty keyboard on the floor and folded her arms. She was in deep thought and pondering on how to proceed and with what language that could be comprehended constructively by extraterrestrials. She knew the universe had a common origin, such as the Big Bang, and the laws of physics were universally true. Therefore, she asked herself, if the extraterrestrials were sufficiently intelligent, they would have discovered the same laws governing our world and universe as their own. Mathematical equations would be the same, no translations required. If you showed the alien the basic numbers or even Newton's universal gravitation equation, aliens would immediately recognise it. Surely this would provide an instant method of communication, a means to bridge two very diverse cultures.

However, she decided that she would not know how sophisticated the alien mathematics might have become, and it could quickly become a one-way conversation. However, she asked herself again whether simple counting systems and hopefully prime numbers would be seen as a sign of advanced intelligence with which communications might be constructed.

She realised probably the best way to start the process was to focus on the basic numbers only. She understood the principles of maths were universal, so it would be a good place to start. Unfortunately, she realised there was no way of knowing just what their normal form of communication might be, possibly acoustic or electromagnetic, or even that prime numbers would be of any interest to aliens. Their technology could be entirely organic, chemical, or biological.

She surveyed the wall and decided that since they had some success in catching her attention with images forming on the wall, therefore, it was probably best to respond back using the same visual language.

'They didn't respond to my verbal screams, so let's try out a new type of correspondence', she said. 'This time I'll try something like purely visual communication'.

She felt that the main problem with communication with an alien life form was that there was no intermediate translator available between cultures. Maybe the translator pens that she had brought with her unintentionally could be utilised as a viable window of opportunity between them.

She knelt and selected a few keyboard buttons and then touched the screen on the wall. She was confirming her translator's recognition of her voice as the valid source. She knew her accent was slightly different to hearing people, but the translator with its powerful built-in computer had made an allowance for it, and it carried out its function impeccably without any delay.

She stood up slowly, taking a deep breath, and looked at the wall where the screen was illuminated. *Well, it did respond to my touch. Therefore, there must be some kind of sensor built into the walls.* She nodded. *Or perhaps all these walls have built-in microcameras? Let's test them . . .*

She slowly lifted her clenched fists in front of her. Then she flicked her one index finger with her voice booming out, 'One!'

Her translator sensed it and projected the text dutifully onto the screen—*ONE*—in a yellowish colour. She nodded, smiling gleefully. Then she held up two fingers and said, 'Two!' And again, the text was conveyed on the screen accurately and faithfully.

She started to increase her numbers, but this time she was signing and using the Australian Sign Language (AUSLAN). She got up to 20 and then went back to the first number, loudly saying every time according to each number. Every time she said it, she nodded as a way of confirming the number was correct. She put her hands down and nodded and said, 'Correct!'

She paused as she was hoping for any inkling of reaction or acknowledgement by the wall—nothing. She sighed and started to repeat the procedure of showing her fingers and signing all over again. Then for the third time, she decided to change her tactics. She held up her three fingers and said, 'Four!' but shook her head and said, 'Incorrect!'

She went through all forms of numbers, switching randomly while reinforcing her stance whether it was correct or not. She was creating a pattern of numbers randomly and then all in order.

After 15 minutes, she was starting to feel despair as there was no response from the wall. She was suffering from the very high humidity and strenuous signing process she was maintaining, and her shirt was soaked through with sweat. She decided to continue signing the numbers but refraining from speaking. She was signing away in total silence. There was no response from the translator, and there was a total blank on the wall. She steeled herself. *Gotta keep going on!*

She held up one hand and spread it showing five digits. Suddenly, the screen came to life and the word *FIVE* in a bluish-white colour came up. The style of the font was different from her translator's type but nonetheless readable. Her eyes widened. *Yes!*

She started to sign the numbers in order, starting from 1. She kept her mouth shut and uttered no sound. She was testing the wall to see if it was responding and understood her signing.

ONE
TWO
THREE

And it went through all the numbers that she signed. She covered her mouth while bouncing up and down; she was so exhilarated. She shouted, 'YES!' while nodding rigorously. Her translator picked up and projected on the wall dutifully, *YES*.

What next? She looked around and picked up the bottle of water. She let a few drops of water fall onto the floor and said, 'That is water!'

Then she tapped the bottle and said, 'That is a bottle!'

She then repeated these words in sign language. A few minutes later, the wall repeated her words.

'Yes! That is correct!'

THAT IS

It flashed the same words a few times. *What? Why is it repeating? Is it trying to ask me something?* She was puzzled and suddenly realised she was speaking and switching into other new words with which it was unfamiliar. It was asking for clarification and definition of these words. *Oh jeez, I'd better be careful with what I am saying!* She paused and pointed her index finger at the bottle. 'That is a bottle', she said, accompanied by her signing.

Then she pointed at the 'rice cakes'. 'That is food', she said.

She started pointing her finger at a few objects around the room and announced, 'That is a belt'. She kept up with signing every time she spoke.

'That is a hole'.

'That is a cup'.

And she kept pointing at the same time. She kept checking the wordings emitted by her translator and was impressed by its accuracy. *So far so good! It's picking things up quickly!*

Suddenly, a new image of a woman appeared on the wall. She looked at it and realised it was a mirror image of herself.

THAT IS

The word had been superimposed on the image of herself. *Perhaps it's asking for my name?* She pointed at the wall. 'That is Emma', she said and then pointed to her chest. 'My name is Emma'.

THAT IS EMMA

She sighed. *English grammar can be so difficult. Okay, let's try and keep it simple.* She looked at the wall and shook her head. 'Incorrect'.

She realised it was going to be a long night, a long night of teaching the wall the use of words in a structured and conventional way.

She sighed heavily. *Okay, here we go.*

* * *

Five hours later, despite lots of hits and misses, Emma was really pleased with the progress made with the wall. She was marvelling at how far 'The Wall' had picked up the vocabulary and some very short sentences. It was getting more and more accurate. She was grateful for the library of photos and pictures stored in her translator that she could access when conveying her point on naming the objects. She had also accessed various boxes of colour shades that had helped her speed up their concept of new words.

She was getting tired and decided she had enough. She switched off the translator to conserve the battery power and lay down on her back in the middle of the room, hoping to grab a moment of eyes shut. It was the power nap that she desperately needed. When she locked her hands behind her head and shut her eyes drifting into a deep sleep, she failed to sense a movement materialising on the floor where her translator was positioned. A small slit opened, and the translator disappeared into it. A moment later, the slit shut, and the floor was back as it was before, with no translator in sight.

* * *

She slept for four hours, and unbeknownst to her, while she was sleeping, the translator was returned to the floor but at a different spot.

She woke up to find her shirt and shorts were still soaked through with sweat. Her bottles had run out of the water. She picked up the cup next to the hole and shook it. It was empty. She looked at the wall and said without much conviction, 'Emma wants more water please'.

She was startled to find the translator was not in the same place as it was before. She looked at The Wall and said, 'Have you touched my translator?'—no response.

She picked up the translator and moved it to the same spot as it was before. She positioned it carefully and switched it on. Familiar holograms of keyboard and TV screen were projected on the floor and the wall. She typed on the keyboard, and the message came up on the wall, 'Have you been toying with my translator?'

CORRECT

'Why?' she typed.

ASSIMILATE EXTRA INFORMATION

She paused as she was looking at it. *Whoa, the language's getting better! It must have accessed the dictionary inside my translator!* She stood up quickly and regained her composure. She perked up and was feeling quite exhilarated.

'Emma wants more cold water', she said. 'I am thirsty'.

Her translator sensed it and conveyed her voice into text dutifully.

MORE WATER YES came the reply.

She placed her two empty bottles next to the hole alongside with the cup and took a few steps back. The corner part of the wall transformed into something. A pipe protruded and inserted itself into the cup and filled it up to the brim and then withdrew into the wall, but it ignored the bottles lying next to the cup. *Well, at least I have more water. Better than nothing.*

'Thank you', she said and signed simultaneously.

She picked up the cup and sipped the fluid. *Ooh, that was really cold water!* She looked at the wall and thought there could be another challenge for her to cooperate with the wall or whoever it was behind the wall.

'I could do with a cooler room!' she decided.

She splashed a few drops from her cup on her face and announced, 'Make the room cooler'.

ROOM COLD MORE

She felt something cool breezing her face. It was coming from the hole. She crawled towards the hole and felt so good when she leant her face next to it.

TEMPERATURE NUMBER QUESTION

She saw it and realised it was asking for what temperature she wanted the room to be set at. She signed the number at the wall without realising she was not speaking at all. She was getting tired with all the mental gymnastics made with the wall, and the heat was getting to her.

22 CENTIGRADE. CORRECT

'Thank you', she signed while speaking without using voice.

YOU SIGN THANK YOU. EXPLAIN

She realised it was detecting her signing without inputs from the translator.

'I need you to know I am grateful for your help', she spoke and was glad to see her translator machine had recognised her distinct accent and adapted accordingly.

YOU NOT EXPECT OUR HELP. EXPLAIN

'I thought you were hostile and would not help me'.

WHAT IS HOSTILE. EXPLAIN

'It means not friendly'.

WHY ASSUME US NOT FRIENDLY. EXPLAIN

Don't tell me I'm dealing with someone like a five-year-old kid with insatiable curiosity! She rolled her eyes.

YOUR EYES ROLLED. EXPLAIN

'Okay, for a start, you hold me here against my will. I am not happy. I feel lonely'.

YOU NOT LONELY

'What do you mean? More people like me on this . . .' She swung her hands around. 'This place?'

YES. FOUR BIPEDAL CREATURES

She paused with her eyes widened.

'Bipedal? Wha . . . erm . . .' She spluttered in confusion. 'What-wha . . .'

'Unable to process your existing speech, please repeat', her translator conveyed the message on the wall.

Upon seeing it, she regained her composure and spoke more forcefully with her voice comprehensively clearer this time. 'Please confirm to me, including me, that there are four human beings at this place? No other bipedal creatures? Humans are bipeds, correct?'

CORRECT

'Then why are they not with me here in this room?'

RISK FROM POSSIBLE HARM

'How come?'

The wall suddenly came alive as a gigantic TV screen, with a clip of filming, could be seen with Nigel kneeling and aiming his rifle at her.

MAN WITH WEAPON AIMING AT YOU

'Oh, I am sure he was trying to save me'.

EXPLAIN HIS INTENTION

'Perhaps he was shooting at your drone to disable it'.

DRONE DISABLED. DRONE FALL ON YOU

YOU HURT

NOT LOGIC

'Perhaps he didn't mean to. His intention and instinct were to save me without realising the consequences'.

HARMFUL AND DEFECTIVE DECISION

'Yes, I can see your point'.

EXPLAIN THIS

Then the wall came alive with other movie clips; this time it was a bird's eye view of people with machine guns shooting at other people. Then another image of fixed-wing planes flying and making a bombing run over a densely populated town.

'Yes, I can see there are lots of conflicts going around in the world, but it doesn't make us all troublesome, warlike people and hostile to one another all the time'.

SEPARATION OF PEOPLE AND YOU ENSURE SAFETY

'Please let me see another person', she said with her hand pointing at her chest. 'Let me be the judge? Is that possible?'

The video images on the wall faded out and were replaced by the familiar glowing lights. Silence. *What now?*

A moment later, she could see the pulsing lights on one wall were starting to become dimmer and transforming into an opaque grey glass wall. She took a few steps closer to the wall in question and cocked her head. The opaqueness in the wall was starting to clear up slowly as if the grey smoke was fading out. Transparency was replacing the opacity, and she could see an image lurking behind the wall metamorphosing into a new image—a smiling human face. The skin was dark, and the hair was short, curly, and black. Emma's mouth and eyes were widening in unison and shouted, 'A black man!' She slapped her hands repeatedly against the wall in a mood of sheer exhilaration. 'Finally, another person! I am not alone after all!'

He sported a few days of beard growth, and he was looking dishevelled and haggard. He was standing behind the wall and waved at her, seemed he was equally happy to see her.

'Helloo!' she shouted.

She could see that the thickness of the transparent wall was about 4 cm of a solid glass-like material. She tapped her clenched fist against the wall and could see the puzzled look on the man's face. He pointed at his ear and mouthed, 'Can't hear you!'

She could lip-read him but decided to shout it louder this time and was practically screaming her head off, 'IT'S GREAT TO SEE YOU! MY NAME IS EMMA! WHAT IS YOUR NAME? WHERE DO YOU COME FROM?'

A puzzled expression could be seen on his face. He shook his head furiously and shrugged and mouthed exaggeratingly, 'WHAT?'

She sighed. What now? How can I communicate with him through this bloody thick glass? She looked down sideways and saw her translator lying on the floor. *Yes, that should work!* She looked up at the man and put her hand up to signal him to wait. She grabbed the translator and lifted it to the level of her chest and spoke in a composed authoritative tone.

'Hello. What is your name? Which country do you come from? Can you speak English?'

Her translator beamed the wording dutifully onto the wall directly in front of the man. The wording appeared in several lines. The man looked at the wording, but his expression still showed puzzlement. It took him a while to work out the wording. *Is he that slow or what?*

Then she realised he was trying to read the wording, which was inverted from behind. She waved at him and pointed her two fingers at her eyes and then at the other adjoining wall. He smiled and nodded with understanding. She put her translator on the floor and repeated her questions. He smiled and spoke slowly. She watched him and beckoned him to repeat again.

She repeated his reply to her translator, 'Did you say your name is Andrew and you come from England? Is that what you were telling me?'

He squinted, looking through the glass wall to the opposite wall, and nodded with a huge smile, revealing brilliant white teeth. She grinned back at him. *We're getting there!*

'My name is Emma, and I come from Australia', she signed and spoke at the same time. 'My parents were originally from England'.

He gawped at her, putting his hands up, mouthing, 'Wait!' He was pointing at her hands.

She turned around and glanced at him.

'So what? I'm conversing in sign language'.

He smiled and started to close his eyes as if he was trying to remember something. He looked at her and started to wave and made a few gestures that were recognisable to her. She stared at him with her mouth gaping.

'Are you kidding me? Are you deaf?' she signed back at him.

He shook his head, took a deep breath, and said, 'No, no, I'm not deaf! But I used a bit of sign language because my parents are deaf, profoundly deaf and native sign language users. Forgive me, my sign language is a bit rusty as I haven't used it for quite a while!' He continued, but the pace of his gestures was much slower than Emma's.

'Hey! You're actually a CODA!' she shrieked with excitement and signed away at high speed.

'What? Please slow down!' he gestured to her.

'Okay, you are actually a CODA, which is an abbreviation for child of deaf adults'. She used her signing at a much slower rate.

He picked it up and responded, 'Yes, that's right, but I mainly used the basic form of British Sign Language'.

'No problem, BSL and AUSLAN are broadly similar in some ways, so we should manage somehow'.

She was hopping with excitement.

'Okay, can you tell me how long have you been in your room? I believe I've been here for about 20 hours!'

'Oh, I am not sure, but my watch tells me I must be here for something like four days!' he said, putting his four fingers up. 'I was forced to watch all those movie images being played all over again and again on the bloody wall!'

His gestures were rather crude, but Emma understood him quite well.

'WHAT? Are you telling me you've been alone here by yourself for four days? Have you met anyone else?'

'No. You have no idea how glad I was when I saw you! You are a picture!'

'Good, let's keep communicating!'

She marvelled at how they managed to understand each other so effortlessly despite the subtle differences in the structure of BSL and

AUSLAN. She took a few steps back and turned facing the wall where her translator was positioned and looked at Andrew.

'I'm going to try to ask them if they can remove that bloody wall between us!'

Andrew looked through the wall to the adjoining wall to where the wording was being beamed by her translator and nodded. She looked around at the wall and spoke in a firm voice while maintaining her signing simultaneously. 'Can you please remove that wall? I can confirm that man is not harmful to me'.

Her hands were pointing at the wall and waved apart as if she was drawing curtains apart. She waited for a few minutes before attempting to repeat her request. Andrew looked at her with a quizzical expression on his face. *Is she expecting too much?*

Then there was an extraordinary occurrence as the wall started to dematerialise. It had simply become liquefied and started to melt into the floor. A moment later, she could see a larger room combining the two former cubes. Andrew was watching the same drama unfolding before his eyes, and his mouth was agape in sheer astonishment. He couldn't fathom how she could have instructed some other being who understood her sign language. She saw the puzzled expression on his face but decided not to tell him that they were residing in a spaceship of some kind—not yet. She could feel warm and humid air flowing from Andrew's area into her area, but she ignored it. Her mind was focussing on joining forces with another human. Her face was beaming with a big smile, and with a spring in her step, she hopped towards the man and flung her arms around Andrew's neck and hugged him. He was taken aback, flabbergasted, as he was not expecting such an enthusiastic response from a complete stranger, never mind such a strikingly good-looking young woman. She let go of her grip and saw she had embarrassed him. She laughed.

'So! You are very shy!'

'Well, maybe!' He looked down at the floor red-faced underneath his unkempt hairy visage.

She grabbed his hand and pulled him towards the middle of her room area. 'Let's sit down! We've got a lot to share, and hopefully, between us, we'll learn something more about this place!'

'Now tell me what's happened to you, and how did you get here?' she said with a quizzical expression on her face.

He started to explain, 'Well, I was in Africa—'

She interrupted him mid-sentence, 'Hang on, let me sort out this translator!'

She scrambled over to the translator. She touched the keyboard and made a few quick adjustments. She was reprogramming it to recognise another new voice. She looked at him. 'Can you please read all these sentences using your normal voice so it can be calibrated to distinguish your speech from mine?'

He looked at the screen on the wall and took a deep breath before he started to speak.

'The blue house has got four red windows . . .'

It took him a good 5 minutes before he completed the exercise. He looked at her askance.

'So how did I do? Was that good enough?'

Her fingers moved quickly across the hologram keyboard, and she was satisfied that the translator had created a new program of recognising another person's speech in addition to hers. Then she replied, with a beaming smile, 'Great! Okay, let's start again—what were you saying about Africa?'

She had positioned herself with Andrew sitting in the middle between her and the translator. She was facing him, but her focus was not actually on his face but just over his shoulder on the screen behind him. She was reading the transcription beamed on the screen by her translator.

'Okay, well, what happened to me . . .'

He started to describe the incident that occurred in Africa. She was smiling at him, but she was concentrating on reading the transcription. Throughout his story being unfolded, she kept interrupting him with questions. He smiled. He did not mind as he was a patient man.

'Oh really, you've got a PhD!' she interrupted him after a few minutes. 'Wow, a Doctor of Science!'

'Yeah, but can I explain my reason for being in the Congo?'

'Sorry, please carry on. I'd better try not to interrupt you too much!'

He nodded and realised it was going to be a long night. He didn't care about that. Why should he? He really welcomed and cherished the moment when he realised he was no longer on his own after four days, as his watch date had indicated, and he was now sharing experiences with another human being. *Absobloodylutely marvellous!*

'Okay, there was a base camp located deep in the rainforest . . .,' he started to prattle on.

He knew he had a thousand questions to ask Emma about her experiences and their current situation, but he decided it could wait until he finished his side of the story. Emma had the same eagerness to ask him for any information that would shed some light on the reason for them being in their current predicament. It was going to be a long night—a very long one indeed.

What was a day, and what was a night, come to think of it?

Chapter 16

30 May 2028

President's Oval Office, White House

Four people could be seen sitting around on the three long settees positioned in a semicircle in the Oval Office. They were the senior members of Pres Rachel Wallace's inner cabinet. Two had arrived by their personal heli-drones on the secure landing area on the roof of the White House, from where they had been ushered into the famous nerve centre. The third had arrived by helicopter. She had summoned them at very short notice to attend this precursive meeting, as she called it, but they knew their president well enough to gauge that it must be a real emergency.

She was sitting on her own at one end of her favourite settee, giving her a commanding view of the other people in the room.

John Campbell, the secretary of state, normally an immaculate dresser, was still wearing his golfing clothes, a clear indication that there was a really serious problem. John was the only person who didn't come in his personal heli-drone but instead by helicopter. He was bemoaning the fact to himself that he had not had either a shower or a set of office clothes on his official chopper.

The director of the CIA, Richard Wagner, was wearing his usual gloomy facial expression. The pressures of controlling the world's most significant intelligence-gathering agency were shown in his fatigue.

Thomas Cooper was the executive director of the White House Communications Agency and after many years' experience in the industry, had been persuaded by the president to join her inner team, to be her government's spokesperson and interface with the press. The third man was sitting well back and seemed to melt into insignificance.

The president scanned her tablet, which displayed an image of the man who was on the edge of her mind and studied it for a few moments to refresh her memory. It was Stevie Ford, and it was he who had used great initiative, managing to bypass the official channels to reach the eyes and ears of the president. Although he was a senior systems analyst, he was also a key public relations officer at the Jet Propulsion Laboratory. He was, however, the cause of the gathering, as he had identified the significance of the apparently disparate abductions in Australia and Africa and the blurred images of what looked like an unidentified spacecraft. *Ah yes, wasn't that same man*, she recalled, coming up on the stage to meet the late Edward Stone and the friendly bear hug between the two men. She was reassured that if Edward trusted him, he was assuredly reliable.

President Wallace reset the tablet, and it came up with a new display. She replayed it a second time. It was a bird's eye view of a hitherto unidentified type of device, shaped like a short and fat torpedo, in the process of winching up an inert young woman.

She turned to John Campbell, who had just slumped onto one of the settees a few moments previously and was breathing hard. He had to walk further than anyone else to the office from the helicopter landing pad. However, during the trip in the helicopter, the Red-Alert-Eyes-Only scrambled electronic message on his tablet had arrived. This showed the apparent abduction of a young woman, which hardly seems sufficient justification to interrupt his personal recreation. After all, it had apparently been carried out in some remote place in Australia. Another set of images came from a source in Africa, somewhere he had never visited. The event had not even occurred in the USA for heaven's sake! He was already quite familiar with several types of human-carrying heli-drones akin to pilotless aircraft that had been developed around the world as a solution to the heavy traffic congestion problems. But he couldn't fathom the urgency of this matter that required him to cut his golf game short. *So what's so important about these damned drones?*

Rachel Wallace smiled at him disarmingly. She knew the crusty old state secretary very well but was quick to disarm him with a 'Thank you so much for coming in at this short notice, John'. Her green eyes were dark with some unreadable emotion.

The president cleared her throat and addressed her advisers.

'You have been called into this meeting because I believe we have been alerted to what are monumental and sensational happenings. First, there was the apparent but increasingly likely sighting of an unwarranted visitor upon our world. Second, there are two abductions at different locations. I might be hypothesising, but there might be more that have not been brought to our attention.

'Individually, they might not be taken as significant, but collectively, they may indicate a major event. I need your considered views'.

She turned on the small display screen in the Oval Office.

'Do we believe there is a real possibility of a connection between these events? And if these can be confirmed in any way, and if so, how? Then what do we do about the whole situation? The possibility of hostile or benign intent may be taken into consideration.

'Do we have to consider to what extent we make this incident known beyond this office? To what extent do we need to involve at least our closest allies?

'Maintaining the strictest secrecy is of paramount importance if we are to avoid global panic, particularly until we have a much clearer view of any intent or confirmation that the three separate incidents are, in fact, connected'.

She paused. Then she said, 'Okay, gentlemen, can we have your best suggestions put on the table? With so many conflicting stories, I'm finding it hard to know where we should start'.

Glancing at Wagner, Campbell said, 'But let's start with you, Richard, do you have any prior knowledge of the drone with its involvement with the kidnappings of the young Australian woman and the Englishman? These two abductions have occurred in widely disparate locations, one in Australia and the other in Central Africa'.

Wagner replied quickly, 'Let me tell you what I've already discussed with Mr Tony Turnbull, UK's prime minister, and with Australia's PM, Mrs Helen Kelly. I've spent a good half an hour discussing the whole scenario with each of them before I came here. I tried to reassure them about what we already knew as factual. In answer to your question, I have confirmed that the CIA has no sustainable knowledge of these drones. They've accepted this. However, they have specifically requested us to cooperate closely with them by providing any further information on the whereabouts of their missing citizens, namely the Englishman Dr Andrew Nelson and the Australian Emma Wilson'.

'Then who the hell operates these drones?' said Campbell. 'Have they been developed by someone privately without our previous knowledge? What is so important about them that you needed me to come here at such short notice? I can't see the importance of things. Kidnapping? Just two foreign citizens, not even Americans, for cripes sake! Big deal!'

President Wallace looked at him quizzically. 'Didn't you get to the final part of the security brief? Especially the part about the drones' presumed origins? The unwanted visitor?'

Campbell looked flustered. 'What origins are you talking about? What final part of what documents? Care to enlighten me?'

The president shot an icy glance at Cooper. 'Thomas, didn't you send him the full information package, including the latest news about the unexpected visitor?'

He shook his head.

'Nope, only the section relating to the drone as I thought it was these that were appropriate issues for him to deal with', Cooper said. 'I thought the second part of the documents was so touchy that I thought it better withheld until it could be brought to his attention when he came here'.

'That is for me to decide!' snapped the president.

'I entered this room looking like I came from another planet, but it seems that it is the right place!'

Campbell chuckled as he sensed the atmosphere in the room was becoming too tense.

'Care to fill me in? What's this second part of the brief that I've missed out on? What unexpected visitor are you referring to?'

President Wallace and Director Wagner glanced at the fourth person who, up to this point, had been sitting unobtrusively on the third sofa. He was in his late 60s and wore a rather ill-fitting jacket and jeans. This was the fashion when the clothes he was wearing wouldn't have looked out of place in the early 1980s. He was assistant to the president for science and technology, director of the White House Office of Science and Technology Policy, and co-chair of the President's Council of Advisors on Science and Technology. These formidable credentials made his opinions on anything scientific invaluable to the president but were almost unknown to the rest of this formidable gathering.

'Doctor Clark is my extremely well-informed presidential scientific advisor, and I am going to ask him to give us the latest information as to what he believes to be the origin of these objects'.

'Yes, ma'am'.

Doctor Clark leant forward and touched his index finger at the edge of the large opaque screen on the wall, positioned for all to see. It sensed his fingerprints and chirped in acknowledgement. Arrays of indexes glowed through to the surface. He selected one, enlarging it until the image filled the screen. It was of a cylinder with a large protuberance from one end, somewhat like an umbrella. The colour of the whole object was mainly matt black, and it was difficult to detect finer details of the silhouette of the object when it was viewed against the black background of infinite space. Only with the help of a slightly stronger light thrown by the sun reflected from the Earth gave a small improvement to the silhouette with an infinitesimal improvement afforded by far-off twinkling of stars against the intense blackness. Doctor Clark manipulated the contrast which helped further improve the image.

'What in the hell is that supposed to be?' said Campbell.

Doctor Clark replied in measured tones, 'Extraterrestrial or alien spaceship. We believe it's where the drones came from. Well, presumably, it is some sort of mother spacecraft. That is our unexpected visitor'.

'Are you having me on?' Campbell's voice quavered as he scanned his peers for their emotions.

Nobody in the room laughed or smiled. He looked at President Wallace, and the expression on her face was sombre. He knew she was not the sort of person to joke with anything. His face whitened as the blood drained from it. A few questions flashed across his mind, but he was at a loss with what to say. He was clearly gobsmacked.

'Yes, I'm afraid it is still up there orbiting as we speak', Doctor Clark commented in a completely unfazed manner.

Finally, Secretary Campbell seemed to pull himself together. 'How long has it been up there? Since when? Has it made any contact with us? What does it want?' He wanted to carry on with questions, but President Wallace put her hand up.

'Those are the questions we all want answers to. That is precisely why we are here. George will fill in for you now'.

'Thanks, Mrs President', Doctor Clark said, looking hard at Secretary

Campbell. 'Okay, John, bear with me, I'll explain as quickly as I can, starting with how it was spotted first, I believe, by the observatory in Chile, probably more than a week ago—'

'A week! How come . . . Why didn't they tell us?' Campbell was clearly intrigued.

'I believe their silence is probably because of the military government in control down there—we don't trust them, and they don't trust anyone else. But we're not sure how long they have managed to keep it quiet and how long the object has been up there'.

The president intervened between the two men and addressed George. 'I think you'd better revisit the incident at the *Voyager* project two years ago at the Hilton Hotel'.

'Yes, ma'am'.

Doctor Clark nodded. He took a deep breath, trying to recollect the incident's details.

'Remember the event at the Hilton Hotel in Las Vegas, where there was a closure of the *Voyager* project . . .,' he started to prattle on.

It took him a good 15 minutes to explain everything step by step, starting with the event unfolding at the Hilton Hotel, leading up to the event where Katie Bond, based at the observatory located in Hawaii, unexpectedly received the photo e-mailed to her from the observatory based in Chile. Then how, in the meantime, a journalist named Brett Fielding, being so persistent, that once he had a journalist's sniff of a scoop, had got wind of the communications? His investigations made over the last two years had resulted in his having a meeting with Stevie Ford. It was he who confirmed his suspicions about the illegible data emitted during the *Voyager* incident two years previously.

Finally, Doctor Clark pointed at the photo on the screen. 'Madame President and gentlemen, to the best of our analytical abilities, we believe that it is, indeed, an alien-manufactured object. However, I cannot begin to guess what its mission or objectives are. That is not a scientific task'.

'If you must know, Doctor Clark has already spent an hour discussing and clarifying this issue with Ford in his office. He is still there as we speak, waiting for our next instruction', Thomas said.

Wagner waved his hands. 'So far, it has been orbiting our Earth at around 20,000 kilometres, well beyond our usual communication satellites' positions, but still has not made any contact with us—yet'.

Campbell responded, 'Why don't we try and first communicate with them somehow and find out what they want? From there, we'll know what next step to take, either militarily or, hopefully, through usual diplomatic channels'.

The president spoke up. 'That is what I wanted to hear! Someone needs to try, in an organised way, to try and contact the alien craft, to try and make some sort of friendly overture, but we do not know what sort of radio dimensions we will have to use'.

Cooper looked down at his watch. 'I will get on to Joanne Thorntons, the director of SETI, to start gearing up their radio telescopes with a view to contact it. We're hoping for peaceful contact'.

The president again intervened. 'Up to this point, there could be other people being kidnapped that we may not be aware of, but for now, with the evidence we have with photos, let's focus on these two people. This abduction might appear hostile, but maybe they have the same problem that we are addressing in that they do not yet know how to contact us either', President Wallace said, shrugging.

Campbell was still silent. He had extensive experience dealing with foreign diplomats with their major international issues but not on this impossibly complicated interspace scale. He was simply at a loss on what to say.

Rachel Wallace sensed it and nudged him with a question. 'John, what's your initial impression of this?'

'The more people on this Earth are aware of it, the less place for the drones to hide or give them no further opportunity to kidnap more people. It would help our people prepare to confront them effectively and perhaps provoke them out of hiding to contact us. If they've hostile intent, then we'll respond with appropriate military action'.

Doctor Clark shook his head vigorously. 'I have to disagree with you there. It's wishful thinking and dangerous thinking'. He took a deep breath and continued, 'By showing up on our doorstep out of nowhere confirms that they have major scientific capabilities way beyond anything we have on this planet—no doubt about it'.

'Your point being?' asked the president.

'Essentially because of that, they're going to be the ones that set the rules or calling the shots, not us'.

'Then what do you suggest we do? Sit on our hands and do nothing?'

'Afraid so. For a start, we don't even know if the operation of this spaceship is manned or unmanned. We'll have to wait for them to make the first move and see what they want from us'.

'That's unacceptable! We can't do anything?! Are you saying we have no choice but to roll over and lie on our backs, hoping they'll tickle our bellies?' Thomas said aggressively.

'Practically', said Doctor Clark. 'That's the conservative view of the scientists saying that once the aliens arrived on Earth, they could undoubtedly conquer the world—that's if they're following the laws of nature as far as our knowledge of science tells us'.

'Care to enlighten us?' Campbell asked.

'I believe that the basic evolutionary fact that all living beings follow is the "survival of the fittest". Hell, that is exactly what we try to do! Compete for access to every source of food or energy and, thus, with the propensity to create a favourable environment to gain an advantage to ensure the survival of their species'.

'Are you saying they're here to harvest our natural resources? Is that what you are saying?' Campbell was clearly unused to this kind of tech-speak.

'They obviously have powerful reasons for being here in our neighbourhood of the universe! They are not likely to want to buy toys for their kids!' Thomas interrupted aggressively with his eyes blazing. 'Then we have no choice but to prepare and consider our next military step to take against them! That's the *only* feasible and logical step to take!'

Doctor Clark responded with a more moderating tone, 'Maybe, maybe not. The problem is we don't really know if we have the adequate military capability to counter the unqualified threats yet. However, the last thing I want to do is to view everything in such a pessimistic way. There is a glimmer of hope—that is, if we can be realistically optimistic'.

'Such as?' President Wallace's eyes widened with hope.

'How about this as a hypothesis—' Doctor Clark looked around to make sure he was getting everyone's attention. 'Let's think this way: If there was no application of what we consider morality in their decision-making, it would weigh *against* them. Therefore, it means it is in their interest to cooperate with us'.

'I still don't get it?' Campbell cocked his head on one side quizzically.

Doctor Clark smiled. 'Less or no morals and ethics would mean less cooperation. Without cooperation, you don't have progress. Any species that do not cooperate would die out or won't make it that far evolutionarily. Lions need to cooperate to hunt effectively. So do other species like ants and bees. In nutshell, no morals mean no cooperation, which, therefore, means no progress being made. Here's what I am trying to say: It should be in their interest to cooperate with us regardless of how grim a situation we appear to be in'.

'So it could be, either way, confrontation or cooperation?' President Wallace pointed her fingers at him in askance.

'Yes, my guess is as good as your guess'.

Nobody spoke a word for a full minute. They all tried to digest the complexities of the unprecedented situation.

'Do we have any form of modus operandi to detect their intentions, or can we set something up with a major defensive programme?' Cooper was looking back and forwards at President Wallace and Doctor Clark in askance. 'Have we got any systems in existence to gauge their intentions?'

'Don't think so, we haven't had any preparation for an extraordinary event of this magnitude. It's only by chance and with thanks to Mr Ford for not giving us the two years' window of opportunity to prepare us to take the necessary steps to deal with unidentified threats we're now facing'.

'Didn't he give you any reason?' President Wallace suddenly stood up and walked around, banging her fist in her hand before sitting down again on the end of her sofa. For a moment, she was silent, and they watched her closely. Finally, she said to Doctor Clark, 'Did you say Ford is in your office at this moment?'

'Yes, I've instructed him to wait there'.

'Good'.

She leant forward and spoke to her intercom, and a female voice came through. 'Yes, ma'am?'

'Susan, I believe there is a man by the name of Ford waiting in Dr George Clark's office in the East Wing?'

'Yes?'

'I want him here *now!*'

'Okay, but I still need to process them through security. It may take a good 15 minutes'.

'No, I said *now*! Pronto! Skip the security procedure!'

'Certainly, ma'am'.

President Wallace broke off the link and glanced at the faces around the room. Nobody had said a word. She looked at the antique carriage clock that stood on her desk. It had originally belonged to George Washington. She loved the tranquilising effect of the clock with its deep mellow chimes and rhythmic ticking. It reminded her that she and her predecessors could not escape from the grip of history from events and decisions in this historic room. She was very aware that every decision she made would have a domino effect down through history. She felt the world's breathing down her neck, reminding her of whatever decisions she made would be profound— for better or worse.

The team helped themselves to the choice of tea and coffee on a table against one wall of the Oval Office while they waited. A few minutes later, Stevie Ford was ushered into the office by the FBI security guard, who saluted smartly and turned and left. Doctor Clark introduced the new arrival who was clearly impressed by the seniority of the assembled team and the president herself, no less.

She invited him to sit down on one of the sofas. Ford was, as usual, cool and collected, even in the presence of the impressive and august seniors gathered around. *The Oval Office!* Not in his wildest dreams had he ever had the opportunity to be face-to-face with the president.

'Let's hear from you, Mr Ford. Correct me if I'm wrong, George has informed me you came across something abnormal with *Voyager 1*'s signals or some kind of irregularity with its transmissions at the time of its communication shut down at the Hilton Hotel two years ago, is that right?'

'Indeed, that is so, ma'am'.

'And you suspected something unusual about it but didn't inform the world, did you? What was your reasoning?' Her eyebrows shot up quizzically. 'Why was that?'

'Yes, ma'am', replied Ford. 'Bear with me. For a start, it was not my intention at all to mislead you all by keeping you in the dark—far from it'.

President Wallace replied with a strong measure of irritation showing in her voice, 'Yes, but why? We could have had two years assessing the significance of the signals ourselves and appropriate measures in place to counter the extraterrestrials, if, indeed, that's what they are'.

'Precisely, ma'am. If you will understand, the information we were trying to analyse was so obscure and faint, it was not possible for us to verify just how significant it was. I can only assume from the fact that you have even summoned me here today that you have had some additional readings, which have raised the significance of the whole scene? I had a good opportunity to discuss our original suspicions in depth with the late Edward Stone, and we were not convinced what was the best course of action to take, given the extremely faint readings emanating from the *Voyager 1*. Even now, we are not entirely sure if the reading was, indeed, the direct result of the external intelligence that influenced it artificially. We have no other supplementary or reliable evidence to back up our initial postulation'.

He took a deep breath and continued, '*Voyager 1* was at its absolute communication limit, and we were about to lose absolutely all contact with it. Our technology was not capable of tracking it physically any further, apart from receiving signals from it. That is it. We had no means at our disposal to monitor it anymore. We were and are completely in the dark as to the real reason for the peculiar readings we received.

'The worst thing we could have done would have been to create a panic based on an uncorroborated occurrence—yes, if we did and opened a can of worms, like the famous event in 1938, when the *War of the Worlds* spoof radio broadcast was aired by Orson Welles, which led to a massive public panic. I am aware of the reality, and the scale of the panic is largely disputed and questionable, but the fact remains that it did happen. Remember also that it was confined to parts of the USA as there was no international dimension to the radio back then. I predict we can expect similar hysteria could similarly arise if we are not careful. As I have been so far, ma'am, mass panic, mass speculation, and mass assumptions made by various cults, no question about that, especially when people start to realise it would contradict all the holy books, which claim God is the creator of humanity. So again, there would be protests by religious groups, and there would be chaos and instability'.

There was a stunned silence while he took another nervous swig from his bottle of water.

'It shows us one thing: No matter how well we prepare or try to reassure the public with carefully worded warnings, I am certain there will be widespread hysteria, such as raiding all the goods from all the shops and trying to flee from the cities. Crimewaves will erupt everywhere as law and order break down'.

The president interrupted, 'That is exactly the scenario that I outlined earlier on in our session'.

Steve Ford continued, 'Probably based on the scares created in their minds after seeing several more recent classic science fiction thriller films, such as *Independence Day*, where we see the aliens bringing a total annihilation to the world's cities'.

President Wallace took a sideways look at Doctor Clark for reassurance that Ford was taking in the gravity of the comments.

'I'm afraid he does have a valid point. There would be an enormous crisis on our country's infrastructure resulting from our National Guard's inability to respond and maintain law and order over such huge geographic areas. Please also remember that this whole threat, real or imagined, now also has enormous international ramifications. We could in no way stand back and think it is only an issue that affects li'l ol' U S of A!' Wagner interrupted. 'But at least you should leave it to us, in the first place, for us to take the initiative, given our huge technological resources, to decide what best options we can come up with very quickly'.

'Prepare for what? How can you decide how our armed forces should react based on such flimsy evidence?' Ford said. He was clearly irked by Wagner's comment and went on.

'You could have a long-winded, ongoing slanging match with Congress, trying to get them to approve a bigger budget set aside for our armed forces without being able to be specific as to what you want the money for. We have absolutely no idea as to what time scale we are facing. Last, we still also need to consider what sort of biological threat humankind might be facing'.

President Wallace retaliated with some vehemence. 'But don't you think we deserve to develop some options for the consequences that may or may not arise—diplomatic, unaggressive, and defensive?'

But Doctor Clark interrupted, 'You really have no idea what you are talking about! I must tell you we need to discard the ideas we have seen in our typical sci-fi films of using our intercontinental ballistic missiles to shoot at the alien spaceship. I'm afraid to say it won't work that way in the real world. Okay, bear with me, I will explain in simple, layman's terms for your benefit. For a start, our intercontinental ballistic missiles are not equipped to tackle a mobile target like an International Space Station or, in this case, an alien spaceship. All missiles are fuelled when launched to lift them into the upper atmosphere. From there, they rely on gravity and free-fall to their targets.

'The biggest ICBMs belong to the Russians, with a range of something like 16,000 kilometres. If we are to adjust the guidance system aboard a standard ICBM and have it launched out into space without coming back to Earth, then, in theory, it can. However, it will burn all the fuel much more quickly when trying to break free of the Earth's gravity into space. Once all its fuel has been spent, it will just float aimlessly, without any guidance from us. Do we really think that the beings on board the alien craft will be unaware of its proximity, and if they are, that they will sit on their bums or whatever their anatomical equivalent might conceivably be?'

This made the atmosphere of the meeting lighten considerably as a few grins appeared.

Doctor Clark looked at President Wallace. 'Mrs President, now you can see my point, and with the greatest respect, I believe you are the victim of it'.

'Which is?' the president asked.

'Bounded rationality'.

Ford turned around pointing his finger as an imaginary gun at Doctor Clark and said simply, 'Bingo'.

'What in the world does that mean?'

Doctor Clark looked up at President Wallace and took a slow inhalation. 'Okay, let me put it this way—bounded rationality is the idea that in decision-making, rationality of individuals is limited by the information they have in their hands, including the cognitive limitations of their minds, and possibly the limited amount of time they have to make a decision'.

'That is exactly the same situation you are in with this ETs spaceship', Ford cut in. 'No matter how prepared you are, the situation remains exactly the same either now or two years ago!'

'Everyone, please keep quiet. I need to think for a moment or two', the president said very sharply.

She swivelled her chair around and faced the age-old clock again, seeking inspiration as to how to progress the complex issues. In the next few minutes, there was almost total silence. Only the soothing rhythmic ticking of the old timepiece could be heard. There were no humans with the specialist knowledge she needed from whom she could get advice. *Bounded rationality*—that really did encapsulate her dilemma.

Then she thumped her fist into a cushion behind her. 'The only way we can unlock this whole can of worms is to find some way to communicate with the aliens. That has to be the priority! Someone, somewhere in the world of communications, there must be someone or a laboratory with the technical skills to open visual and radio signal dialogue with this spacecraft? We have all been looking to an aggressive solution, but we have no idea what they may actually want'.

Finally, without warning, President Wallace swivelled back into position in front of her large desk and spoke to her desk mic, which instantly recognised her voice. 'Call Aaron Schmidt, Secretary for Defence, security code red 1'.

She waited for a moment before an image of a man with short goatee beard appeared on the big screen.

'Hello, Mrs President. What can I do for you? Security code red 1? It must be a real hot potato, ma'am. I should tell you that I have, by chance, Admiral Andrew and General Norman with me at this moment. They are, of course, cleared for SCR1'.

'Aaron, we need to have all the armed services on standby at level 3. Encoded confirmation will be on its way within an hour. I'll explain it to you when I see you, and you'll find out the full picture in two hours' time, when I make the announcement to the world. All I am asking you is, how soon can it become effective when we have decided to implement it?'

'Which of the military do you want on standby? At this level 3, it is 15 minutes' readiness'.

'All of them'.

'Oh my god, that's bad! Well, it can be done within 10 minutes or so'.

'We can make it in two hours when I make the public announcement. Once I have done that, I'd like to have you come here to my office immediately'.

President Wallace looked back at Cooper and said, 'Can you arrange a list of questions for your friend Brett Fielding to pitch to me at the news conference, and I must have drafted answers for me to use in response to his questions. I will focus on Brett more than other reporters'.

She pointed her finger.

'Stevie and George, I think you'd better go with Thomas and work closely with him and prepare any technical advice that I could use for my press release. Make it simple and clear for the public to understand. No need to frighten them with jargon. Have it ready in an hour'.

'No problem', Doctor Clark replied and stood up and left the meeting.

Without pausing, she looked immediately at Campbell. 'John, I'd need you to contact the top 20 countries in terms of economic muscle and military strength and invite them to hold live videoconferencing with me.

Also, I want a team of advisers to be present in the cabinet room. I will leave it to you who you co-opt, but I do not want any waffles. How soon can that be arranged?'

'Given the different time zones, it's probably more practical to hold the meeting in two days' time. We need to get them updated first with the latest information prior to the meeting'. This was the sort of pressure that Campbell thrived on.

'Make it so. First, I must have had direct links with two prime ministers from the United Kingdom and Australia. They need to be informed first since it is their citizens who have been abducted. A closer communication relationship with them takes precedence over other countries'.

'Okay, but what about Chile? Should we declare we got our information from them?' Campbell queried.

'Forget it and say nothing about them. We will say we found it through our observatory based in Hawaii. I simply don't trust the Chileans, and they probably have had some ulterior skewed motive for information censorship. There would certainly seem to have been an unauthorised leak to Hawaii, which probably puts a question mark on the safety of the communicators' lives at their observatories. We need to take a precautionary path by taking the pressure off them'.

'Got it'.

The president stood up slowly. Her steely eyes roved round all the men in her office. 'Any questions?'

Ford responded, 'Yes. Just one. Why set DEFCON at level 3? I understand that we want to make sure that we get a sense of urgency, but at that level, will it be just as likely that it will in itself create panic?'

She drew in a long breath and spoke in an unusually deliberate way. 'We are all facing what is a totally unforeseen set of circumstances. We have absolutely no experience on which to base our reactions or to guide mankind. Hence, it is my destiny to show them that I am still in absolute control with my own decision-making. I am not subjected to the realm of bounded rationality. It is called leadership, and it is what I was elected to do'.

She shifted her eyes to the image of the alien spaceship. The room was engulfed in total silence. A moment later, it was broken by President Wallace's quiet voice. She simply muttered, 'So God help me'.

The clock chimed 11.

Chapter 17

The Gathering

Emma Wilson was sitting with her legs crossed on the floor in the centre of the area. Andy Nelson was pacing around the room restlessly, not exactly in circles but more of an oval pattern governed by the shape of the space. The two cubic-shaped rooms had been joined to make one larger rectangular area.

Andy was in deep thought, agitated by the information Emma had been able to glean, based on her acute observation that they were nowhere on Earth but rather residing deep inside a spacecraft in outer space. She had previously spent time in deep discussion with him, exchanging all her useful information and opinions.

'Unbelievably, unfuckingably incredible!' he kept muttering to himself.

He stopped in his tracks and looked at her. 'Emma, did you say there are four of us in this spacecraft? If so, where are the others?'

'Well, that's what I believed the wall had communicated to me. As usual, my translator had functioned so flawlessly, but could we check again'.

She stood up decisively. 'Okay, let's ask the wall'.

She took a deep breath and spoke in a louder-than-usual tone, and her translator picked it up and projected her bluish text on the wall.

'There are four people like us here in this place, is that correct?'

CORRECT came the reply on the wall in a reddish colour.

'Then please show us the two other people'.

ATTAINABLE QUESTION WHEN

'How about now?'

REQUEST ACCEPTABLE IF PEOPLE NOT HOSTILE

'I have faith in them being not hostile'.

The two walls at both ends of the joined room simultaneously started to become first opaque and then appeared to melt into the floor, exposing two new figures, a man and a woman. Andy and Emma gaped at the sight of the two extra humans. They had no idea that these two humans had existed in such apparent proximity to their own limited domain.

The man was wearing a traditional Arabic dress, a white *thawb* with a black keffiyeh on his head. He was sporting a thick black beard but was cleanly shaven around his lips.

The second person at the other end of their enlarged accommodation was a woman dressed in a simple grey nun's habit, in Mother Teresa's style. She also wore a simple headscarf. She had an oriental face, accentuating her large brown eyes.

The attention of the original two occupants was immediately arrested as the figure in the Arabic attire began to shout and gesticulate excitedly, his eyes gleaming and wide open, revealing his dark brown fanatical eyes, and he began shouting, with his hands waving in the air, 'Allahu Akbar! *Anaa hurr!*'

Emma tried to lip-read him, but she could not understand what he was saying. She looked at Andy and shrugged.

'What's he saying?' she mouthed.

'I think he's speaking Arabic, and I believe he was glad to know his God has been merciful to him'.

She turned around and faced another woman. Her face was very rounded, and the shape of her eyelids revealed her identity as Asian, possibly Chinese, Japanese, or was it Vietnamese? Whatever it was, Emma could not pinpoint her origins. The woman's dress was of no help to Emma either. This Asian woman was, nevertheless, looking very shocked at the sight of three other people in this even bigger room. She immediately clasped her hands together as if praying.

'Excuse me, can you speak English?' Emma pointed at her own mouth.

'Ye! Yaggan!' She was smiling and nodding.

'Say again?' Emma was puzzled.

'Oh, a bit!' This time she spoke more slowly and deliberately in English with her index finger and thumb closing together in a gesture.

Then Emma realised that she had been thrown off course as the first words from this woman were distorted by her excitement and what she meant was 'Yes, I can!'

'Great, what is your name?'

'Gyeong Lee'. The woman was smiling. 'But you can call me Gillian Lee'.

Emma's translator failed to pick it up. Instead, it bleeped and projected sentences on the wall. *'New voice detected. Unable to comprehend it. Requires new configuration'.*

Emma read this and decided to ignore it. *Not essential for the moment*, she now thought. She felt more confident as she was able to lip-read Gillian quite well.

'You speak good English! I think you said Gillian?'

Gillian nodded vigorously. 'I was fortunate to learn it at my school as part of compulsory learning'.

Emma looked at Andy asking him to repeat what she was saying. He repeated it slowly for her benefits.

'Okay. Where do you come from? And how did you end up here?'

'Oh, originally, I came from South Korea. But I was sent by my Christian mission to serve God in Mongolia'.

'Mongolia? You mean the country between China and Russia?' She was double checking her.

Gillian tilted her head, trying to fathom Emma's peculiar accent, but she got it nonetheless. She smiled and nodded.

'What were you doing there?'

'I was part of a strong missionary team sent on a mission to aid a small town recently ravaged and flattened by a major earthquake'.

Emma again got lost here and looked at Andy in askance. Andy took a few steps forward and said with few augmenting gestures, 'She's part of the missionary team. It makes sense to me as she comes from South Korea, which is reputed to be in the top five countries with the highest number of missionary teams'.

Emma smiled and assured Andy that she followed his explanation. She looked at Gillian. 'Wow, but how come you're here now?'

'Well, I was taking a long break from all the hard work assisting the people at the village next to the town and took a long walk on my own up the hill to seek some form of spiritual solace'. She paused and closed her hands together. 'I was seeking to strengthen my spirits and get some guidance and meaning to . . .' She paused as she couldn't find a better word to complete her sentence, but she gave up and continued, 'Anyway, I was meditating on my own when, out of nowhere, came this strange object—it flew over me. I thought it was an angel sent out to guide me in response to my prayers, so I was not frightened and did not run away'.

'Then what happened?' Andy asked.

She looked down sheepishly. 'Yes, I was spreading my arms out, making a welcome gesture to it, but it stung me!' Then she looked up in bewilderment. 'I blacked out, but then the next thing, when I woke up, I was here in this strange environment! I don't recognise the place here! Where am I? Am I in heaven?'

'Afraid not, far from it. I think we're in some form of a spaceship—an unidentified flying object, if you care to call it that'.

'UFO?' Gillian took one step backwards with a look of horror on her face. 'So it was the devil's way of tricking me into it?'

'Nope, we're all in the same boat, regardless of our backgrounds'.

Andy pointed his finger at Emma. 'For a start, her name is Emma, and she's from Australia. My name's Andy, and I'm from England'. Then he realised he was ignoring the other person still standing quietly in the far corner and waiting to be introduced. 'Uh, hello, can you tell me who you are?'

'Ana la 'afham'. The Arabian man shrugged.

'Can you speak English?'

Again, the noncommittal shrug and headshake.

Andy looked at Emma. 'I think we may have a problem. He can't speak English. What can we do about it?'

Emma looked at her translator and smiled. 'Maybe I can use my little box of tricks again!'

She took a few quick steps, grabbed his hand, and pulled the yet unknown man towards the translator.

'Come on, I think there's a solution!' she said with careful attention to her pronunciation.

The Arabian was flabbergasted at the way she had held on to his hand. He was clearly not accustomed to the idea of a scantily clothed woman, not of his own family, invading his personal space. No woman in his own environment could be so crude to touch him without his consent. He snatched his hand away with his eyes blazing angrily, shouted in Arabic, 'Where are your manners? How dare you touch me!'

This violent and unexpected reaction stopped Emma abruptly in her tracks. She looked at him in amazement and then looked at Andy, seeking his advice. 'What's the matter with him?'

'I think you need to be reminded about his culture. They don't like to be touched, never mind being bossed about by any women!'

'Ah! Okay, my apologies!' Emma bowed slightly at the Arabian and gestured to him to come to the translator.

He was still looking at her with disgust on his face, but it took him a while to cool down before he grudgingly consented. He nodded and moved slowly towards the area where the translator was positioned.

She sat down on the floor, crossing her legs. Her fingers danced and skipped over the keys as she exhibited her extraordinary dexterity around the hologram keyboard on the floor. It took a while before she stopped and looked at him while he was still standing next to her. She pointed her two fingers at her own eyes and beckoned him to look at the screen already formed on the wall, but the configuration guidance was now written in Arabic. He knelt and started to read it. He smiled and started to speak quickly in his native language. It took him a good 5 minutes before coming to a halt. Finally, Emma typed in a few more instructions into the translator to programme it to recognise the new source of speech. But this time the difference would be automatically translated from Arabic into English text and vice versa.

She looked at Gillian and beckoned at her to come over, and Gillian did with some nervousness. Emma went through the procedures all over again. Finally, she looked up at the other humans.

'Okay, I think that should do the trick. My translator is indeed a lifesaver for us all!'

She stood up and looked at the Arabian in his white *thawb* and said, 'Okay, can you please at least tell us your name and where do you come from?'

He failed to notice the slight impediment to her speech. He had no idea as to which particular language she was using. The translator picked up her speech and projected her words onto the wall, with one line in full English while the second line underneath in full flowing Arabic script. The bearded man's eyes widened in acknowledgement.

'Alrrbb ladayh rahma!' he shouted. 'Ma 'arwae shay' hu'.

'God have mercy' appeared above the Arabic line. 'What a wonderful technology this is!'

He dipped his head to the others in acknowledgement. 'My name is Rahman Hussain'.

He looked at Andy, ignoring the other two women, and started to explain what had happened to him. 'Well, I drove out deep into the desert on my own, enjoying my sport with my wonderful Talon'.

'Talon?' enquired Andy.

'My name for my *saqr falcon*'.

'Ah, hunting the birds with your bird of prey, the falcon?'

'Nem fielaan!' he pronounced, but the translator simply came up with one word: 'Yes!'

'So where were you, and what happened?'

Hussain began to explain, gesticulating while he was speaking, to emphasise his meaning. 'I come from Port Sudan, which is on the coastline of Sudan, my home country. A few days ago, I drove for three hours or so west into my beloved desert with my superb Talon. Then I came up to a large sand dune to gain a better view for hunting purposes . . .' He suddenly paused. There was an expression of disdain on his face.

'Well?' Andy prompted him to continue.

'I know for a fact there's a large American aviation military base across the Red Sea at Jeddah, which is about 300 kilometres away on the coastline of Saudi Arabia. Out of nowhere, there was a large drone! It came over me, and I had to shield my eyes against the wind blowing sand into them caused by this drone device. Then I couldn't remember what had happened afterwards, but I must have blacked out!'

'Well, you were probably stung. Were you?'

'Ah yes! I do remember now. It was on my forearm!' He rolled up the sleeve to expose his forearm, revealing a purplish bruise the size of a large coin. 'Ah, there it is!'

'We are all aware of that as we have had similar experiences'.

'Must be that unholy great Satan! The Americans must have sent out their drone and abducted me! I saw it with my own eyes! Allah is my witness! They have brought me here!'

'But it was not the Americans!' Andy tried to assure him.

Hussain retorted, yelling excitedly, 'So typical of the CIA to send their latest spy drone to kidnap me! Why can't the world see how scheming they can be with their new technology?'

He looked at them and noticed all their eyes were wide open. They were all still focussed on the wall reading the text as his story was unfolding.

'Ah! Did you all have the same experiences?' Hussain said, raising his voice even more. He was still aggressive, but his intensity was lessening.

'Well, that's exactly what has happened to us all. But . . . hang on . . .,' said Andy.

'We need to stand up to the Americans, God willing!' snarled Hussain.

Andy interrupted him, 'Hang on, Rahman. By the way, is it okay for us to use your first name? We do not want to offend you, but we are not sure what the correct manners should be for us to use when addressing an Arabian gentleman'.

Hussain was taken aback and visibly wilted because of the courteous attitude of the Englishman.

'Erm . . . I suppose you may use my first name, but the women should not', he responded somewhat hesitatingly, having been wrong-footed by this very diplomatic man.

'Thank you for explaining things to us'. Andy gave a furtive wink to Emma. 'Anyway, going back to what we believe to be the situation we all seem to be in, we don't think it has to do anything with the Americans. It's absurd they would go to such lengths to abduct us! On what grounds would they do that? It will achieve absolutely nothing for the Americans. None of us can have any scientific knowledge or any other skills that would benefit them'.

'Then what, in the name of Allah, do we provide and to whom?' Hussain challenged Andy, completely ignoring the women.

At this point, Andy realised Hussain had not been brought in the picture with his latest dialogue with Gillian and Emma. Andy would have to break the news to him about the notion of them being stranded in an unspecified environment yet to be fully understood. He took a short breath. 'Rahman, you may have your opinion, but can we at least forget about America for a moment? Can't you see how strange our surroundings are? Just look at the structure and material of the wall and floor? And how did the wall manage to melt down before our eyes? I don't believe there's any technology like that exists in our world, do you?'

'Come on! You should have known that! Don't be hoodwinked by this stylish environment! That's exactly what they want to disorientate our minds! That's their sole purpose of disconcerting us to control us like puppets!'

Up 'til then, Emma had remained sitting on the floor in silence.

She was still watching the captions flashing up from the translator and absorbing the conversation unfolding between Andy and Hussain. She realised that she must remember to call him that. *Enough! He's just not getting it!* She thought.

She suddenly stood up and with one hand, nudged Hussain's right shoulder gently as a means of gaining his attention. Even this simple gesture had the opposite effect on Hussain. It irritated him even more. He reacted violently, turning around, and slapping the back of his hand squarely on Emma's cheek, sending her sprawling backwards. Fortunately for her, Andy caught her in his arms. Hussain was still glaring at her unapologetically.

Emma reacted automatically going towards Hussain, rubbing her slightly bruised cheek. She was not hurt very much, but her sense of dignity inflicted really stung her ego. With her eyes blazing and clearly incensed, she took a few threatening steps towards Hussain.

'How dare you do that?' she shrieked at him.

He did not understand her verbally. He had failed to see the captions flashed on the wall. Or rather, he did not want to. He was still rooted to the same spot. *How dare she think she can argue or even challenge me!* He was furious, still reeling with anger from the previous incident.

'You have no reason to hit me! I will have none of that!' She took another step closer to him. 'Only cowardly men like you who do hit women because you think we are weak and cannot retaliate, and in your society, you can get away with it!'

She tripped up, and her face was now inches away from his. She was challenging him to take another swipe at her. Andy stepped in swiftly and quickly pulled Emma back. He positioned himself between them. He had managed to grasp her shoulders and muttered to her, 'There's no need to provoke him anymore! He's not worth it'.

Emma did not understand his words because he was too close to lip-read easily, but his intervention was enough to cool her down. She realised that no good would come from any confrontations amongst the 'earthlings'. They were all in this mess together. She exhaled and took a few steps backwards and signed, 'That's fine, Andy, I'm okay. But I think it's time for you to convince him what we already know about how we all came to this situation'. She was calmer now.

'Why me?'

'Well, for a start, you are a man, and he has already said that men pay more attention to men. That means Gillian and I are second-rate citizens to you men'. She gave him a surreptitious wink. 'Go on and tell him', she signed.

This was the first time she used signing instead of speaking since the encounters with the two new occupants.

'Righto'.

He turned around to face Hussain and found him with his mouth agape. Hussain was startled to see Emma signing at Andy.

'Asamm 'abkam?!' he shouted while pointing at Emma. Captions flashed on the screen: 'Deaf-mute?!' He had failed to notice this as she had been speaking orally all the time. She had given no indication of her deafness.

She saw the caption and rolled her eyes. Her level of anger had hiked a bit and took another step of confrontation towards Hussain. Again, Andy blocked her pathway and said simply, 'Please!'

She sighed and shook her head. 'Well, that is still offensive! You still need to educate him!'

'Okay! We are all being stressed by circumstances that no other humans can have endured!'

'Rahman! Yes, she's totally deaf, but the last thing you need is to call her mute in any form! That's uncalled for. The deaf detests being labelled "dumb or mute" as they are certainly not!'

He took a few steps away from Hussain and Emma and searched around for a better position to talk to them all. He decided the spot next to the translator and captioning wall should be good enough. He took a deep breath. 'Rahman. Okay! I understand the problems that have faced us all from the beginning'.

He checked the flashed captions and was satisfied with the accuracy of the translation provided in English, but he assumed the Arabic script flashed underneath would match it, regardless if he did not understand even a word of it.

'We all have had the same basic experience', he continued, 'which we now know is that we have been stung or injected and abducted by the drones—that's absolutely certain. However, what we don't really know definitively is the origins of drones or whatever they are, especially where they came from and their overall purpose in abducting all of us from widely differing locations'.

Only the two female heads were nodding. Hussain said nothing.

'Okay, that's for a start, but with thanks to Emma's perseverance and ingenuity, she was able to build up some rapport with the wall or whoever or whatever it is behind it. She has already explained it to me, but I think it's better if she can tell you in her way. Can you please tell them exactly what you've explained to me—from the beginning, when you woke up in your own room, 'til now—and what you have concluded, based on your reasoning with the creation of artificial gravity on the floor of our original cube-shaped rooms and so on, would you mind?'

'Fine. Please be bear with me as I will try to do my best and explain it orally in plain English rather than using sign language, which I normally prefer to use because I am deaf, not dumb as some of us believe'. She looked directly at Hussain, and she was unable to resist an opportunity to put in a jibe at the Muslim. She was also watching the captions. They matched word for word with what she had said.

She took a deep breath and began. 'Okay, I still had my working helmet on my head when I woke up . . .'

It had taken her more than 20 minutes to convey everything that had happened to her, from the moment she opened her eyes in this strange room. She continued every subject she could think of during her brief stay in her cubic room: food, hole, floor curved, the flow of water on the floor, wording on the wall, her video playbacks on her helmet, the clue with the lifespan of her hearing aid battery. Then she went on to explain how she built up the conversation and increased the vocabulary with the wall. At one point, she held up her communication device to show the lack of homing signals as part of her emphasis that there should not have been any black spots in Australia.

She took great care, concentrating more than usual to ensure that her speech would be accurately replicated by the wall. There were a few times when she paused when she needed to take a few sips of cool water, which also gave her some breathing space while she considered what she was going to say next.

'That's how I managed to request them to remove the walls between us all, allowing us all to meet for the first time'.

'Well done, Emma', said Andy. 'You've done brilliantly, and I can tell you what, I've been watching the captions throughout and pleased to say your translator had worked perfectly!'

'Now there you are'. She smiled and searched for their reactions. 'That's how I came to my initial belief we're somewhere inside an alien spaceship. Any questions?'

Gillian was obviously completely overwhelmed and at a loss for words, except she kept muttering to herself, 'Oh, Lord, preserve me!'

Hussain was still looking impassive and unreadable. He still had not said one word. He was obviously trying to comprehend all that was being explained but was obviously out of his depth at the scientific aspects as explained by 'that woman'.

Andy detected his unwillingness to be included in the same boat. *If he's that stubborn, then it's going to be a challenge for us,* Andy thought. *What was his reasoning?*

'So, Rahman, it looks like you are not buying it, are you?' Andy asked. 'Any particular reason that you think Emma's story doesn't hold up? If so, what part?'

'I'm still not convinced'.

'Then would you care to share with us your line of thinking?'

'For a start, we know how desperate the Americans are, with the knowledge that Islam is already spreading out successfully and about to surpass the Christians as the de facto and next premier religion of the world. That's the fact we know already'. He put up his index finger to reinforce his point.

Andy narrowed his eyes but said nothing. Emma rolled her eyes and said nothing. Gillian said nothing as she was totally at a loss to understand any of the explanations so carefully construed by Emma. Her core religious beliefs had not prepared her simple existence for such extreme concepts.

Hussain continued, 'They want to throw everything at us by experimenting with us using their latest technology as a means of mind control! We are here as their guinea pigs! They want to throw mind-boggling technology at us to see if we can be moulded into their line of world domination. Alien? Get real!' Hussain folded his arms to show them that by his stance, he was not to be swayed.

Andy sighed. He knew it would be hard to reason with someone like him who was so devout and unswerving in their beliefs. No matter how logical your reasoning was, that person was not open to dialogue. Then he had a eureka moment—an idea to counter the illogical brick wall.

'Rahman, that's fine. I know I cannot "prove" anything to you, except in mathematics and logic. Proof doesn't exist outside deductive reasoning. So based on this, would you like to see evidence?'

'What evidence?' Hussain challenged him.

'How about us seeing the extraterrestrials themselves in person for the first time? Would that convince you, for real, that we are riding inside their spaceship?'

'Maybe. Maybe not. Why didn't they present themselves at the first opportunity? Why hide behind the wall?'

'Well, you've got a good point, but I wouldn't like to meet them, and given the chance, I would avoid meeting them in the flesh, if at all', Andy said.

'Why not?'

'If you're familiar with our human history, often it was the native or indigenous tribes of America and Australia, and not to forget the Māori of New Zealand, that was largely decimated, not through warfare, but mainly by diseases brought into them by the first contact with European settlers.

'In fact, more than 90% of them were wiped out by common pathogens, from which they have basically no immune system to fend off what to the Europeans were often not lethal. Whereas, the common cold amongst others, like smallpox, influenza and so on, frequently became epidemics and death sentences to them.

'From my scientific standpoint, it would be an absolute nightmare for us to be in physical contact with these extraterrestrials, not knowing what type of infectious viruses or alien microorganisms to which we would be exposed'.

'Perhaps they know this and got us immunised while we were in our sleep?' Emma Wilson interrupted. 'There's another puncture bruise on my forearm!'

Andy smiled and shook his head. 'Possibly! But I wouldn't bet my life on it as there are, indeed, thousands of viruses to reckon with! It would be a logistical nightmare to produce full vaccination on this scale!'

'You never know, with their superior technology at their disposal, they could make it a child's play to immunise us'. She was trying to sound optimistic.

'If possible, I would try to keep the wall in place between us and the extraterrestrials! We can view them through the transparent wall and see it for ourselves! It's much safer that way!'

'Well, can we try to ask them to present themselves to us through the wall?' Emma positioned herself in front of the wall.

'Would that convince you, Hussain?'

'No! They could have created images through computer-generated imagery and fool us again!'

Emma rolled her eyes again. 'Okay. Have it your way! I'm not going to give up and will ask them to show themselves to us!'

She looked at the wall and signed while speaking, 'Have you been following and understanding our conversation?'

It took a few seconds before a new caption came on in English.

YOUR SUPPOSITION CORRECT

There was another line of script language flashed beneath it, but it was in full Arabic language.

She felt motivated. 'Then you know we wanted to ask you why you cannot present yourself before us?'

WHEN YOUR REQUEST GRANTED YOU CONSIDER COOPERATION QUESTION

'Of course, we'll consider cooperating with you as long as it's reasonable'.

BUT RISK CONSIDERATION

'Risk of what?'

RISK PERTURBATION TRAUMATISE

'We'll be shocked to see you?'

POSTULATION CORRECT

'Okay, thanks for the warning, but we'll be prepared to face you and do our best not to be alarmed by your appearance'.

She looked at others. 'Can you assure me you will not be frightened by the extraterrestrials' appearance?'

'I will have my God as an inspiration for my strength'. Gillian bowed. 'But I'm ready'.

They all nodded, except for Hussain. Emma ignored him and looked at the wall.

'There you go. We're ready'.

The atmosphere in their room was turning into something they had not experienced before—major apprehension.